'A protagonist who complains about British weather is one thing, but one who feels the Thames would be much improved by a few crocodiles is something else!'

'Some genuinely laugh out loud moments plus a really engaging cast of characters, and a meta plot that has me hooked! Cannot wait for the next one!'

'...a fun take, with engaging characters and good writing.'

'... funny, bloody hilarious in places. Its characters are well written. I think, if the next one is as good, it will be the start of a bloody good series of books.'

Amazon

'A very entertaining, action-packed read with excellent characters and several good jokes - and no doubt some more I missed :) Reminiscent of *Ash* by Mary Gentle and the *Rivers of London* series.'

'...a delightfully fun read.'

'St. John does a great job of weaving in real history with fiction and an alternative history. So much fun!'

'It started interesting and just got better. The twists were unexpected and added to the story, can't wait for the next instalment.'

'Enjoyable and quirky.'

Good Reads

By Eva St. John

THE
QUANTUM CURATORS
AND THE
ENEMY WITHIN

EVA ST. JOHN

MUDLARK'S PRESS

Cover art by Books Covered
Map by Damijan Jerič

First paperback edition 2020

ISBN 9781913628031
(paperback)

www.thequantumcurators.com

For Mum.
Thank you for all the stories. Here's one in return.

Map

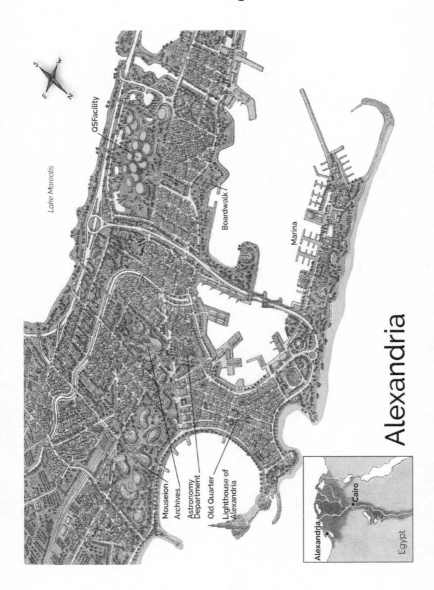

Lake Mareotis

OSFacility

Boardwalk

Marina

Mouseion

Archives

Astronomy
Department

Old Quarter

Lighthouse of
Alexandria

Alexandria

Egypt

Alexandria

Cairo

#1 – Julius

My name is Julius Strathclyde, and I might be dead. This is my story.

I waded through the freezing water. People surged past me crying, others grabbed my arm demanding to know if the way ahead was blocked. Their voices bounced weirdly off the rising water levels and flock-lined corridors. An old lady in a flimsy pink gown held a small lapdog aloft, a fur stole wrapped around the top of them in some futile attempt to stay warm in the icy water. I removed my dinner jacket and draped it over her shoulder, tucking the stole underneath. The dog snapped at me, but she scolded it and pleaded with me to help. As we made our way to the outer deck, I remembered my mission. I wasn't here to save people; I was here to save a book.

Her bony fingers dug into me, begging me not to abandon her. I had to harden my resolve to ignore her cries as I turned and fought against the tide of other first-class passengers struggling through the water. This was the hardest aspect of any mission, not the potential threat to life and limb but ignoring the suffering of those around me. A man shoved me out of his way, ushering his wife and children along. Clearly, he had mistaken me for staff. He looked the sort. Or maybe I was doing him a disservice and he was panicking? Personally, I thought it was the former. As our eyes caught he frowned, perhaps he didn't like my expression. Here we were on the Titanic as it began to sink, and he was putting himself first.

I struggled past the crowd until their voices fell away and the corridors emptied. As I walked through the water I counted off the doors until I reached my destination. Twelve, thirteen, fourteen, I was getting closer to my goal when the floor shuddered and I felt the boat tilt further. I could hear distant screams and shouts, somewhere a violin was playing, but here in this corridor, all was quiet. Just strange mechanical groans echoing along the structure, the water muffling everything else. The leather soles of my shoes slipped on the carpet and I had to grab onto the balustrade; my arm plunged into the water, and I could see goose fleshed skin through my sopping sleeve. As I got to cabin 15, I tried the door, but ridiculously it was locked. Who, whilst fleeing for their life on a sinking ship, locks the door? I went to pull out my lock picks and realised with horror that they were nice and safe in my jacket pocket, which was now on its way to the lifeboats, draped over the shoulder of a little old lady and her pet dog.

'Hello, Cadet. Do you need assistance?'

I jumped. The disembodied voice of the AI support chirped in my ear. No, I did not need any assistance.

'Disengage.'

'Are you sure about that, Cadet? You appear to be struggling.'

Great, mocked by a computer.

'Disengage now.'

Feeling furious with myself, I saw I would have to open the door with brute force. I would solve this problem myself and not reply on the wrist brace. Running at the door wouldn't work as the water was now waist level. I tried the door handle again, just in case. Definitely locked. The lights in the wall sconces flickered. Trying to do this in the dark would be a pain until I remembered my wrist brace and flicked on the torch. When the lights went out, I would be ready. I looked up and down the corridor, trying to find a solution within the rising water. Strange items floated on the surface, a hairbrush, a child's doll, but nothing I could pick a lock with. At the end stood a solid metal fire extinguisher. *Only to be used in case of an emergency.* Well, I think this counted.

I hitched it off the wall and returned to the cabin. Heaving the extinguisher out of the water, I smashed it into the door. It resounded with a dull thud but remained very much shut.

'Hello, Cadet, do you—'

No, I bloody didn't. 'Disengage until reactivated by me.'

When I got home, I was going to have to ask the boffins to change the voice. This one reminded me of a paperclip I used to know. I picked up the fire extinguisher again, considered where the weakest part of the door frame was, and smashed the metal cylinder directly against the lock.

In a rush, the door gave way. I fell into the cabin as the water from the corridor surged past me, pouring into the room beyond. My ribs thumped into a table and I ended up in a heap on the other side of the room along with the other furniture that had washed forward in the wave of water. By the time I got to my feet, the water had levelled out and was now up to my chest. I cursed myself; I hadn't anticipated that the door would have kept out so much of the water. My entire body was shaking with the cold, but I had to get to the book. I looked around the suite. A large bed was in the far corner and water lapped at the sheets, a little writing table was on its side and a stool bobbed in the water. What had been the height of opulence less than an hour earlier was now a dishevelled mess. I pushed one of the floating chairs out of my way and headed to the far wall where the safe should be.

The *Rubaiyat of Omar Khayyam* was a collection of Persian poetry. There were many versions of it in print, but this one was known as the Great Omar. This was due to the wealth of its binding by the renowned Sangorski and Sutcliffe bookbinders. They had made the book in 1911 and it was a masterpiece. The front cover depicted three peacocks; the back board featured a lyre. All images were made in a marquetry of various leathers and ivory and encrusted with over a thousand gems. These emeralds, diamonds, and rubies were then set in gold, with further gold thread embroidery decorating other parts of the cover. It had taken the binders over two years to make, and the glorious cover was then protected in an oak slipcase. We weren't saving the contents of the book as much as its wrapping.

There was a distant metallic groan as the ship twisted further. The floor was now almost at a thirty-degree angle and water was pouring in through the door. The water was deeper at this end of the room. I bobbed and swam to the far wall, wrenching the painting away from the wall safe. With shaking fingers, I removed my wrist brace and, activating its magnet, placed it against the wall of the safe and turned the dials. The brace confirmed each click. Opening the door, the surrounding water poured in and hundreds of dollar bills floated out. Grabbing a velvet bag, I shoved the Great Omar in my retrieval pouch to protect it from any damage and sagged with relief. My mission was a success.

'Thief!'

A hand grabbed my collar and a heavy body slammed me towards the wall, my chest and shoulder hit the metal door of the safe forcing the wind out of my lungs. I tried to duck, but the person behind me had their hand in my hair and their other hand bunched around the neck of my shirt.

'I wondered what you were doing heading away from the lifeboats, and I was right. You're nothing but a dirty little thief.'

Releasing my collar, he grabbed for the book, but of course, this was a mistake. Unpinned and recovering a few seconds of breathing space, I fell in a dead weight. As I did so, I kicked out my back leg and twisted against his.

The two of us fell into the water. He hadn't been expecting that, and it gave me a couple of vital seconds to turn and face him.

It was the man from the corridor that had barged past me earlier. Doubtless, he had got his family onto the lifeboats and then returned for his treasures. I couldn't imagine greater stupidity, although as I looked over his shoulder and saw my wrist brace stuck on the edge of the safe, I realised my stupidity outstripped his. Without my wrist brace, I was dead. I was an idiot. How could I get past him, get the brace, and get out of here? I thought I'd try the truth.

'Sir! Listen to me. I'm trying to save it, not steal it.'

He lunged towards me with a roar. So much for trying to reason with him. He was much larger than me, but whilst he moved and fought like a street fighter, his dinner jacket suggested that it had been a few years since his ill-gotten gains had elevated him from the alleyways to the opera houses. Scratch a gentleman and you'll often find dirt and corruption under your fingernails. That said, I still needed to get past him and escape.

I ducked under his fist and stepped to one side. Fighting in deep water was hampering both of us, and the angle of the floor was lending him a slight advantage. Smashing a punch to his nose, I wasn't quick enough to avoid a ringing clout to the ear and slipped under the surface. Seconds later, he grabbed my hair and wrenched me upwards. I tried to pull free but as I did, the ground under my feet shuddered. He released his grip as the ship itself tipped and we were both suddenly swimming. The lights flickered once and then went out. I heard him shout in alarm.

'Where's the door? I'll let you keep the book if you get me out of here.'

I stayed silent, trying to conserve my energy. He was already lost; I didn't want to join him.

The water level was rising quickly and in the pitch dark, I was blind, no longer able to tell whether it was a floor, ceiling or wall above my head. I needed to find the safe and get my wrist brace. Swimming forward, I decided that feeling the surface in front of me I might be able to orientate myself. The ship had stopped filling with water and was now sinking to the bottom of the ocean. Time was running out. My head hit the top. The room was now almost totally full of water. I felt above me, and my hands touched an ornate picture frame. This was the one opposite the safe, I was sure of it. The water now rose around my face and I could feel the onset of panic. I was freezing cold and blind and knew that my life was being counted down in seconds. Taking a deep breath, I duck dived and tried to swim down towards the safe and my wrist brace. Ahead of me I saw the torch beam of my brace and knew it was just within reach. My throat was becoming painful and my eyes were bulging. I kicked my legs again, forcing myself down through the icy water to the brace. Every stroke was getting harder and harder. My kicks seemed weak and uncoordinated. I thought my lungs would explode and I drew in a desperate, involuntary breath of water.

#2 – Julius

'And you're dead. Class, what did Julius do wrong?'

I lay on the ground of the holosuite, a large plain white box of a room, the bright ambient lighting and warm dry air a disorienting change. The rest of the class were sat in an adjoining room divided by a glass viewing wall. Those that weren't grinning were looking concerned, and every one of them had their hands raised. I tried to stand up, but I was still feeling slightly discombobulated by my drowning. Instead, I sat up and took large gulps of lovely dry air. Everyone died during training, but this close to graduation, deaths were rare.

Six months ago, I had unexpectedly arrived on this earth and had fallen in love with an awful lot of it. What's not to love? A society based on science and academia rather than religion and commerce. Their shining achievement was the quantum technology that allowed them to open a portal to my earth and save treasures just before they became permanently lost or destroyed.

Not knowing quite what to do with me as I fell through the quantum field with Neith, they had allowed me to join their final year students who were preparing to work as quantum curators. Not all would pass, but their skills would be utilised elsewhere. No one's talents were ever wasted here.

Professor Hu's voice droned on as my mind drifted. He was the perfect lecturer for this class, and he had a very high pass rate. Over the years the weaker candidates had been weeded out, moved into more suitable career paths. Early failures in academic lessons helped thin out the crowd, as had simulation scenarios. Students, obviously, weren't allowed to step across to the real Beta Earth and had to train in the holo suites. Unsurprisingly, I was top in my class at fooling the computer algorithms into thinking I was a Beta inhabitant, which was hardly surprising, given that until six months ago, I was. The rigours of an academic life also went in my favour. Six months of daily exercise routines and an overhaul of my diet also meant that my general fitness and strength levels were dramatically increased. But in simulated retrieval events, I kept making stupid mistakes and dying.

My fellow students now looked at me nervously; soon one of them might be partnered with me. If I passed. I could see that they were all weighing my positive attributes against my startling ability to die. My own death would be regrettable, but they may be less sanguine about their own.

'Yes, Sabrina.'

Sabrina, the smartest girl in the class, or certainly the loudest and first to have her arm in the air.

'Paragraph 1. Sub-Section 1. Clause 1. A quantum curator must never remove their wrist brace under any circumstance whilst on Beta Earth.'

I continued to look at the ceiling. Obviously, I shouldn't have removed my brace. But what else was I supposed to do?

'What should he have done instead?'

'He should have activated the remote listening function and focused it on the safe dial. We practised this in Years Three, Four and Five.'

You may have done, I sighed inwardly. I may not have had it drilled into me for years, but I had read the manual. I'd just forgotten that feature. There were a lot of features. I decided that if the wrist brace was so smart, it could do with a built-in help feature. Ha! See, they didn't think of everything these Alphas.

'Cadet Strathclyde didn't attend those years,' continued Hu. 'What else could he have done?'

'He could have interrogated the brace and ascertained which functions could help him.'

'Yes, well done, Sabrina.'

Bravo, Sabrina, I thought sourly. Now I could go home and recuperate and maybe bang my head against a brick wall. Like I said, there were a lot of features. Too many. How annoying to have missed such a vital one.

'What else did he do wrong? Beyond switching off the virtual assistant. One at a time please.'

I groaned and sat up, smiling at the jury. I was happy to see them smiling back. I did like my fellow students. My hope was to become a quantum curator along with them, but first I'd have to stop dying. A voice interrupted my musings.

'He shouldn't have given his jacket to the old woman.'

'Correct.'

No, I wasn't going to let that slide and interrupted the dissection of my failings.

'I disagree. She was shivering.'

'She wasn't real.'

'No, sir, but none of it was, and yet we need to act as though it were. I would always give my jacket to an old woman, standing in icy water, fearing for her life. But,' I paused and nodded my head, 'next time I'll clear my pockets first.'

'Hmm.' Hu didn't sound impressed by my explanation and turned back to the class. 'Any other problems?'

'He did spend a bit too long in the salon. I didn't understand. Was he trying to gather intel?'

Gather intel? I was standing in the salon of the Titanic, seconds before it struck the iceberg. I wanted to look around. In fairness, maybe that was a problem. But these holo-simulations were just so lifelike it was utterly fascinating. I tipped my head in Kamil's direction. He always delivered his assessments with manners.

'Cadet Strathclyde. What exactly were you doing in there?' asked Hu. 'You appeared to be playing cards. Were you, in fact, gathering intel?'

'Yes, sir.'

'And was the nature of that intel, who had the five of hearts?'

'Yes, sir.'

The class laughed and I smiled, I was unused to being the centre of entertainment and found I rather liked it. Or at least I liked it when they were laughing. Less so when they were staring in horror at my latest faux pas.

'In my defence, sir, could I say once more how incredibly impressive the holo suite is and how the mastery of your engineers is to be applauded.'

'You may, Cadet Strathclyde, but you also said this when you died on the Serengeti Plains, at the Mongol uprising, and in the seventeenth century Doge Palace. I am concerned that you are still dying too frequently, and this fact distresses me.'

I shared his concerns. I too found these death events deeply unpleasant. The rest of my squad thought this was very amusing given how much unnecessary death there was on Beta Earth. I tried to point out we still only died the one time and the holo-deaths were very realistic. Still, they didn't mean to be heartless. They had all done their share of dying in the holosuite and had been smart enough to stop doing that. For the first time in my life, I was proving to be less than bright.

Leaning down, Hu offered me his arm and pulled me to my feet. I stood up and left the room as Diane, the next cadet, walked in. Like me, she was barefoot and dressed in a simple lycra bodysuit from head to toe. All the better to project the holo-clothes onto. In a real-life step, we would wear genuine clothing, but for these practice events, we wore bodysuits. I was the only person who appeared to find these outfits mortifying. No one appreciates their crown jewels being moulded so graphically. It was just another aspect of my new life that

I couldn't get used to, their utter disregard for the human form. Nakedness was absolutely not a thing, and it had taken me weeks to try to explain what swimming trunks were and why I wanted a pair. I joined the other cadets in the viewing gallery as Diane stood motionless in the holosuite. A Dresden sitting room rose around her as the bombs started to fall, and her simulation began.

'Move over,' I said as I came and sat down next to Jack and Stef. I shared most of my lessons with these two, except for the science-based ones where I was practically in the remedial class. Stef was in the middle stream, and Jack was so bright that there were only three others in his class. I was pretty certain that Jack would make a great quantum curator, but he was here because they considered him a bit of a child genius in the science fields and he had a particular ability in quantum maths. Hence, he was here, seventeen, and brimming in confidence.

Stef, on the other hand, was a rock-steady pick for QC all day long. The guy was six foot five and would have made an excellent second row. He playfully knuckled me on the head and offered to buy me a beer later. More evidence that he was a loss to rugby teams everywhere.

As they shuffled along they caused Sabrina, who had been taking notes, to tut in our direction. I whispered an apology, but she told me to be quiet, so I just grimaced at Jack and continued to watch Diane execute a perfect retrieval of a small Rembrandt.

As the day wore on, no one else died, although a few failed to retrieve their specified object. One or two nearly blew it by acting incorrectly and I winced when someone said, "Wotcher, Guv'nor" at the Royal Opera House in 1852.

When Hu asked the class why this was wrong, no one put their hand up. I expected Sabrina to leap in, but she didn't know either. I was about to raise my hand when Hu called on me.

'Cadet Strathclyde. Explain.'

'"Wotcher, Guv'nor" is an East End form of address; it should also be pronounced differently. It would also not be employed by anyone in a dinner jacket.'

'I thought that was a tuxedo?' Sabrina chipped in.

'Not in nineteenth-century England it's not.'

It didn't seem hard to me to understand the difference between British and American terminology, but I suppose I had grown up with it and these guys weren't just learning British/American differences, they were learning the nuances of an entire world. They were incredible, and yet some of them still had an overwhelming urge to boast.

Sabrina piped up again, eager to show her superior knowledge and attempt to trip me up. I always hated this moment. She was determined to show she was better than me at Beta history and customs. I have no idea why she competed against me so aggressively, and I felt like a churl when she failed.

'Sir, I think Cadet Strathclyde may be mistaken. The "East End" is only three miles from Covent Garden. It seems unlikely that the vernacular language and pronunciation would be so different.'

You see, that was the problem with the Alphas, they just couldn't properly grasp class structure.

'Incorrect, Cadet Mulweather,' said Hu dismissively. He didn't mind interruptions, but only when they were correct. 'This is an example of societal structures and cultural dialects. Best brush up on that section before our next class. In fact, as none of you raised your hand on that point, we'll run a test on it next week. Class dismissed.'

Everyone groaned except me.

'Cadet Strathclyde, please stay behind.'

Now it was my turn to groan.

'See you down at The Last Bar in a bit?' said Stef as Jack stood beside him looking concerned for me.

Telling the others I'd catch them up, I waited to be bollocked in a considerate and empowering fashion. As was the way here, as was everything, it was all thoughtful, intelligent, caring and attentive. Who'd have guessed that that led to awful boredom? But equally no famines, genocides or pandemics. You pays your money you takes your choice.

'Look, Blue,' said Professor Hu. Inwardly, I groaned. It was a terrible sign when a professor used a student's nickname.

When I had first arrived, everyone kept overreacting to my name. Julius Caesar had set fire to their library block and they were still twitchy about it. And, of course, it was that one act that separated our two worlds. In my world, Julius Caesar sailed away and created the Roman Empire and the rest, as they say, is history. In this world, his boat sank in a storm. At the same time, the Egyptian people decided that they really valued their library, and a world based on science and the betterment of humanity developed.

So, they didn't like the name Julius. They tried to shorten it to Julie, but that wasn't going to happen. Only Charlie called me that. And Charlie had been killed by one of this lot, so no, they didn't get close to being able to use Charlie's words. Instead, we settled on Blue in honour of my one blue eye. My other blue eye was now residing in Neith's face. One of the charming side effects of a step gone wrong. Some splices were a lot worse; I was lucky. Apparently.

Incidentally, I didn't have a gaping socket where my other eye should be, that was filled with Neith's brown one. Not the most obvious of mementoes, but I was beginning to get used to it. Hu continued.

'We're concerned about you. For obvious reasons, you score better than your fellow students in a vast majority of fields. You turned out to be surprisingly proficient in weapons deployment, but the minute we put you anywhere interesting, you lose focus. It's basically the most important aspect of the job and you drift off. We've been discussing it and we think you would make an excellent lecturer, probably the best, on Beta studies. Or we could offer you a post in our England—'

I shuddered and quickly interrupted him. 'Not there, sir, they're bizarre. They keep crying and taking part in mass poetry recitals. And what's with all the televised yodelling?'

Hu smiled gently and continued, 'Very well, but if you bow out now, that would be the sensible thing to do. We don't understand why you persist with this. An Alpha would have acknowledged their unsuitability by now. They would stop wasting resources and—'

This was not going well for me. A lot of the time I felt like I was being indulged, a circus curiosity walking amongst the enlightened. And yet they were still prepared to let me try, like a lab rat. It seemed inconceivable to them that someone would waste their time and energy on such a futile course.

'Am I wasting resources, sir?'

'No, not yet, but you will be when you are on active service and fail your brief or endanger your teammate through your sudden fascination with how a lute sounds or what twelfth-century bread tastes like.'

I broke in, keen to fight my corner. 'But think in all the ways I could improve things. With the right partner, Sabrina, for example.' Inwardly, I shuddered. 'They would help me focus and I would help get us to our goal with the fewest number of mistakes or misunderstandings.'

It was a weak argument and a selfish one; I was unlikely to bring anything special to the table. Eighteenth-century Germany was as alien to me as it was to them, but it was all I had to go on.

'Very well, if you are determined to continue training, you may do so, but you have nearly reached your death quota. If you exceed that, it will be an automatic redistribution of skills and talents.'

In other words, I'd be off the course and brushing down my favourite lecturer's outfit.

#3 – Julius

Having been dismissed, I headed to the lockers and changed into a long cool robe, relieved to be out of my lycra bodysuit. Men's clothes were far looser here, which was understandable in the heat. We often wore long, or short, robes called chitons, similar to kaftans. It had taken me a while to get my head around the fact that no one thought I was wearing a dress or a skirt. Finally, when I was happy that I was correctly dressed—they were fussy here about the oddest of things—I left the changing rooms. Instead of the pub, I decided to head home. I was tired and in no mood to celebrate. This world was bewildering, and just when I thought I had got a grip on it, it would slip out of my fingers.

Six months ago they had murdered my best friend. I had been in a fight in a graveyard, held at gunpoint and shot at. This all ended when I was dragged through into a parallel world. For obvious reasons, I'd spent the last half year trying to blend in and not draw attention to myself. Someone tried to have me killed once, and I was paranoid enough to wonder why they had stopped trying. Or if indeed, they had.

I walked towards the central plaza and stepped out into the heat as the tinted glass doors slid open. Of all the madness that I had come to terms with in the past six months, it was the heat that I found hardest to reconcile. It didn't help that Egypt was now in the height of its

20

summer. Some aspects were wonderful as every building was beautifully air-conditioned through intelligent architecture and smart technology. Outside, the pavements and roads were coated in a membrane that absorbed heat, micro lattices ran through the substrates, wicking the heat away and converting it into energy elsewhere. Large multicoloured fabric sails billowed from the tops of buildings, offering shade and catching the tiniest of breezes. Through careful placement, they then funnelled those breezes down to floor level. As the heat engulfed me I was glad I was in a robe, I cannot begin to describe how lovely a cool breeze can be in the right location.

In many ways, Alexandria felt very Northern Mediterranean in temperament. I knew the Sahara was in the background, but it was a good hundred miles away and wasn't pervasive. The streets weren't sandy, there were palm and date trees everywhere, and pink bougainvillea tumbled down city walls. People were sitting out at tables either eating and drinking or reading and writing. Some people played cards when the breeze didn't flick along the streets, and when it did, they turned to chess. On either side of these streets were the buildings of the mouseion itself. I left the teaching block and headed home.

To all intents and purposes, the city of Alexandria *was* the mouseion: the archives, museums, teaching wings, the library, the conservation labs, and the quantum stepper. A giant city-sized campus.

Over the centuries, Alexandria had become a global power. Whilst Cairo was very much Egypt's capital, it was Alexandria that everyone revered. The training campus for cadets was a short distance from the mouseion itself, but I could still catch glimpses of its towers and minarets overhead. All around, the buildings were a blend of ancient, medieval and modern. This society may have been weaker in its artistic endeavours than my own, but its engineering and architecture were awe inspiring. Glass walkways, high above my head, connected red sandstone towers and minarets clad in shining blue tiles; as I watched, citizens walked across them, enjoying the breeze.

I stepped out from under the shade of the atrium's canopy into full sunlight and sneezed.

'Attention, Citizen.'

I jumped as an overhead voice hailed me and I craned my neck to see a tay-tay gently glide down to rest beside me. A uniformed custodian stepped out and my shoulders slumped.

'Hello Custodian Shorbagy.' Shorbagy looked to be in his late twenties, with a solid square jaw and a crooked nose. His black hair was shaved down to his scalp, and no doubt felt good under his helmet, which he now clipped to his belt as he tapped on his wrist brace. He had the air of what I considered to be a good policeman. He was alert and attentive, but the pastel yellow uniform seemed incongruous.

We had first met when I had been reported for scaring children. Apparently, saying "boo" to children whilst being in possession of a dodgy heritage was a no-no. Within minutes a custodian had arrived to give me a stern talking to.

The custodian had introduced himself as Custodian Shorbagy. People here were sticklers for their designations. It was all very polite and formal. For the first minute, he explained the importance of his role within society, the next minute was taken up with my role in society. He then suggested we both recite the daily affirmation together, and I pushed the sunglasses up off my face, resting them on my head. Once he had composed himself and apologised for the small cry, he said it was an honour to meet me and left. We've met each other a few times since then and he even smiles now when he sees me, and sometimes that smile even reaches his eyes.

This time his smile seemed relaxed. He was finally getting used to me.

'Ah, Cadet Strathclyde. Yes. I see. May I enquire where your handkerchief is?'

'My hanky?' I wish he hadn't asked as I then had to listen to a lecture about the dangers of wantonly endangering humanity by spreading viruses and general bacterial lurgies. I cut him off apologising for my grievous neglect and promised to deploy a handkerchief in all future infractions. He wasn't wrong, I just felt glum for having to be told off about something so basic.

Having put his mind at rest, I asked him how his monthly quota was going and was pleased to discover that he was leading the board.

Normally the mouseion complex is considered a plum position, with lots of prestige and easy pickings from boisterous students. However, since I had arrived, it was now viewed as high risk.

'And how's Custodian Farag doing?' Custodian Farag was Shorbagy's arch-nemesis. Although of course, they have no such thing as arch-nemeses, just valued teammates. Some a little more valued than others, some a little less.

'Slipped to third position. Incorrectly filed the last batch of paperwork. Used the wrong dating format if you can believe that?'

I laughed. 'What an idiot.'

Shorbagy laughed along with me and then remembered himself. Clearing his throat, he put his notebook back in his pocket, reminded me to purchase a handkerchief and left with a small wave.

I was beginning to have a bad influence on him, fancy laughing about the misfortune of a valued teammate. The horror!

Six months, 185 days. Not that I was counting, but it still felt wrong as I watched his tay-tay rise and join the other flying traffic zipping overhead.

#4 – Julius

The following morning I opened the window and smelt a change in the air. With relief, I felt that the temperature had dropped and if I didn't know better, I could swear it was going to rain. Rainy days here were few and far between, and I loved them. Instead of an hour's study before breakfast, I slipped on my running shoes and headed out along the boardwalk. It was often full of long-boarders, skaters and other runners, but I was banking on the fact that few others would be out enjoying the rain.

I knew I had miscalculated at the seven-mile mark. The rain was torrential and whilst I didn't think I was in trouble it would slow me down. I'd miss breakfast, and at this rate, my first lecture as well. Skipping lectures was not considered acceptable. I laughed, remembering an old girlfriend who'd found most of my life unacceptable. I wondered what she was doing now. Did she think about me? Had she even noticed I was gone? Our breakup had been somewhat abrupt, but nothing in our lives overlapped. Perhaps I had been reported dead? Although I think you have to be missing for seven years before you can be declared legally dead. This was something that bothered me from time to time.

In the early weeks, when I was trying to get my head around what had happened, I asked if my body was left behind. Was there an empty shell of me lying on King's College lawn? I had to endure a rather patronising explanation that this wasn't astral projection, nor was I a snake that had shed its skin. I was a human being and wherever I went I would take my body with me. When I asked how my absence would be explained on Beta Earth, their lack of knowledge became clear and their know-it-all attitude was replaced with a dismissive air. Those were my first introductions to the Alpha attitude towards the Beta Earth. Parental at best, derogatory at worst. When I tried to ask again what it meant if I just disappeared, they said that people in my world disappear all the time and no one seems to care. Why did I think I would be any different? I have to confess, that stung. Maybe people would assume I'd been bumped off in an attempt to grab the priceless Fabergé egg. Neith said they had placed a large cash deposit in my bank account to apologise for all the inconvenience. It was standard procedure, but of course, she had done that before the showdown on the college lawn, when I was yanked through to this world.

Maybe the police would find the money and decide it lent greater weight to the fact that I had been done away with. Especially as no one was spending the money.

There hadn't been a Live Event in the past six months, so there was no way for me to return or even to ask someone to drop off a postcard to my folks. A Live Event was when the quantum stepper calibrated a precious item becoming available in real time. Our worlds ran on the same timeline, so if it was Wednesday here, it was Wednesday there. Generally, the stepper opened into moments in the past but occasionally, once or twice a year, it opened in real time.

It was the rain that made me think of home and my state of existence. So, like I said, maybe I was "dead".

I pushed my wet hair back off my face and turned to face the onslaught and was caught out by just how much water there was in the air. I know we Brits like to go on about the rain, but this was monsoon-like. Yes, with this wind I was definitely going to be late. I'd have to go back to my dorm to change, grab some fruit to last me until lunch, and then spend my lunchtime trying to catch up on the first lesson. Thank God it was early European faith-based systems. A lesson I could probably deliver myself. The problem was that my lecturer might think the same thing and assume that's why I had skipped his class. That would be unforgivably rude of me. I upped my pace and decided I would run straight to the lecture. They might laugh at the foolish Beta arriving dripping wet, but at least my lecturer would know I wasn't slighting him.

A car overtook me, and its brake lights shone through the spray from the road. The rain was so heavy now that the rest of the car was barely visible. It made a U-turn, passed me on the other side of the road, and a few moments later pulled up alongside me and the window lowered. I jogged over and saw with dismay it was Chancellor Soliman Alvarez.

'Hurry up, man, get in the car. You're letting in all the rain.'

I thought that was a little unfair, but I could hardly debate the point and got in, my wet clothes sliding on his expensive leather upholstery.

'What on earth are you doing out in this?' He smiled at me with an avuncular air and then returned his attention to the road ahead. The force of the rain was making a mockery of his wipers, and the road was filling with surface water.

'I just felt like a run in the rain,' I panted with an apologetic laugh and wiped my face. 'Didn't realise it was going to get this bad.'

'Ah yes,' he said, 'what is your saying, "mad dogs and Englishmen"?' He laughed at his own joke and I refrained from pointing out the lack of a midday sun. 'Tell you what, why don't we get you back to the dorm, you can get changed and then join me for breakfast?'

Inwardly, I groaned. Since I had arrived, I supposed I was one of the chancellor's pet projects. I didn't know if he found me a curiosity or a threat to his establishment, but he would regularly invite me out for a meal, or a coffee and a chat. Once a month he invited me to a poetry recital, which was possibly the most excruciating thing I have ever endured, and I have sat through an entire production of the Ambelforth WI's Mikado. Having watched Soliman declaim on Ovid and football, I decided to apologise to the Women's Institute. Happily, though, I had a perfect excuse to turn him down and explained I had lectures first thing.

'What have you got this morning?'

'Religious studies.'

'A-ha with old Peepee. I bet you know more than he does.' He laughed a little cruelly and slapped the steering wheel. I rather liked Pierre Rigaut, and we often shared a drink in the bar. I was fascinated by his culture's belief systems, which he tried to insist were few and far between, and he loved to hear more about mine. It was always an enjoyable evening. He had an enquiring mind that was ready to acknowledge a point if well-argued. He was also happy to defend a principle to the last of his breath.

'That's as may be, sir, but still, it would reflect poorly on everyone if I failed to attend a lecture, no matter how,' I paused trying to think of a suitable adjective, turgid, dreary, asinine, 'interesting the alternative.'

He beamed at me. 'Good call. You know I wasn't sure about you when you first arrived, but you are definitely one of us, aren't you? I like the cut of your jib.'

Where did he get his language from? It was as though he had been raised on a diet of Biggles and Shelley. Rami had told me that some people were total betaphiles and had little cliques within that. The chancellor appeared to be a fan of late Colonial England; what-what, toodle pip and tally-ho.

I smiled weakly and insisted that I couldn't miss my first lecture. I checked my wrist brace; given this lift, I could get changed and make it to the lecture on time.

'Tell you what, I'll come with you. Get changed and then we can arrive together. If you're late I can say it was my fault. I need to speak to old Peepee, anyway.'

I thanked him as sincerely as I could, which he seemed to accept, and thirty minutes later we hurried in through the plaza to the lecture hall. I had made it just in time, although I noticed that the room was only half full and others, like me, had wet hair. Some who didn't live on campus were looking decidedly soggy, others were slipping off their sandals and wringing out the base of their trousers or kaftans by the front door.

As each one rushed in, they all had a uniformly alarmed expression as they noticed their chancellor sitting on the edge of a table, giving them jovial smiles. Now and then he'd offer a little quip about a well-prepared curator would not arrive wet or late, reminding them that a good curator is a prepared curator. I stood beside him cringing, I wanted to join the others, but he kept asking me questions and it was clear that he wanted everyone to witness this favouritism.

A door banged from the other side of the lecture hall and Professor Rigaut arrived, heralded by a gust of wind. He smiled at his class, laughing at the drama, and then his face fell as Chancellor Alvarez's voice boomed across the lecture floor.

'Pierre, dear boy, how good of you to join us. I was just telling your young charges here how important it is to be prepared.'

'Well, yes, this is quite the squall, isn't it? I apologise for being late, I—'

'No matter, no matter, I have no doubt young Strathclyde here could have taken the lecture himself and probably a lot better. Yes?' He boomed with laughter, making everyone feel desperately uncomfortable, or maybe that was just me. Still, no one else laughed.

'If you'll excuse me, sir,' I said to the chancellor, 'I'll just go and take my seat but thank you for the lift.'

'Any time, dear boy, any time,' he said in a voice that carried to the back of the theatre. 'Let's do lunch. Okay, pip-pip. Pierre, I will catch up with you later, I wouldn't want to delay your class any further. Besides which, I'm meeting the pharaoh in a minute. He needs my advice on a few matters of state.'

With that, he quit the lecture hall and left behind a general air of awkwardness.

The lecture was an enjoyable discussion of the Christmas customs and whilst Rigaut and I generally cantered back and forth, with the rest of the students jumping in with questions, my heart wasn't in it today. I felt I had been used to somehow belittle him and I felt uncomfortable. It was a double session with a halfway coffee break, and I'd stood up to try to grab a drink and some breakfast when Rigaut came over.

'Are you okay? You seem quiet today?'

'I just, well this morning, I didn't want you to get the impression that I thought I could do your job better than you.'

Pierre Rigaut rolled his eyes. 'Of course you could. Or you certainly could for parts of it. It would be the act of a fool to think otherwise. And it would be the act of an even greater fool if he thought he could use a student against me, to try to belittle me.' He arched his eyebrows and then smiled.

'Go grab a coffee and when we get back, I want you to explain why you eat coal at Christmas.'

The coffee here was delicious, and I was about to take a sip when Sabrina came over. Here was a girl that would never miss an opportunity to advance herself.

'Why did the chancellor give you a lift in? You live here in halls.'

'I was out running and got caught short by—'

'Fine.' She cut across me. 'Don't tell me then. I just wasn't aware you and the chancellor were on such good terms.'

I couldn't tell if she was offended or appalled, but she obviously didn't believe anyone would run in a monsoon. At least not voluntarily.

'Honestly, we aren't on good terms. I barely know him. I was just out running, and he saved my bacon.'

'You had breakfast together?' she asked, confused by my expression.

'No, it's just a saying.' I regretted it as soon as I had said it as she tapped on her wrist brace. They love storing up idioms.

'To save another person's bacon. This is a Beta saying that means...?' She looked up, enquiringly.

'It means he got me out of a sticky wicket.'

'Sticky wicket?'

I sighed, my coffee was going cold and I still hadn't grabbed any sort of breakfast, real or metaphorical.

'He helped me out of a difficult situation. I would have been late without his assistance.'

She repeated what I had said into her wrist brace and then looked up at me again. 'And what is a wicket and why is it sticky?'

I glumly explained as I sipped at my coffee and thought about lunch instead.

The second half of the lecture was much more fun as the students pitched in with questions from their studies. We were having a great time until I mentioned that in Beta England we had once banned Christmas carols during the Interregnum. The class suddenly looked awkwardly at the floor, or the ceiling, or anywhere but me.

'Did I miss something?' I asked. 'Is this one of those, you know something and I don't moments?'

'Have you looked through your Temporal Anomalies textbook,' said Rigaut apologetically.

As we broke for lunch, my mood was much improved and Rigaut asked me how my projects were coming along. As well as an end-of-year exam, each subject had a project to complete.

Over the past six months, I had been taking end-of-year exams every month. I was only covering the basics each time, but it meant my workload was enormous. I was now theoretically on the same level as the others, although there were still gaping holes. One area of study I was enjoying though was the final year project, as it meant I had time to do research rather than pure revision. I was doing a piece on the Romans and their lack of dominance.

The division point between our two worlds fascinated me, and I wanted to explore it as closely as I could. Interestingly, the people of this earth were far less interested in the Romans than I was. However, I had run into a curious issue with dialling up exhibits.

'Actually, you may be able to help me with that. I was trying to look up an exhibit and Tiresias directed me to the Level Five vaults, but I don't have permission for that.'

The professor looked at me and cocked his head. 'Why ever are you bothering with the originals? Pull up a holo.'

'That's the issue, apparently, there isn't one?'

That caught his attention and he beamed at me, full of eager curiosity. 'Whatever are you trying to view?'

'Some Roman artefacts.'

His face fell into polite disinterest. 'Oh. Oh well, yes, I suppose there is a limit to what is copied. Still, if you are interested in them…' He broke off and tapped on the screen on his lectern. 'There you are. Access granted.'

I thanked him and headed off to the archives. At this rate, I wouldn't be eating until supper.

#5 – Naga

Naga O'Reilly looked around the room for a final check. Each place had pens and paper. The chancellor liked a secure method of data storage. At the end of any meeting, he would either put the notes in his briefcase or insist they were incinerated in front of him. Naga mentally added a note to switch off the fire alarms. Chancellor Soliman Alvarez was hosting today's meeting and as his assistant, it was Naga's job to ensure everything was perfect. Especially as today, he wouldn't be the most important person at the table; far from it. Today was the annual quantum review and all the senior figures from Egypt would be present, as well as representatives of other international mouseions.

The seating plan had been a nightmare. All forty viziers had naturally been invited, but not all were active or interested, so they had seats around the outside edge of the room where they could watch or take part or fall asleep. Then Naga had to balance all the other functionaries. Chancellor Alvarez, as host, sat in the middle of the table. Opposite him sat Pharaoh Tarek. The current pharaoh was coming to the end of his ten-year term and as no one could be pharaoh more than once, a new face would soon govern Egypt. Seating the pharaoh, the viziers and her chancellor had been easy. It was fitting in the others that had been tricky, and she had needed to remember which way the current alliances were running.

So long as she kept Chancellor Shan out of Alvarez's sight, life should be easier. Shan was the chancellor of Cairo University. He was an intelligent and highly respected official and it was his burden that Alvarez, a more bloated fool than one was ever likely to meet, was in charge of the quantum facilities. The mouseion itself was under the care of Chancellor Chen, but Naga saw that she wasn't here today. She rarely was.

In any other country, the leading university's chancellor would be the most senior academic figure. Unfortunately, in Egypt, because of the stepper, it was complicated. It might be easier if Alvarez didn't enjoy lording it over his contemporaries so much. Naga sighed. If only chancellors were elected rather than appointed.

A door banged and the catering team arrived with jugs of iced water, nibbles and chilled fruit. Naga strode over and ran through her checklist with them and, happy that everything was in order, she returned to her desk. She could hear noises from Chancellor Alvarez's office, and she realised his door was open and he was getting ready to greet his guests. Naga checked herself over and took a deep breath as the door swung open.

'Ah, Naga, there you are. You weren't at your desk?'

'No, sir.' She gulped. 'Just checking everything was in order.'

'Well, you failed there then, didn't you?'

'Sir?'

'Because when I came out of my office to ask you how things were shaping up, you weren't here to tell me, were you?'

'No, sir.'

'No, sir, exactly. Your job is to be here, you are my personal assistant. What is the point of having a personal assistant if she isn't there to personally assist me? Right. Come along, we don't want to keep my guests waiting because I had to remind you how to do your job.' He looked back over his shoulder. 'And don't forget to deduct a half days pay for sub-standard performance.'

Naga kept her face blank as she rushed to keep up with him. Her salary was good, so a small drop in income wouldn't affect her, but the black mark against her monthly earnings would be noted on her CV. Since working for the chancellor, her CV looked like it had been attacked by ants, there were so many little black notations.

Looking around the room, Naga saw it was going to be busy. Pharaoh Tarek was over in the corner chatting to friends, and most of the chancellors and directors were already here. There were more viziers than was normal, but then events hadn't been the same since the Fabergé Incident and the arrival of the Beta male. The room was heaving with academic and political personnel. The pharaoh ruled over all of them, with the civic directors and academic chancellors answering directly to him. In theory, they were equals, but the chancellors considered themselves superior. This was not an opinion shared by the directors.

Naga stood at Chancellor Alvarez's shoulder. As the delegates arrived, she would lean in and whisper a little bit of trivia about each guest to him. He had seen it done on a Netflix show brought across from Beta Earth and thought it was a clever thing to do. Naga tried to point out that everyone could see her doing it. Wouldn't it be better for her to brief him earlier, so it appeared to be him that knew these things? He had looked at her like she was a fool and asked how she possibly expected him to remember all these facts about people. That had been another ant day.

'And how's little Xavier, I hear he passed his music exams?'

As the small talk flowed, Naga made mental notes of all the delegates' comments to add to her database later. Everyone had a file that she used to make the chancellor's job smoother. When to send flowers, who to ask after, who not to sit together.

Finally, the point of tedium was reached when no one could any longer pretend to be interested in their colleagues' offspring, and they moved through to the meeting room.

As they churned through the agenda, glasses were filled and emptied, the clock ticked on, and doodles filled the jotters. Finally, they arrived at Item Seven, Classified. Pharaoh Tarek thanked Soliman and then, following a sip of water, cleared his throat.

'Engaging protocol Gamma Five.'

38

All assistants put down their pens and switched off their recorders. Four assistants left the room, leaving only those with adequate security clearance.

Al-Cavifi stood up. 'Engaging protocol Gamma Six.' Naga looked about, it was unheard of for a director to overrule a pharaoh, but they had the authority. This wasn't some feudal dictatorship. Pharaoh Tarek nodded his head in acceptance of the suggestion and waved his hand to dismiss the majority of the room. Of all the personal assistants, only Naga remained in her capacity as record keeper. Gamma Five meant that the subject matter was not suitable for casual discussion and might alarm the general population. Gamma Six meant it definitely would.

As the doors closed Director Giovanetti, head of security, placed a device on the table and a faint static buzz emanated from it. This raised more than a few eyebrows.

'Come on now, you don't think this room is bugged, do you?' asked Chancellor Alvarez.

'Standard Gamma Six protocol. No insult is intended. And forgive me,' said Giovanetti as she turned to Director al-Cavifi and the pharaoh, 'but I felt we would be happier discussing the following topic with as few as people as possible.'

Naga shrank as Giovanetti glared at her, but finally, she nodded her head in acknowledgement of her presence. Al-Cavifi cleared her throat as Giovanetti told her it was now safe to proceed.

'Thank you. This year's exams are now upon us, and we find ourselves in a quandary. Chancellor Alvarez, would you care to explain yourself?'

The room stirred. For some unknown reason, al-Cavifi had always supported Alvarez, even up to the position of chancellor, which many had found difficult. He was a remarkably good bureaucrat but had no personal shine. The director had rebuffed all criticisms, saying that she would prefer a dullard who was capable, over a brilliant failure. But now she appeared to be ready to haul him over the coals. Naga winced, maybe she should have left the room. Was this why Giovanetti had let her stay? So her boss couldn't pretend it hadn't happened. So that every time he saw Naga, he'd be reminded of this meeting. If that was the case, the head of security had misjudged Alvarez. It was time for Naga to brush up her CV.

As she watched, Alvarez launched into his standard bluster.

'Explain myself? I'm afraid I don't follow?'

'You assured us that the Beta individual would not pass the exams and here we are with him predicted top of the ranks.' Al-Cavifi pulled up a screen and presented it to the others as she continued talking. 'With his marks and profile, he is the perfect candidate for the position of quantum curator. One of the best this year. You were at great pains to tell us that this wouldn't be the case.'

'Indeed. I have been most surprised by his success as well. Although I would draw your attention to his "death rate" whilst in the simulations.' Alvarez pointed at Julius' termination frequency. But al-Cavifi wasn't impressed.

'I have spoken to Professor Hu,' said al-Cavifi as the others watched on in glee. 'He assures me that Julius could ace the simulations if he chose to. It is Hu's opinion that he still views this as a very sophisticated game. He also said he felt his assessment had been confirmed by Julius' flawless performances since his last death during the Titanic simulation. Hu is of the opinion that unless we drop Julius in the middle of a volcano, he will not suffer another death within the simulator. So, I repeat, what do you propose we do with a Beta quantum curator?'

'As I said,' stammered Alvarez, 'his achievements have been impressive, but I feel certain that he will fail his exams. Until now he has just been lucky.'

Naga watched the room and couldn't help noticing a flash of utter pleasure on Chancellor Shan's face, as Alvarez began to squirm.

'You were only boasting the other week of how he was something of an acolyte of yours,' said Shan, 'attending all your poetry recitals and dinner parties. His achievements should not have caught you on the hop.'

'Well, yes.' Alvarez cleared his throat and turned towards the pharaoh, refusing to acknowledge Shan's existence. 'It became clear that he would be an excellent student early on, despite his obvious problems.'

'Which are?' continued Shan. 'I'm sorry, Soliman, I don't remember us recording any obvious problems.

Some obvious advantages certainly, given his splice with QC Salah.'

'We had concluded that those splices would be a hindrance to him.'

Before Shan could come back, the pharaoh stepped in. 'As you all remember, I was eager to give the young man some hope and a place within our society. I know that some of you were against this, but what are we, if we are not welcoming and benevolent? I was assured that he wouldn't qualify as a quantum curator, but that he would make an excellent archivist or lecturer. Now it seems this is unlikely to be the case.'

Naga groaned inwardly. If the pharaoh was now arguing against her boss, surely his days were numbered. Tarek's voice was calm, almost contemplative. He came across as a nice man. The citizens loved his steady management, but now Naga was beginning to see why he was such a good politician. He didn't lose his temper, he let people try their best, and he was prepared to come in and clean up after them. Point by point, he showed Alvarez where he had made mistakes.

'It seems he assimilated those splice advantages quickly and then learnt to master them, wouldn't you agree? In effect, the things you promised would trip him up, served to improve him, make him better and faster and gave him the skill set of a highly skilled QC operative, giving him a significant advantage over his fellow students. So, what then were his obvious disadvantages?'

'Well, that he's a Beta, of course,' replied Alvarez with an air of pointing out the obvious.

The pharaoh paused and looked at Alvarez and then took in the rest of the room.

'If I may, sir?' Shan looked toward the pharaoh and as he inclined his head, Shan turned to Alvarez.

'Soliman, you say that he's Beta like it's a natural disadvantage. But he is a highly educated individual with specialist knowledge and a natural understanding of the Beta culture. Is that what you meant by disadvantages?' Shan's voice positively dripped with disdain as he peeled a satsuma, his boredom and derision emanating from every action.

'We all know what savages Betas are,' protested Alvarez as he looked around the room, several heads nodding in agreement.

'Does Strathclyde strike you as particularly savage?' This time Shan arched his eyebrows as he popped a segment in his mouth.

'As it happens, no. Why just this morning we were chatting about one of my recent recitals. He really is quite a cultured individual. As I said, I have been monitoring him.'

Shan paused and chewed whilst making a point of looking thoughtful. The rest of the room waited to see who was going to win this exchange, although by now no one was going to bet against Shan.

'Is it possible that you have completely misjudged his potential and are responsible for the quandary we now find ourselves in? You promised us that no unstable Beta would have access to our quantum technology and we're about to give him the bloody front door keys.'

Naga saw Shan's mistake as soon as Shan did. Swearing and raising his voice was not likely to win any argument, and Alvarez pounced.

'I think you are getting a little excited, dear boy. I know you have no concept of running the quantum facility, but trust me, here we anticipate every eventuality. It's pretty much what we are.' He gave a little chuckle and Naga memorised his words so that she'd be able to recite them back to him later, praising his wordplay. 'Honestly, Shan, you worry too much about things you don't understand. Besides which, I have a plan. I have the perfect partner to team him up with.'

The rest of the board sat back and listened carefully as Alvarez outlined his proposal and shimmied away from the bear pit that Shan had set.

interlude 1

The following text conversation was retrieved, during a sweep of the ghost files of the Q Zone security system. It has been added to the evidence report for Case No: 234530/H. The sender is yet to be identified.

— And what do we make of that then?

— Soliman is a bloody fool.

— Yes. But that wasn't what I meant. We should have got rid of that Beta the minute he fell out of the stepper.

— You've changed your tune. Better to play the long game, you said. Wait until the fuss dies down, see if he blends in. Those were your exact words.

— I am quite aware of what I said. I think you'll also remember that I argued strenuously that he shouldn't be enrolled into the cadets.

— According to Soliman he's going to fail. And if he doesn't fail, Soliman has a Plan B.

— A Plan B that sounds even more dangerous to us than letting him live in the first place. With those two curators working together, our plans could be exposed. I may have to step in and veto this, and I really don't want to be seen interfering. It will draw attention to me.

— It's bad enough that we've had to stop all orders, because of the Fabergé failure, but now we have a quantum anomaly running around.

— This again? We've had angels on Alpha for years, nothing has ever gone wrong.

— Angels at the end of their lives. Angels that can't have children and continue their dirty little genetic markers.

— Look, it's been discussed. If that becomes an issue, we kill him. Agreed?

— Agreed.

— And if he passes the exams and Alvarez puts Plan B into operation?

— Then we can say they killed each other.

— And you-know-who agrees with this?

— Who knows what's she's thinking? All I know is that Julius Strathclyde is running out of time.

#6 – Julius

I headed over to the main archives. They were about a half hour walk from the university section, so I caught a hover-scooter and zipped past the pedestrians. These scooters were like a surfboard with a handle and were great fun, although their speed within the city was regulated.

Jumping off, I walked into a stunning geodesic structure that would have made Zaha Hadid weep with joy. It looked as though a shoal of flying manta rays had leapt out of the water in a long continuous pod of fish, leaping in and out of the waves below.

In this largest section of the complex, there were six floors above ground looking out over the Egyptian landscape from their beautiful, billowing walls of glass and steel. Below ground, there were a further eight floors. This was where the Beta artefacts were stored in a vast labyrinth of perfectly controlled environments, and all the lower floors had restricted access.

I made my way to the lifts and pressed the R button; the screen asked me to present my brace for authorisation. Every time I'd tried in the past, I had failed to be admitted. I mean, I knew those levels were restricted but hey, you can hardly blame a chap for trying. The concept of there being a library or museum to which I wasn't permitted access was an anathema to me.

This time though, the light blipped green and the lift gently descended. I stepped out into a well-lit corridor with a large reception on the other side. I walked across to the receptionist who had watched me step out of the lift and anticipated my enquiry. As I approached, I watched the familiar alarm cross his face and then it turned to peevish annoyance. Was there ever going to be a day when I wasn't immediately profiled? Oh look, it's the Beta. He's obviously stupid or dangerous or lazy. Choose your stereotype and run with it. For God's sake, don't wait for me to open my mouth so you can actually get to know me.

'Cadets are not permitted down here. Please return to the upper levels.'

I guess it was his tone, or his sneer, but I was fed up. It was lunchtime and so far today I'd had the sum total of half a cup of coffee, got soaked, and been nannied by the chancellor. I wasn't in the best frame of mind, and now some jobsworth had decided to get officious.

I leant across his desk smiling widely and raised my wrist brace for inspection.

'It is not socially correct to move so closely towards another individual.'

I leant further across. 'Sorry, what did you say?' I spoke slowly and loudly. 'I don't understand good.'

'I said move back. Now.' He stood up himself and took a step backwards. It was churlish, but it made my day. Receptionists the two worlds over fell into the same two camps. Those that saw their role as helpers, keen to get you to the right place quickly and efficiently, and usually in a friendly manner. If you have a well-run business, chances are you have a good receptionist at the desk. The other sort are the types that view themselves as gatekeepers, none shall pass until they have deemed you worthy. If you notice that your clients are short with you, if everything seems a bit of an effort, if morale is low, investigate your reception. You may have a gatekeeper.

I stepped back and stopped the dumb show. 'I'm here to examine exhibit RR3789782.'

The man behind the desk glared at me, aware that he had been goaded into acting foolishly and now primly hit a few keystrokes.

'Oh, right,' he said as the item flashed up on his screen. 'I suppose someone has to look at them occasionally. You'll need a scooter. You do know how to use one, don't you?'

'Move in a straight line, avoid the walls?' I paused, winding him up further. It wasn't very grown-up of me. 'But I'll walk, good to have a bit of exercise.'

'As you wish. Follow the green line.' I turned and saw bands of colour along the wall of the corridor in either direction. I found the green dashed line and, thanking him, headed off. Just as I got to a distance whereby he had to shout quite loudly to be heard, he called out,

'It's four miles.'

I counted to ten and returned to the desk. I had deserved that.

'In that case, I think I will borrow a scooter.'

Five minutes later I was zooming through the long empty corridors. Occasionally I would pass another researcher on a scooter and we would nod and smile as we passed at speed. Once I was out of sight of reception I stopped the scooter and worked out if it was possible to tell it where I wanted to go as I did on the street ones. Sure enough, tapping in the item's code number worked and soon I was zipping along the electromagnetic strips in the centre of the corridor. At some junctions there was no slowing of speed, at other times I came to a complete halt as another board shot across my path. Clearly, all the traffic was centrally controlled. I passed a few smaller reception desks but continued until my board slowed down. Which was a good thing because it was also the end of the corridor. The light was no less bright here, and the walls were just as clean and white as at the main reception, but there was a sense of dust out here in the furthest reaches of the deepest corner of the Mouseion of Alexandria.

I stepped off the board and pushing it towards an empty rack walked across to this section's reception desk. There was no one around and no obvious way to make my presence known. I knocked on the desk and then after a few minutes called out. There was nothing for it but to walk behind the desk, which I did with a certain amount of caution. No matter which type of receptionist you have, neither of them like strangers behind their desks. There was a door leading off the reception and I pushed it open, calling out again. As I did so, I startled a woman who had been peering into a magnifier, lost in her own world.

I braced, waiting to be shouted at, but her entire body language changed and she jumped forward, shaking my hand.

'Professor Julius Strathclyde! It is my honour, my absolute honour. This is the correct term of address, isn't it? Oh, I've been practising so much, but I wasn't certain if using your academic nomenclature would be correct. Please sit, sit.'

She was a short wide Asian lady, in her late sixties if I had to guess, with hair dyed in long green strands pulled back and woven into several long plaits of green, black and silver-grey hair. As she looked up at me with twinkling blue eyes I was put in mind of Mrs Tiggy-Winkle and smiled back. Dashing around to my side of her desk, she shooed a beautiful long-haired cat off a chair, which made me raise an eyebrow. These guys never inconvenience cats.

'May I offer you a cup of tea? You do like tea, don't you? And a marmalade sandwich? Oh dear, you haven't said a word. I'm rabbiting on. This is the stiff upper lip, isn't it? Oh, how incredibly rude of me. You must think I'm a boorish idiot. I have been waiting for months to meet you, desperate to not be one of the hordes clamouring to meet you and now when I do, I act like a teenager.'

I held up my hand and she stopped abruptly, placing a finger on her lips.

'I'm silent because this is the first genuinely friendly treatment I have received since arriving here.'

She looked at me in astonishment.

'Honestly, most people look at me with either fear or distrust.'

'Not here on campus, surely?'

'No, here on campus they mostly look at me as though I am a fascinating lab rat.'

'But that's awful. I could have met you earlier.' She laughed. 'There's me wondering what you would think of us, if you would consider us thieves and monsters, and now you probably think we are uncivilised as well.'

'You have the advantage over me, I'm afraid. You seem to know everything about me, but I don't even know your name.'

Her face fell and she began apologising again and asking if she had breached a form of etiquette. Having reassured her that I was in no way slighted, she introduced herself as Minju Chen, although some people called her Sherds. A nickname based on her spending so much time fiddling with broken bits of pottery. 'It's a hobby of mine. I enjoy fixing things.' She paused. 'But I think I would prefer it if you called me Minju. That is what my closest friends call me.'

'Why do you think I would call you thieves and monsters?'

'Because we remove your artefacts but fail to save lives. What is more precious or unique than a human life? It is a problem I have wrestled with my entire career.'

I thought about it. Her point was valid regarding a saved life, surely at the point of certain death, they could save people? Maybe they did, maybe I didn't know about it, but as regards the artefacts there was no doubt in my mind.

'You aren't thieves, you are saviours. Those items are about to be destroyed and you rescue them. I'm just grateful that they still exist. I mean, there are shades of Elgin and it would be nice to have them back, but they are at least preserved.'

Minju groaned. 'You see, we are monsters. I don't think we even fully appreciate them as much as you do.'

'I think you're being a bit hard on yourselves.' I looked around the room feeling uncomfortable. I could have done with that cup of tea but she seemed to have forgotten her offer. 'Why do you say you don't appreciate them as much?'

Minju then went on at length to explain her philosophy. Beta creations were so much more exquisite because we suffered more. I wasn't sure about that. That we could appreciate beauty more because we lived with squalor on a daily basis. Really, these chaps had a poor view of us. The genius of Beta Earth was its resilience and was tested in the fires of their history. I had to interrupt her.

'You know, for the most part, we live totally normal lives. Just like you do. Beta days are mundane, happy, tedious, frustrating, exciting. Just like yours. I know we have more sudden deaths and diseases and violence and inequality, but generally, our days are humdrum.'

'Unless your lives are directly affected by all that you just listed.'

'Fair point. But those people are also just struggling to survive. None of us stop and test our genius in the forges of history.'

'You're mocking me.'

'Not at all. It's just odd to see us through your eyes. You see us very differently.'

I watched Minju as she considered my words and then she jumped up in alarm.

'I haven't even made you a cup of tea.'

I could see the conversation had upset her and, honestly, it had alarmed me as well. It was the first moral or philosophical discussion I had had, and it went straight to the heart of my existence.

'So, no one has looked at you with the eyes of a friend or a colleague?'

'Oh, the other cadets are fine. It's not them, it's me. Fish out of water, so to speak.' I watched as she quickly scribbled "fish out of water".

'The one person who has treated me as an equal so far has been Rami.'

'QC Ramin Gamal? Lovely man.'

I paused. That too was odd. Since he had been placed on sand leave, it was as though Rami had developed an unpleasant smell that no one wanted to acknowledge.

'You know him?'

'I know all the QCs. Retired QCs always take a keen interest in who is filling their shoes. But please, as lovely as he is, I would rather talk about Cadet Strathclyde.' She finished with a smile and a small bow. 'You will have to learn to forgive us, we aren't good at change and are cautious by nature. It has made us safe, happy and prosperous, but it does leave a large proportion of the population somewhat skittish. Like a horse in spring.'

I laughed and thought what a good description that was of her fellow man.

'But you're not?' I said.

'Too long in the tooth to waste my time jumping at shadows, besides look at me, you don't see me doing much jumping, do you?' As she turned to put the kettle on, I was startled by a long, thick striped tail that hung down to her knees. I was still staring when she looked over her shoulder to ask if I wanted milk or lemon, and I flushed in embarrassment, stammering an apology.

'Badge of honour, nothing to apologise for at all. When we see someone that's been spliced we look on them as pioneers and heroes. This is what I got in the early days trying to save a snow leopard.'

'I don't think anyone's looking at me like that.'

'Well no, because they aren't really reacting to the splice but to what it means. Only two people in the entire world have your particular splice. One is the renowned and most decidedly female QC Salah, and the other is the terrifying Beta. Excuse me, their term, not mine. I've always disliked this Alpha Beta nonsense. So dismissive. I much prefer the term Other Earth. Sugar?'

As she presented me with a beautiful blue and white porcelain cup and saucer, I could have wept. I had given up on anyone viewing my earth as a worthy equal to their own. Certainly, we had wars and famines and plagues and poverty and inequality and the more I listed it, the worse it got; but we also had beauty and excitement and joy and wonder. Beta artistic achievements made theirs look like a damp squib. But here was this total stranger treating me as someone that she clearly wanted to know. It was lovely.

'So, and please forgive me if I'm speaking out of turn, is it acceptable to mention or acknowledge a person's splice?'

'Of course. Our splices after all were gained in the line of duty and are a public declaration of bravery. The public is a bit caught out by them, body deformities and injuries are rare here, but splice injuries are harder to fix. Here within the mouseion, we know what they imply.'

'Is it like war wounds?' I mused.

'Elaborate.'

'Back home, soldiers would come back from a conflict, injured and maimed. Everyone knows that this means they were involved in something terrible. The public is either embarrassed or angry by the sight of the injuries and doesn't know how to talk about them, but other soldiers see them for what they are and can even have very dark humour about them.'

56

'I think so.' She paused reflectively. 'Although, from what I have read and watched, you guys really do dark humour to a shocking extent. Here the public isn't embarrassed by physical defects, just startled. I mean, it's hardly the individual's fault. Is it?' She laughed and I sighed. They seemed to approach everything better but with a poorer sense of humour.

I sipped my tea and smiled, it was very good.

'Is it okay? I've tried in vain to find out what builder's tea might mean. It seems so popular in your programmes, but I'm at a loss.'

'Trade secret, I'm afraid.'

'Yes, of course, how rude of me.'

I groaned. No one got my sense of humour. I apologised and explained I was trying to be funny. 'I will happily tell you how to make it, but you aren't likely to be impressed. Not having poured something this delicious.' I was gratified to see her smile and relax, and then she picked up a pen and a notebook. 'So, builder's tea?'

'It's usually a blend of Indian leaves, usually sold under a brand name: PG Tips, Typhoo, something like that. You then stew it. Leave the teabag in the cup for a long time, pour in a little milk and add two spoons of sugar.'

She looked at me with a dumbfounded expression on her face. 'I thought that was a joke. I tried it once and it was so revolting I was certain it was some arcane humour.'

'Nope, builder's brew, milk and two.' And then I felt the need to apologise and change the subject before I destroyed any more of her illusions. 'But look, I've popped down here in my lunch break to have a closer look at an item. I just misjudged how far away it is and I might need to come back on the weekend.' As I handed over my enquiry chit, her face lit up.

'Romans. Oh, I love the Romans. No one ever pays them enough attention. Understandable, I suppose.'

I wasn't sure why it was understandable, but she didn't say any more and I left her tapping away on the screen. In the silence, my stomach rumbled alarmingly. I tried to pretend I couldn't hear anything, but she simply got up and beckoned me over to another room with a viewing platform. Through the glass wall, I could see a cavernous warehouse below me.

'The item you seek is at the far end. We have no conveyer belts in this part of the system so it's all manual retrieval, which means that to go into the warehouse you will need to change into protective clothing and undergo a full decontamination shower before you enter. I would advise you set at least two hours aside for your study and also to prepare a fuller list of items that you would like to study to save time.'

My heart sank. There was no way I could manage that and make afternoon lectures.

'May I make a suggestion?'

I nodded glumly.

'Would you do me the very great honour of sharing my lunch with me and allow me to bore you silly with questions about your earth? Then tomorrow, as it's

Saturday, the vaults open at seven am, and you can come and spend as much time as you wish?'

It seemed a perfect solution, and as she bustled around the little kitchenette, I helped her prepare some sort of sushi and vegetable dish.

As we sat down, I decided to ask about Neith. Over the past months, I'd been told I asked a lot of questions about everything. But surely that was the mark of a good student? I had learnt quickly that asking questions about the Fabergé mission or team was a strict no-no. So, I proceeded cautiously, I was enjoying myself and didn't want to spoil things.

'You indicated you knew QC Salah?'

She paused and placed her chopsticks back on her plate and raised an eyebrow. I decided that was a positive step and continued.

'Have you seen her recently or spoken to her? Only, well, I wondered how she's doing.'

'The elusive and brilliant Neith, who foolishly lost her team.'

I bristled on her behalf but tried to keep my reactions to myself. I knew I was walking across slippery stones; one misstep and I'd fall into the water. She waited for me to say something and the silence continued as I picked up my chopsticks, carefully trying to phrase my next question.

Her brace buzzed and she let out a deep sigh; the difficult moment broken. 'That, I'm afraid, is the alarm I set so you would have enough time to return to campus without being late for the next set of lectures.'

It was a thoughtful gesture, and I was grateful, although I still felt uncomfortable about how the conversation had ended.

'Am I still welcome tomorrow?'

She looked at me, shocked. 'You are always most welcome. I am already looking forward to it.'

'I just thought. My question about Neith...'

'It was a good question. But a good question rarely receives a satisfying answer.'

#7 – Neith

Six months and a week and I was back in Alexandria.

I had left six months ago, having tried to settle Julius Strathclyde in during his stay on our earth. God knows what he had made of his brief time here. How long had he waited for a live window to send him home? I hadn't followed any quantum news, it was far too painful, but I hope the kid got back safely. Not that he was a kid, he was a grown man in his mid-thirties. I just viewed all Betas as kids, they were so naïve. Still, whoever had taken him back would have adjusted any police records and created a convincing digital trail for his temporary disappearance. His involvement with the egg would also have been expunged, and then there was a bank account full to the brim of their precious money. So, at least that had all worked out. My own acclimation was taking a little longer.

Cairo had been lovely, but a girl can only do so much cataloguing. In fact, for the first three months, I was pretty much in a fugue state. My best friend was dead, my lover was a traitor, and my oldest friend was… The truth was I didn't know what to think about Ramin, so I didn't. Instead, I just drifted around like an automaton. Subu, my therapist, said this was a normal grief response and I wasn't to let it bother me.

At three months, Sam Nymens, my boss at the quantum facility, asked if I was coming back to work.

Now that did bother me. I didn't think I was grieving. I thought I was hiding from my failure. Going back to Alexandria would force me to deal with that. Sam tried again a month later, but it wasn't until last week when Chancellor Alvarez told me to get back to work, that I did. Alvarez may be a pompous fool, but he was a pompous fool that was in charge. So back I came.

As I left the quantum facility, I leant on the door and breathed a sigh of relief. I had avoided seeing anyone I knew as I signed back in and collected my house keys. Now I was going to go for a run. My fitness levels weren't where they needed to be and if I was going back into active service I needed to shape up.

'Good morning, friend.'

I looked up and saw a middle-aged couple walking towards me. They were wearing long multicoloured robes that suggested they came from southern Africa. Her red and green batik dress perfectly matched his kaftan, and I wondered if that had been deliberate. His hair was tied in a complicated braid structure, but hers fanned out in a magnificent black cloud framing her face. Golden chains pinned most of it back off her face. They were clearly tourists. Alexandria was the pre-eminent cultural centre in Egypt and probably the world due to the Beta exhibits; tourists flocked to it.

I smiled at the sight of them and offered the traditional greeting.

'Health to your hearth and home. May I help you?'

I tried to treat them like normal citizens, but the sad fact was that since I had returned from Beta Earth, I still felt like I was on a mission. My sense of alertness hadn't decreased, and I was seeing enemies everywhere. Subu said this was also natural and would calm down in time.

The man pulled a map out of his pocket and unfolded it. His wife tutted and rolled her eyes.

'Yes. If you would be so kind. We are trying to make our way to the harbour, but we've got lost.'

The woman gently swatted the map and turned to me.

'I told him, just consult Tiresias,' she said, referring to the online AI system. 'He'll tell us how to get there. But oh no. Not for Adebayo. He wants to be traditional.'

'Hush now, Momo, I just feel that here in Alexandria, it seems fitting that we revere the older technologies.'

I smiled, taking pity on poor Adebayo. 'Keeping it old school, I like it.'

They both looked at me and Adebayo suddenly burst into laughter.

'Using the Beta vernacular "Old school". How wonderful. You see, my dear,' he said as he turned to his wife who was also looking impressed. 'It seeps out everywhere. This is going to be the start of a very wonderful holiday. If we can only find our way to the waterfront.'

I hadn't expected to make their day so quickly, but it made me feel good. I stood alongside the couple and we all looked at the map.

'Right, you are currently in the university section for the quantum stepper.' I pointed to the east of the city. 'If you head that way you should get to the mouseion itself, can you see that big silvery waving roof? That's the central mouseion and over to the left where you can see those minarets? That's the astronomy department. I'm not sure if they admit visitors, but of course, you can visit any of the public galleries.'

The woman rummaged in her handbag and pulled out two paper tickets.

'Yes, we have booked to visit all floors.'

'But not the archives,' said Adebayo disappointedly. 'I hear they travel for miles underground?'

'They do indeed,' I said. 'In fact, we are standing above them right now.'

The couple looked at me shocked and then smiled delightedly, staring down at their feet.

'So, if you keep the mouseion to your right and the minarets to your left, you will soon get to the harbour.'

'We have tickets for the lighthouse and the original library as well.'

I inclined my head gently. 'You are well prepared to have a wonderful time.' I wanted to head over to my apartment, but Adebayo was looking over my shoulder towards the building I had just left.

'It is a great shame that we can't visit the quantum facilities though.'

His wife shook her head at him, the golden chains moving in agitation. 'And risk death or injury? We would not be so foolish.'

Adebayo looked like he would very happily choose to be foolish, but he kissed his wife's hand tenderly instead and smiled at me.

'A wise man listens to his wife.'

'And a wise woman loves her husband,' she said as she kissed his hand in return.

I cleared my throat. 'If it helps, it's not terribly exciting. It's just basically a white wall. And when you step through it, it just makes you feel awful, so you really aren't missing anything at all.'

The couple looked at me in silence and then looked at each other, their shocked faces mirroring each other.

'Friend. Are you a quantum curator?' asked Adebayo with almost reverential awe. I was embarrassed; in trying to reassure him he wasn't missing anything, I had somehow elevated myself in their eyes. I hurried to downplay the situation. Momo again opened her handbag and this time pulled out a pencil.

'Can you sign our map?' she asked breathlessly.

I laughed. This wasn't the reaction I had been expecting, but it was a good one and I was happy to oblige even if I felt like an idiot. As soon as I had signed their map, they bowed towards me and having apologised for interrupting me they hurried away. What a story they would have to tell when they got home.

I was about to head to my apartment and see if any of the plants had survived when I noticed a lad out of the corner of my eye. Nothing about him was remarkable except that I had also seen him earlier in the day when I stepped off the felucca. He wasn't much past a teenager, still a bit self-conscious, limbs slightly awkward.

I made a display of limbering up and then started running. I headed towards the boardwalk, turning right and following the route back towards the heart of the city campus. As I got to a bench, I stopped for some lunges, carefully looking around. The stranger was no longer in sight. I laughed to myself. Subu was right, I was jumping at shadows. I got up and continued my run, taking the path out of the park and towards home. As I crossed the road, I saw him again. He had been waiting by an orange juice stand and had now slipped back into the shadows.

There's a Beta Earth saying that goes, 'Just because you're paranoid, doesn't mean they aren't out to get you.'

I jogged on a bit and then stopped to touch my toes. Whilst my hair obscured my face, I asked my brace if my location monitor was switched on and when it said it wasn't, I stretched out. Whoever was following me was of a decent standard. He had anticipated my direction rather than risk being spotted in the boardwalk's open location. He hadn't relied on following my brace, so he had skills. But he had two massive problems. The first was that he wasn't that good—I had spotted him twice—and secondly, he was on my patch. I had grown up here and trained here. I knew every alley and every back door. If he wanted to follow me, he was about to discover how woefully underprepared he was.

I set off on a light run towards the mouseion complex. I wanted to know a bit more about who this young man was. A trip to the art galleries would do the trick. Everyone entering the building was scanned. This was less to do with security and more to do with statistical retrieval, but no one got in without dinging the system. It would then be a simple matter of me dialling into the records and finding out who he was. The joy of public access databases. I upped my pace, but I did nothing to throw him off my tail. I needed to know who he was.

I came in via one of the quieter side doors and then had to drop to a walk. Quantum curators were tolerated in most things, but not taking a jogging circuit through a collection of Beta masterpieces. I made my way through the crowds passing by Titians and Raphaels. Large holograms were projected in front of the paintings, highlighting particular features, and it was impossible not to walk through someone's view. It was all very chaotic. I headed to a set of central benches in one of the larger galleries. This way my follower could conceal himself in the crowd and relax. Theoretically, he should have known I knew I was being followed, but who knew. I watched surreptitiously as he entered the room and then turned away. I dialled up the entry figures and found my own access timestamp, I then checked to see who had come in next. The records were empty. Whoever was following me was able to erase their movements from the database.

Either they were very clever, and so far there was little evidence of that, or they were working for someone powerful.

All my rage over Paul's betrayal and Clio's death came rushing up. Whoever had been responsible for Paul's actions was still active. I decided to confront my follower, draw him to somewhere quiet and find out who he worked for. If I had known what would happen next, I would have acted differently.

#8 – Neith

I was wearing my Beta security combats under my running clothes, and now I activated them. My robe adjusted itself as the armour stiffened underneath them, but as far as anyone could tell nothing had changed. When I had picked them up at the quantum department, I had decided to wear them rather than carry them. It looked like my instincts had been ahead of me. Now I stood up and briskly made my way out of the gallery. I noticed a kerfuffle as my follower was blocked by a group of annoyed tourists. Never get between a matron and her photo opportunity.

I started to move in earnest. I needed to get out of sight, where I could interrogate him without witnesses. According to my brace, the third avenue was closed for repairs. That should do nicely. The avenues were aerial glass corridors connecting the towers and minarets. We used to run along them as children trying to keep up with the birds. We were never at any risk as the safety barriers prevented anyone from falling.

Once I got to the building's exit, I started to run back towards the towers, knowing from the shouts behind me that he had broken cover and was actively pursuing me. Maybe his intention hadn't been to simply follow me? Maybe he was here to kill me? The idea was shocking, but someone had killed Clio in cold blood. I sped up. No wonder he didn't care if I spotted him. I tried to think what my chances were if I headed into the main mouseion plaza. The place would be heaving with tourists as well as staff. Would he risk it? Could I risk him hurting someone else? I was confident that I could outsmart any Alpha operative so the aerial platform it was.

As I got to the base of the tower, I realised I would have to use the stairs. The lift wouldn't stop on the third level. Wincing, I began to run. Six months of inactivity were making themselves known as my thighs began to burn and shake. I could hear him below, and I realised he was gaining on me. I cursed my arrogance and continued up. I burst out through the doorway and removed the warning signs that the walkway was closed, then I stepped out onto the avenue.

Thankfully, there was only a light breeze today. I could see the sides of the walkway flickering, the force field shorting in and out of action. Clearly, this was why this avenue was closed. A fall from this height would be fatal. I took a few steps out onto the walkway and flicked on my perception filter. I didn't want anyone to notice me and raise the alarm. The views from up here were spectacular. Looking down towards the harbour and the whole city campus, from the ancient lighthouse and back towards Lake Mareotis. Today though, my eyes were firmly fixed on the doorway that suddenly flew open.

The look of alarm on his face was priceless as he ran through the doorway. He had to pull himself short as he saw me standing just a few metres away. It told me everything I needed to know. He wasn't an assassin. He was an incompetent agent trying to follow me. No doubt he thought I had already run across the passageway and was hoping to lose him in the towers.

Now he had a problem, and it was clear from his face that he didn't know what to do. I spurred him into action as I held up my brace and captured a hologram of him.

'Who are you?' I asked. He was barely more than a kid. Maybe I could bluff him out of this.

'You shouldn't have done that,' he panted.

'What? Take an image of the person following me. I repeat. Who are you and who do you work for?'

Taking the photo was a mistake. He was agitated and I could see he was beginning to panic. He took a step towards me.

'Stop, the barriers are broken. Look.'

He paused but continued towards me. I took a step back as I saw him slip a knife out from his sleeve.

'Put the knife down. Stand still and I'll destroy the image.'

'How do I know you haven't already uploaded it?'

I hadn't and said so, but I could see he didn't believe me. I tried again. I flicked up the hologram of the brace and went to erase it. At the same time, he lunged at me and slipped. I grabbed at him and pulled him back from the side.

'Don't be an idiot. The barriers are broken.'

He tried to pull away from my grip, but now I couldn't let go of him. If I did, his momentum would throw him towards the rails.

'I can't fail.'

'You don't have to fail. Just walk away. I'll delete your photo. We can act like nothing has happened.'

He struggled some more, but now I had his arm up behind his back.

'I don't believe you.'

'On my honour as a quantum curator.' I wondered what else I could say to reassure him but realised he had gone still. I let go of his arm and took a step away from him.

He turned to face me and stepped back. We were now about three metres apart, out towards the middle of the avenue.

'Mind the edge!'

His inexperience and nervousness were making him forgetful. I needed to calm things down as fast as possible. He stopped, his eyes wide as he realised he had been about to lean on the rails.

'I'm going to walk away now,' I said, not taking my eyes off him. 'I've already deleted the photo. Now we just pretend this never happened.'

'Give me your wrist brace.'

I shook my head. 'Not going to happen. This is a quantum wrist brace. We don't hand these over. I'm going to leave, but on my word, I have deleted your image.'

He nodded and wiped the sweat off his face as he tried to recover his breath.

'Okay then,' he panted. Relieved that I had defused the situation, I relaxed and made a critical mistake. I turned my back on him.

I heard his feet on the walkway as he charged towards me. I don't know why he did, or why he was so driven. All I knew was that I had turned my back on a desperate youngster with a knife in his hand. As I judged his pace, I ducked at the last second, and he tripped over me and flew forwards, smashing through the barrier and plunging over the side. I lunged out towards him, but my hand grasped at thin air.

Shocked, I watched as he fell screaming and then hit the marble floor of a small, pleasant concourse. People had already been alerted to his fall by his screams and had started to converge around him.

I ran back into the stairwell and jumped over the bannister. The suit broke my fall and then I legged it out of the tower, switching off my perception field as I headed towards the concourse.

'Move!' I shouted at the gathering crowd. 'Call the custodians and medics.'

There was a lot of blood, but his eyes still flickered in confusion.

'I'm sorry. That wasn't meant to happen. Hang on in there. The medics will be able to restore you. Hang on.' I was blabbering trying to get him to hang on. Around me, people were screaming and crying. Such violent acts were incredibly rare. To witness one was unheard of, especially involving such a young person.

He gripped my hand and tried to speak. I leant closer as his voice bubbled through the blood.

'Not your fault. Mine.'

His face twisted and he coughed up more blood.

He tried again. 'Death to the angels.' His head lolled to one side and his hand fell limp. I had seen enough dead bodies to know that the medics wouldn't be restoring this one. I slipped into the crowd and walked back to my apartment.

interlude 2

The following text conversation was retrieved, during a sweep of the ghost files of the Q Zone security system. It has been added to the evidence report for Case No: 234530/H. The sender is yet to be identified.

- I was slightly distressed to discover that when I suggested you keep a quiet eye on Salah, you chose to dispatch a total idiot to follow her who only succeeded in alerting her to your surveillance.

- She'd have recognised anyone with a skill set to match her own.

- Why were you even following her?

- You said to.

- I said to keep an eye on her. Surreptitiously. Check her e-mails, see who she met. Not play peek-a-boo. Now, on her first day back, she knows that someone is watching her. Did his brace catch what he said at the end?

- No. I suspect she had her hand over his recorder.

- Of course she did.

- Do we let people know she was present? Maybe start up a whispering campaign against her that she's unlucky?

- We're not superstitious Betas. Neith Salah is a hero, and any attempt to vilify her will backfire on us. This really is tedious. I am going to have to justify your actions to my colleagues, having just convinced them all to leave you in place following the Fabergé fiasco.

- And I am very grateful for your support. I promise you nothing like this will occur again. I have someone watching Julius, and he is utterly unaware of that fact.

- Is he still meeting with QC Ramin Gamal?

- Yes.

- That is annoying, and now that Neith knows she is being watched, she's going to become a problem. Okay, we will have to wait until the time is right. I think we now need to dispose of all three of them. For now, please don't do anything else that I am going to have to cover up, or I'll be disposing of you as well.

#9 – Julius

I woke up with a start. The cotton sheets were soaked with sweat and tangled around my legs. Another forgotten nightmare. My nightmares were fewer now, but they hadn't left me yet and I wasn't looking forward to today. I wasn't sleeping well at the best of times; I couldn't sleep in the heat, I couldn't sleep in the air conditioning. At my weekly check-up, the doctor kept mentioning that my brainwave functions were sub-par. I don't think he meant to be insulting. He prescribed something to help me sleep, but it made me feel very disconnected, which in turn set off a panic attack. I was already feeling pretty bloody disconnected. I didn't need any artificial help with that.

Getting out of bed, I headed to the shower cubicle. I'd smiled when they first showed me my student dorm. Everything was state-of-the-art, no nailed down rug over centuries-old oak floorboards, splintered and dusty with woodworm. One entire wall was a white screen for the projection of holograms and I remembered my old pinboard that had been propped up with a brick back in my Cambridge halls. I also had a self-catering pod, so no need to hang a plastic bag out of the window to try to keep my food cold. Now I had everything stored in perfect ambient zones though, despite our little kitchen pods, we would mostly congregate in the large open dining plazas.

I also had my own en-suite shower room and loo, but my dorm rep had been shocked when I asked about a bath. They're not big on individual baths here, everyone shares large public baths. They are mixed sex and naked. I have become a fan of showers.

Stepping out, chilled and refreshed, I gathered my kit together and headed to a shaded spot under a date tree to have breakfast. Stef joined me as we tucked into hummus and olive oil, some salted tomatoes and a hard-boiled egg. At first, this breakfast had seemed bizarre to me, but now it was my favourite meal. There was a small breeze coming in off the sea and it was making the heat tolerable. I knew that by ten, the breeze would have dropped, and the waves of heat would engulf me again in sweat and exhaustion.

My phone buzzed and I saw a text from Rami.

Usual Spot 7 pm.

I smiled. Finally, something to look forward to. Thursday was a solid maths and science day, and I was so far behind the rest of the class I was practically sitting in the corner with a cone on my head.

Eventually, a breeze and faint chimes played through the rooms, signalling the end of the teaching day. Some students sighed regretfully, and I was genuinely pleased that they loved what they were studying so much. I just wished I had that level of enthusiasm for maths and science.

I placed my tablet into my bag and beat a hasty retreat before my tutor held me back to discuss my utter inadequacies. I headed off towards Lake Mareotis. I would need to run if I was to get there by seven, but that was probably the point. It would be no doubt classed as a warm-up exercise. Six months ago, this would have killed me. Now it was something I enjoyed doing, especially as the heat of the day had receded. I ran along the footpath, lizards scuttling along the sandy kerbs ahead of me and off into the rough grass and succulents lining the edge. As I left the buildings, the sounds moved from those of a busy cityscape to the evening cries of frogs and crickets. A breeze was blowing through the irrigated wheat field, and I watched as the crop waved like ripples on the water. This was not an Egypt teetering on the brink of desertification, the Great Saharan plain was far to the west and the neighbouring countries remained fertile through centuries of clever land management. During decades of low rainfall, they simply changed their crop production. Early Nabatean technology for moving water around deserts had been developed and improved. On my home earth, the Nabateans had been relegated to ancient technology. Here, they were the pre-eminent global hydro engineers. Looking at the cornfields, I remembered that my Norfolk was said to have less annual rainfall than many desert states and was termed as being in constant drought. But you would never know it as you sailed on the Broads or walked under oak trees alongside wheat fields.

A glint of light ahead of me said I had arrived at the lake sooner than I expected. I was getting a little faster and a little stronger every week.

As I got to the lake's edge I was alone. I threw my shirt and satchel on the ground and ran into the water, diving under the surface and then swimming out to a sandbank. The sun was casting long shadows, and I enjoyed the breeze drifting in off the lake.

'Watch out for flesh-eating crocodiles,' shouted a voice from the bank and I laughed at Rami.

'You're never going to tire of that, are you?'

When I had first arrived, I was somewhat concerned by the number of people bathing in the waters. This had caused initial indulgent amusement at my expense. I don't know, maybe they thought people from my earth didn't swim or something? When I stressed my concern was more to do with crocodiles, they sniggered and some just roared with laughter. The idea, apparently, was so preposterous that they thought I was "adorable" and "precious". I thought they were smug arses. That was pretty much a daily occurrence for the first few months. After that, I just kept quiet and watched. The thing with the crocodiles was that they had been relocated and tagged, and then baffles were placed downstream to prevent incursions into the population centres. There were central channels in the river that the crocs could use, but I tried not to think about those. Something like the Australian shark nets, I supposed, although I was never certain how they worked either. I had no intention of travelling to Australia and even less of swimming in water that may or may not have a great white in it. But that was on my earth, and here I was on theirs and it was boiling, and no one who had been swimming in a safe zone had been attacked by a crocodile in the past fifty years. So, I had gingerly entered the water, having first secured bathing trunks.

Now I loved being in the water. By the end of each day, I was gritty and sweaty, and I loved the feel of the cool water washing me clean. I was finally beginning to really appreciate some of the early religious cleaning rituals and ablution ceremonies. I had considered writing a short thesis proposal and then realised that I had no one to submit it to.

'Hey! Stop loafing and get back over here. See how far you can manage underwater.'

More training. I grinned. I looked forward to boasting about how long I could hold my breath on the Titanic before I died, and I walked back into the water. Running in would place an additional burden on my lungs. See, I was learning. I broke the surface about halfway across, definitely an improvement, but I couldn't see any approval on his face as he was standing in front of the sun. I walked out, pleased as ever to see the only person who had kept me sane during these past six months.

'You're improving, although I heard you screwed up the Titanic scenario.'

Damn. I was hoping to lead with that as evidence of improvement. Not evidence of failure.

'The thing is, Rami. If we ignore the death bit I was actually doing pretty well. And I haven't died since then.'

'You took forty-five minutes.'

'Yes, but I had to look around.'

'Why? Why did you have to look around? How many times are you told that time is a variable?'

This was exactly what my instructors kept saying, and they weren't wrong. The more time you spent in a timestream the more chance there was of things going wrong. It was the standard butterfly effect.

Rami continued whilst I re-evaluated my performance. 'The fastest that simulation had been done in is three minutes.'

'Three minutes!' I was stunned. That was ridiculous. 'No one can do it that quickly. I mean, the family would have still been in the stateroom.'

'So what?' he chided. 'Who were they going to tell? None of them survived the sinking. Our curator knocked on the door. When it was opened, they threw in a stun bang, stepped over the unconscious bodies, opened the safe, removed the book, closed the door and left. As the occupants regained their senses, the boat hadn't even struck the iceberg. That was a textbook retrieval.'

Yes, an extraction where no one had been hurt and no one was aware of the theft was pretty perfect.

'I suppose that was you, was it?' I said with a weary sigh. Rami was an excellent curator by all accounts, his recent situation excepting.

'No, I took five minutes. That record belongs to Neith.'

Her name fell heavily between us.

'Have you heard from her?' I asked, but Rami snorted.

'You are more likely to hear from her than me. Don't forget I'm a traitor in her eyes. A murderer. A…?'

I watched as his face twisted in pain and I felt guilty for asking. I hadn't brought her name up in the past month and I was distraught to see I was the source of this fresh pain.

'Right. Enough of her then. Ask me a question.'

After Neith had left to nurse her guilt and grief, QC Ramin Gamal had got in touch. He wondered how I was doing, and did I need a hand with anything? It was that call that saved me. We would meet up after class and run through the day. In the beginning, he just helped provide a small sane bubble. None of my classmates had ever actually visited my earth and spent most of the day casting me surreptitious glances.

It was tedious; only Rami treated me like a human being. After a few weeks, he began to help me with my training. The academic lessons were easy, well some of them. But the physical training sessions were an effort. Turns out that spending years playing Assassin's Creed was not an actual substitute for really jumping from roof to roof. I have to say, their infirmary here is first rate. If they had a loyalty card, I'd be on my hundredth free cup of coffee by now. For the record, their coffee is also excellent.

On top of all that, I was lonely. Having no one to socialise with meant I could devote more time to my studies, but it did make Jack a dull boy. That was the other reason I appreciated Rami's company so much. We were the same age and had a similar sense of humour. I think he was also lonely. His boyfriend had very politely walked away after they placed Rami on sand leave. It was depressing to see the two worlds over that some people won't stand by you when times get tough.

We would chat about our favourite books and TV shows. It seems he consumed more than me and was disappointed when I couldn't explain the deeper meaning behind The Archers, but we both loved reading the same sorts of books—all Beta stuff, naturally. I had watched and read some Alpha stuff, but it was dire. One day I took a day trip to Cairo and went to visit some of the art galleries, but they just missed a certain something. I'm not an art historian and I couldn't tell you exactly what was missing, only that something was. I mooched around the temples, which were in gorgeous condition, and then returned to Alexandria. After that, I stuck to the art department of the mouseion which displayed Beta exhibits only, and they were glorious. Rembrandts, Goyas, Hanchens, Dürers, the finest collection of art in the world, though surprisingly there was nothing by da Vinci. No doubt the great man's stuff didn't get lost.

Clearly I was drifting off because I was hit in the face as Rami threw a towel at me and so the tests began. He would shout questions out at me, as we ran spot runs, did press-ups, one-handed no less, climbed trees, and jumped down from the branches.

'How old was Napoleon when…?'

'Who was on the throne in Thailand when the Boxer Rebellion broke out…?'

Happily, I dodged the trick question. It was important to know broad local knowledge, not just detailed stuff. I raced him to the rocky outcrop, shouting out the answer. I hoped I had bought some time, but he was straight in with the next set of questions.

'What is the currency in New Zealand?'

'What is the best way to store vellum?'

'How much stun gas is required to disable a room twelve foot by twenty foot, with two people in the room?'

I paused. 'Any animals?' and was rewarded with a big smile.

'Four guard dogs.'

I replied and smiled without waiting for Rami to tell me I was right.

Rami stopped doing press-ups and waved at me to stop, I wheezed in gratitude. I'd got fitter, but guessed that he could carry on doing press-ups through the night if he felt like it. He tossed me a bottle of beer and I gratefully prised off the cap and glugged it down. It was a ridiculously small thing to take pride in, but I'd never managed to open a beer bottle with just my hands before.

Rami took a swig with a satisfying gasp and then looked at me. 'Any idea who you will be paired up with if you pass?'

Neophytes were normally paired up for their probationary year and assigned a mentor to oversee their field training. Sometimes, when there were uneven numbers, or a neophyte that required one-on-one attention, they would work alone with their mentor.

'I'd like it to be Stef. He's quick in drills and has a good eye for details. Plus, he's looked out for me ever since I arrived. Unlike Sabrina.'

'Sabrina?'

'She's the one I was telling you about the other week.'

'Ah, the overachiever? Yes, well, that's who I would pair you with.'

I spluttered in alarm. Spending a year with her as my partner filled me with dread.

'But she'd always be critical of me. Nothing I did would be good enough.'

'You'd raise your game. Sounds like you and Stef are too well matched. Plus, it would only be for the year. Neophyte partnerships don't always continue into full curator status. Mine didn't.'

I took another glug of beer and wondered just how I was going to manage it but decided that was a problem for tomorrow. This evening I'd just enjoy the company of a friend and listen to the cicadas as the shadows lengthened, and the night creatures began to stir in the fading warmth.

If I had known that someone was deciding whether to kill me or not, I may have been more alert.

#10 – Julius

'Blue, help us out with something?'

My heart sank. Today we were doing our final step exercise. It was a group retrieval, in teams of four. We had done lots of these to see how we managed in teams and who worked well together. Today was special, today we were doing a simulated retrieval in the Library of Alexandria as the Romans set fire to it. Obviously, we could never visit it for real as the two earths didn't split until afterwards, but it was a way of signing off our course.

I had just entered the staging room where Stef, Sabrina and Jack were waiting for me. From the looks on their faces, I knew this was going to be some stupid Beta culture question. No matter how hard they tried to understand our movies and TV, they just couldn't quite get a grip on the fact that they were all pretty much a fantastical portrayal of our world. Not an accurate description of reality.

'If The Archers had to go and rescue the hostages in the Nakatomi Plaza who would be their lead warrior?' asked Stef.

See? I just didn't know where to begin. I mean, I could see Eddie Grundy in a vest, but that was as far as it went. I tried to reply, thinking that Lynda's Nativity might be a bit spicier than normal. Then decided against it. Now was not the time to discuss whether or not Die Hard was a Christmas movie.

Happily, I was saved from trying to explain once again that The Archers wasn't real, as Hu arrived and told us our exercise would begin in five minutes. This was ten minutes shorter than the customary fifteen-minute staging and caught all of us on the hop.

'Okay. Team up,' began Sabrina. 'We work as a four, but if we need to split up; Blue, you're with me. Jack, Stef, you happy with that?'

Both guys nodded, but I looked at Jack's face. He seemed nervous, and Stef tended to be overly boisterous. I didn't think they were a good fit. At least not today. I knew Sabrina was doing this because she viewed me as the weakest link and she was the strongest, but today I didn't agree with her assessment.

'I'd like to partner with Jack. I think we worked well together on a previous step, but I'd like to improve on some of my issues. I think Jack can help me.'

Sabrina looked at Jack who shrugged, but I think she saw what I did and agreed.

'Okay. Stef, you're with me?'

Stef whooped and gave her a high five salute, 'Dream team, baby! Now let's go kick some Roman backsides.'

I rolled my eyes at Jack, who grinned as Sabrina and Stef high-fived each other. The four of us walked into the holo suite as a voice on the tannoy counted us down.

'Five, Four, Three, Two, One.'

For a second I was startled and confused. This was the most realistic simulation yet. I was standing in a stone passageway; the smell of smoke was pervasive, and my eyes were watering. In the distance, I could hear screaming. Doubtless, the university saved their hardest step for last, and it was certainly disorienting. I could see the others, but they looked equally unsettled.

'Team! Group up.' I ran over to them, giving each of them a shake. There was a room behind Jack, the door was open, and nobody was inside, I pulled them all in.

'Come on, Sabrina, snap to. Use your eyedrops.' Quickly chivvying them along I got them all to focus and clear their eyes and, with a shake of their heads, I could see that they were all adjusting. Although Jack seemed very twitchy.

'Is this real?' asked Sabrina. 'Are we on Beta? Everything seems more vivid.'

I shook my head. I couldn't explain it, but I knew this was still just a synthetic version of my planet.

'No. Check your brace.'

With embarrassed grins, Sabrina and the others looked at their braces and relaxed.

Jack laughed. 'For a minute there, I thought we had actually been sent over. This is one hell of a simulation.'

Sabrina took a deep breath. 'Okay, not the best start, but we can only improve. We each have to get a wax tablet and return. Anyone whose tablet melts loses their team marks. Blue?'

'Yes, Sabrina?' I asked innocently. I knew her last comment had been a warning to me not to screw up. She looked at me but decided to let it go.

'According to our briefing notes, we are likely to encounter Romans. We are encouraged to avoid direct contact. They are wild savages and will attack without warning. Their goal will be to kill us and anyone else that tries to stop them burning down the library.'

This was part of the briefing that I didn't quite understand. As far as I could see the fire had started by accident, and any soldiers still in the building were either trying to put the flames out or fleeing from the fire. This portrayal of savage vandals seemed at odds with what I had learnt about this incident.

'This is a short exercise. Fifteen minutes and we're out. Agreed?'

We all nodded at Sabrina as she led us out of the room and along the corridor. Jack and I followed, and Stef covered the rear. I looked back at him and grinned. The guy was in his element. God help any Roman that ran into him.

According to the braces, we were heading towards one of the main archives. There was screaming ahead, and I was beginning to feel deeply unsettled. Why was there so much screaming? A woman ran down the corridor towards us. Her gown was torn and covered in blood, the top half had been ripped off and she was naked from the waist up. As she ran towards us she made no attempt to cover herself; in her terror, I wasn't even sure if she was aware. There was blood running from a wound on her scalp and her ear was bleeding from where someone had torn out an earring. She ran straight past the three of us and flung herself at Stef.

'Save me! Great Ra, protect me!' She started sobbing incoherently.

Stef pulled her towards him and told her she was safe now. Sabrina shouted back at him that she was a simulation, and to point her towards the exit.

We moved forward, disconcerted. There had been no mention of civilians in the briefing notes. And from what I could remember of my history, I couldn't work out why there would be a woman in here at night. Maybe a librarian's wife?

The noise of the fire could now be heard beyond the screams, and we could also hear the shouts and laughter of soldiers. We edged toward the end of the corridor where a heavy door was hanging off its hinges.

'Everyone get your guns out,' ordered Sabrina. 'Immediate incapacitation and shoot first. This sounds ugly.'

We quickly slipped into the room, but at first, no one noticed us. It was a scene from hell. The room was the size of the grand hall in the National History Museum in London, but that building had never seen such devastation. The room was full of citizens being attacked by Romans. The shelves of books and scrolls crackled in the flames behind them.

We watched in horror as a soldier dragged a baby out of its mother's arms and drew back his sword. Sabrina fired her gun at him but nothing happened, and the soldier finished his action. Jack vomited. The soldier now advanced on the woman and the three of us fired our guns at him. Again, nothing happened.

'Why aren't the guns working?'

'A glitch?' shouted Stef.

Sabrina shook her head. 'No, most likely this is a test. Right, ignore this room, it's a diversion. The wax tablets are located further along. With me.'

She and Stef immediately left the room, but I saw that Jack was still transfixed by the unfolding horrors. He had now slid down the wall with his head tucked into his knees and his hands over his ears. I ran over to him.

'Jack. It's not real. This is fake. This is just a bloody clever illusion.'

Behind me, I could hear the roar of fire and a man screamed in pain as the flames caught him.

'This isn't real,' I repeated, trying to shake the teenager out of his terror. Someone lunged towards me and I flinched, ready to protect Jack as he rocked back and forth.

'Blue. What the fuck are you doing?' shouted Stef. 'Get out of here.'

'Jack's frozen. I'm staying with him.'

'That's not the mission.'

'Sod the mission. Jack's more important.'

'No, he's not, Blue,' insisted Stef. 'The mission is more important.'

I turned and glared at Stef. Now wasn't the time to fall out, but how could he not see the distress that our young friend was in? I watched as Sabrina ran back into the room. A soldier tried to stop her, but she simply grabbed his arm, pulled him towards her, then flung him over her hip. As he fell, she grabbed his sword and plunged it into his throat. Pulling it out, she sprinted over to where we were huddled down by Jack.

'What's going on? Why the hell are you all still in here?'

'Jack's bugged out and Blue won't leave him.'

I could see she was conflicted. 'But the mission?'

'Sabrina, look at him. This is torturing him. Are you really prepared to put a training exercise before his mental health?'

I knew she agreed with me and was about to say so when Stef tried again. 'We don't treat these as training missions, Blue. We treat them as real events. That's what this is all about.'

'And in a real event, you would leave your partner behind?' I asked incredulously.

'That's the mission. That's what we do. We Preserve.'

'Bollocks. We preserve *life* where I come from.'

'Don't make me laugh,' spat Stef. He had stood up now and was pacing back and forth. 'You lot spend all your time killing each other.'

This was getting us nowhere, and Jack was beginning to moan as a baby started to wail.

'That's it. I'm out,' I said.

Sabrina nodded. 'I agree. This is a team decision. Blue, step back with Jack. Stef, you're with me, we'll pick up four tablets. Now go.'

I hit Jack's brace, then my own, and we were back in the holosuite. Sabrina and Stef were still moving to one side of us and I dragged Jack to the exit where he was quickly helped by medics. Hu came over to me looking grave but he shook my hand and told me to wait for the others in the changing room.

#11 – Julius

Jack had been given a restorative and Hu told us that as a team we had passed. He didn't give us any feedback on our individual performances, but we were just grateful for the pass. Stef and Sabrina said they were going to the pub and insisted we all celebrate together. Stef seemed uncomfortable by our falling out, and I was eager to put it behind us. Jack was particularly bouncy, and I wondered what they had put in his restorative. Whatever it was, I was glad that it helped.

'Did that scene with the Romans strike any of you as odd?'

They looked at me, gave disinterested shrugs, and continued getting dressed. I tried again.

'I mean, did the Romans really act that way? And why were there so many women and children in the library? Who were they?'

Again, the other three just looked at me. Finally, Sabrina replied as she zipped up her sports bag.

'The Romans were monsters, Blue. Everyone knows that; it's just a bit shocking to see it first-hand.' She paused and straightened up. 'Look, I'm sorry it must have been tough for you to see what your earth is based on but I'm just very thankful that mine took a different path. Yallah. Let's head over to the pub, have a drink and celebrate our final exercise.'

Jack and Stef both agreed fervently, and I realised that none of them was prepared to engage in discussing what they had witnessed.

Turning down the offer of a lift, I said I would meet them there and walked instead. I needed to clear my head. Something about that Roman scene stank. I know indoctrination when I see it, and this time I'd witnessed it upfront and personal.

The Romans had been portrayed as animalistic. Their brutality was over the top, and whilst I wasn't going to pretend that Roman soldiers were pussy cats, I was pretty certain they hadn't acted like that during the Alexandrian fire. It had been so blatant. Library good. Romans bad. They'd even chucked a naked woman at Stef to puff up his ego. Protect me, protect me. Ugh. Honestly, it was all a bit embarrassing, but I realised that I was the only person who saw it that way. For the other three, it solidified their previously low opinions of the Romans, and I suppose everything that the Western Beta Earth was founded on.

A flock of parrots swept past me, and I treasured the flash of colours as they flew from tree to tree. It shook me out of my low spirits as their calls mingled with the shouts from the agents offering tours of the mouseion grounds and vendors selling hot food and cold water. It was a busy and colourful city, the heat of the day now dissipated as evening fell. People were leaving work and chatting to friends as they strolled along the streets.

I headed to The Last Bar, which appropriately enough sat on the far end of the harbour wall. The views over the Mediterranean were glorious, and it was one of the few locations where I could pretend that I was still at home. As I watched the waves roll in and listened to the clink of the yachts and feluccas in the marina behind me, I could pretend I was on holiday.

I walked into the bar, and a big shout went up as my class saw me arrive.

'Blue! Blue! Blue!' I smiled self-consciously and headed towards the long table. Jack was clearly not the only cadet to have received a restorative.

Not everyone here was going to be a quantum curator. Three-quarters of this table would head off to other departments: conservation, cataloguing, security, medicine, research, science, engineers. All for the greater good of the quantum step and society at large.

Jack was leaning forward, his hand around the neck of a bottle, when Diane, almost certainly destined for the medic corps, called out, admonishing him for being too young to drink.

He took a quick glug and placed the bottle back on the table, looking over at Diane innocently. 'Sorry, what did you say?'

'Jack, that's a code violation.'

He grinned at her. 'I was accepting a gift. My good manners made me forget myself.'

Diane glared and beckoned a waiter over to remove the offending bottle.

'Waste not, want not,' I said and picked up the bottle before the waiter took it, and started to drink from it.

Stef roared with laughter, and Jack looked on admiringly. Sabrina muttered under her breath that I was a dick, and Diane looked alarmed at my lack of hygiene protocols. They weren't wrong. Honestly, this place was bringing out the worst in me. Maybe it was part of my splice with Neith.

I tried to change the conversation and congratulated Sabrina on a great quantum session the day before. I was reluctant to bring up our last session and I noticed that no one else was talking about the Romans either. It was still too raw.

Mollified, she conceded she had performed with great skill and accuracy and the tension at the table eased as some of Sabrina's acolytes began to unwind.

'You did pretty well yourself in yesterday's defence and attack class,' said Sabrina to me. It was a kind gesture from her, given my appalling performance today, and I was pleased to let bygones be bygones.

'He can hardly claim any credit for that, it's almost cheating,' said a voice, jeering from the other end of the group.

A silence fell along the table, and I placed my hand on Stef's forearm, but surprisingly it was Sabrina that came to my defence.

'Bollocks, Diane,' challenged Sabrina. 'When you use a neural download to pick up a new language that's not considered cheating, is it?'

'That's not the same thing at all.'

'No, it's not, that's even easier. Blue's splice with QC Salah meant that he got fragments, and fragments imported into a body that didn't have the muscles to make use of it. He's had to train harder and faster than any of us to make use of those splices.'

She wasn't wrong, I was just surprised that she had noticed. Since Neith and I had stepped through the quantum field together, some of our memories and knowledge had become muddled. Nothing appeared lost from our own memories, but we had gained knowledge, habits, and thoughts from each other. Apparently, they would calm down, as all memories do when not used, but it wasn't an exact science. It did however mean that I had a mind that knew exactly how to deliver a heel round flying kick, but a body that fell over when I actually attempted it.

My trainers kept telling me to slow down, but I couldn't. I only "knew" how to do it quickly. The only solution was to make my body faster and stronger, and eventually, I was flying through the lessons. I could strip a gun down in five seconds if I closed my eyes. If I looked at it, half of my brain freaked and blocked the part that was trying to operate my hands.

I raised my bottle to acknowledge Sabrina's compliment, if that's what it was, and she continued.

'QC Salah went to considerable risk to bring Cadet Strathclyde back through. He didn't ask for it. He was pivotal in saving the Fabergé egg and in return he lost his whole world. If you think he somehow cheated, then you don't deserve to be working for the Mouseion of Alexandria and you don't deserve a place at this table.'

A second silence fell over the table as Sabrina stared at her, until Diane awkwardly stepped back from the long bench and grabbing her tote bag, stormed out of the bar.

The tension was uncomfortable, and I tried to change the mood of the room. 'Look, we're all jumpy this close to end of term exams. Let's just relax. I'll buy the next drink for anyone who can tell me exactly how many times I've died so far.'

With a united roar of "thirty-two" I winced and wondered just how far my credits would get me.

The atmosphere finally began to unwind and, yawning, I pleaded a headache and headed back outdoors. The sun had sunk into the Med, leaving a faint orange glow on the far horizon, and the water was lapping soporifically along the harbour wall. It was almost a little too perfect. There was a storm coming, I just didn't know when it would break.

#12 – Neith

Okay, girl. Deep breath. I looked in the mirror, bothered that the face that looked back at me seemed calm and composed.

Last week a man had died in my arms. Someone was having me followed, and I had no idea who they were. I didn't know who to talk to about it. News reports had mentioned a tragic accident and left it at that. The man was supposedly one of the city cleaners, which I knew was ridiculous. Someone was going to great lengths to cover this up.

And, despite all that, I still had to go back to work and pretend that nothing had happened. I didn't know how I felt about today, beyond terrified. Time to buckle up and face my demons. The public saw me as a hero. I saw myself as a failure. I had no idea how my colleagues saw me, as I'd been avoiding them.

Curators get damaged, die, disappear. That's the nature of the job as far as most people are concerned. During the Fabergé mission, we had successfully saved a priceless treasure, so it was a success. But would other curators see my mission in the same light as the public? I certainly didn't. I had been duped by Paul, and it had cost Clio her life. Paul died a traitor, Clio died a hero, and Ramin survived as... I paused, what exactly had Ramin's role been in that shitshow of a mission?

I lathered up a flannel, scrubbed my face and gave myself one last look in the mirror. There's lovely, I thought, and paused. There was nothing lovely about what I saw, and I wondered why I'd thought it. I headed out the door. Today people had better get out of my way. Today, Neith Salah was back in business.

I walked into the central briefing room and nodded to some of my colleagues but didn't go over and chat. What was the point? It would either be fake platitudes or prurient questioning. I'd had enough of both over the past six months. Nothing could bring back Clio, and I could never forgive myself that Paul had evaded proper justice. All of that was my fault, and I just had to learn to live with it.

A few weeks ago, however, I had received my next assignment. Apparently, it was time to get back in the field. At first, I have to confess I was excited and then nervous. The chancellor himself had said he had a special mission for me, and I was flattered until I found out the nature of my special assignment.

I was going to be a "neophyte quantum curator mentor". A sodding wet nurse. Me! Well, that put me in my place. From one of the leading quantum curators to a bloody nanny. Not that I was dismissing nannies—well, I was—but at this stage, I was so cross, I wasn't being fair. But what a total waste of resources. I was the worst person for the job, I knew it, and probably everyone else knew that right now. In one mission I had lost two team members and had harboured a traitor. It was the single biggest scandal on record. My head was not in a calm, nurturing mindset. My mindset tended more to the cataclysmic rage and self-loathing, shouting in pubs, vomiting in gutters, walking out into the wilderness to sleep under the stars for days. I was not someone I would consider a safe pair of hands for a new recruit.

Looking around the room I noticed Sam watching me, and as our eyes met he smiled and nodded. As my boss, I should have acknowledged him, but I simply stared at him and then continued to look around, glaring at anyone else that tried to make contact. I was done with pity and done with recriminations. I was on my own and a new Neith Salah. They could all get used to the new version.

Still, the assignment had said that they had a cadet that would benefit from my unique perspective, and if that didn't sound like blatant flattery then I don't know what did. Was there a bigger screw-up out there than me? And a single neophyte, not a pair. Clearly, this was one messed-up individual if they didn't trust them with a partner yet.

The volume rose around me and I realised we were going through to the neophytes' lecture hall. I remembered my first assignment with Clio. We had stood there quietly, full of terrified pride, desperate not to giggle or jump around. I think we'd have held hands, but our palms were so sweaty that neither wanted the other to know how nervous we were. Like the other neos, we stood whilst the senior QCs entered the room and then pairs were allocated to a named handler.

Clio and I got an old guy called Ben. We looked at his age, at least fifty by our reckoning, and decided that we could run rings round him. We would be the first to lose our trainee status and be fully graduated curators. Our names would go on the roster as the fastest pair to ever be promoted. People would nudge each other as we walked past, full of respect and admiration.

Ben was perfect for us. He was slow, kind, calm and took not one ounce of bullshit. How quickly he punctured our ridiculous daydreams. He would drive us nuts, abandoning missions, returning us all back through the stepper every time we made a transgression. At the beginning, our failure rate was abysmal. Mortifying in fact, but gradually I relaxed into it and began to assimilate better. Clio began to relax and assimilate less. Great Ra, if there was a street fight or an opportunity she would go in swinging. Bast, even when there wasn't an opportunity, she would go in fists first. I, on the other hand, would stand back, assessing, evaluating and monitoring. Basically, failing to interact in case I disrupted the timeline and shattered the entire fabric of space and time.

Through Ben's tutelage, we eventually settled down and whilst we weren't the fastest to ever graduate—hell, we weren't even the first in our cohort to graduate—we did eventually become one of the top Alpha teams, with an almost perfect record of retrievals.

Wiping the smile off my face, I followed the other curators into the assembly rooms. Whoever my neophyte was, I didn't think they were going to enjoy the experience. I wasn't here to make friends or babysit anyone. I was here to prove my worth as a quantum curator and, if I had to start from the very beginning, I would do it for Clio and remind everyone of how great we once were. I looked across at the latest set of neophytes. All standing prim and proper, waiting with dutiful expectation. Silent and respectful.

'NEITH!'

A neophyte stepped forward and ran towards me, picking me up in a massive hug and swinging me around. As he put me down, I looked up at the blue, brown eyes of Julius Strathclyde and felt tears form in my eyes. The evidence of my greatest failure was standing right in front of me.

'Fuck no. No fucking way.'

I turned and walked out of the room as fast as I could without actually running, I headed through the reception and as I got to the corridor, I was sprinting down the hall towards the exit when a voice rang out behind me.

'Quantum Curator Salah. My office now. Or consider yourself fired!'

I came to a halt, not turning round. I could continue to walk out the door, but then what? What was I if I wasn't a QC? I could work as a curator or a bodyguard, and could probably name my price. God knows I'd had enough offers over the past few months, but then I would never go through the stepper again. And that was one loss too many.

Turning, I saw the corridor was empty. Sam hadn't even waited to see if he would be obeyed. I wiped my face and headed towards his office. As I entered I saw he was already sat behind his desk and Julius was seated to the side. This time he wasn't smiling. He looked healthier than I remembered, his skin was tanned, and his dark wavy hair seemed glossier in the sunlight, he had also bulked up a bit. Which was hardly surprising, given the fitness requirements for a QC. He must have been working so hard.

'Sir, respectfully, does he need to be present? He might not like what I have to say.'

'I couldn't give a rat's arse. Respectfully. We are going to sort this out, right now, here in this room, and then that will be an end to it. When you leave this office, it will either be as a mentor or a civilian. Is that clear?' When I nodded he continued. 'Make all your objections now. Ask any questions and we will deal with it all, here and now. Proceed.'

I didn't want to do this in front of Julius, I didn't want to embarrass him, but he was clearly being used as some sort of token. A poster boy or something. But the risk to him and his partner was incredible.

'Is this a publicity stunt? How has he actually made it through training?'

Sam looked at me calmly before speaking. 'You're a smart person. Or at least you used to be. Why don't you try to answer that yourself? I'll help you. How do you think he did at Beta Current Affairs and Beta Social Customs?'

I paused. Obviously, he'd have aced them, and probably most of the historical modules as well. Oh, and the social customs. And of course, he was some sort of religious lecturer, so he'd have that covered. In fact, I couldn't think of any academic subject that he would have had problems with. Well, maybe science? Thinking about it, which was probably something I should have done before I opened my mouth, he was probably top of his class.

'What about physical combat? Weapons training? When we last met, he didn't even know to duck when the bullets were flying and when Clio kicked him in the gut, he just sat there looking like a winded football.'

I'd made my point with probably more flourish than was necessary, and I was disconcerted when Julius nodded his head in acknowledgement.

'May I?' he asked Sam, as he turned to me. 'It seems I had a few other splice issues when we stepped through together. I gained some muscle memory and some core drills from you. It turns out that I "knew" how to use all manner of weapons: swords, Glocks, crossbows. If you want me to point a weapon at someone and be effective, then it appears that I am your samurai.'

I was staggered. It hadn't occurred to me to investigate the level of splicing "gifts" I had received from Julius. After the sock folding and the strange verbal mannerisms, I had actively blocked any impulse that felt out of sorts. I decided to think about that later. They may even be a bonus, tidy! Ignoring Julius, I looked back at Sam.

'Can I see his assessments?'

Sam flicked up the holo-screen and we all watched as I scrolled through his attainments. He was impressive for someone that had only been in the system for six months but as Sam said, he did have a rather unique head start. I suddenly came to a halt as I was scrolling through.

'Thirty-two deaths? In a final year student? Cat's teeth, Sam, are you kidding? Thirty-two bloody deaths. And you think he's fit for active service? That would look bad on a novice report, but on someone who's about to graduate?'

The average for a final year cadet was ten. Mine had been none. Clio's had been one, but she blamed the trebuchet for being temperamental. Personally, I don't think hiding in the bucket was the smartest choice. I also don't think kicking it in annoyance had helped.

'The figure is high, but it has to be remembered that Julius has only been doing this for six months. He has had a remarkable learning curve. He hasn't just had to learn how to be a quantum curator, he has also had to learn how to be an Alpha citizen. Hell, Neith, seven months ago he wasn't even aware of alternate realities.'

'But thirty-two deaths!'

'Are you scared this may end in failure?' asked Julius.

'Of course, I'm not bloody scared.' I was terrified.

'Only, I'm scared. And excited. The idea that you were going to be my mentor was incredible. I was so worried that I was going to spoil it for another recruit. Or a different mentor but—'

'But I'm already spoilt, so what does it matter. Is that what you were going to say?'

'No, you stubborn mule, I was going to say—'

'NQC Strathclyde, you do not address a senior officer as a stubborn mule. Show the proper respect,' I barked.

'When you earn it,' he replied mildly.

'I earned it when you asked to join the quantum department.'

'And what else was I going to do? I didn't ask to be dragged into an alternate reality. This wasn't my choice, remember?'

'I was saving your life!'

'Thank you. But now you're acting like a spoilt brat.'

'ENOUGH!' roared Sam, and we both fell quiet. Julius was flushed under his tan and his face was set in hard angry planes, his eyes firmly locked on Sam. It was only as I looked at him now that I realised how angry he was. His words had been infuriatingly calm, and I had mistaken his emotions. 'QC Salah. Will you take on this assignment or not? We believe Strathclyde has the potential to be a valuable asset, and you were selected to ensure that potential is realised. If you feel incapable of doing it, I will take him on myself.'

That made me pause. Sam had been an incredible QC and still went out into the field every couple of months to keep his hand in. If he was prepared to devote the time to one-on-one mentoring of Julius, then the mouseion must have really wanted Julius to work out.

'Very well.' I turned to Julius. 'Meet me outside the gymnasium at five tomorrow morning.'

'He has passed all the required assessments,' said Sam.

'If I am to be his mentor, I need to see for myself what he is capable of. Also, can you send me the footage of all his deaths? I need to see what his weaknesses are.'

Sam agreed and then dismissed Julius, telling him to enjoy his graduation evening with his fellow cohort. Julius stood up and gave Sam the customary salute and then turned to me. Calling me ma'am, he saluted and never once made eye contact as he left the room, quietly closing the door behind him. I felt rebuked a thousand times over but could find no fault with a single action.

'What the hell is wrong with you, Neith?'

I looked back and saw that Sam had relaxed and was now making two cups of coffee.

'You've been impossible for the past six months and now you are acting like—what did Julius say?—"a stubborn mule". I like that phrase, by the way. That guy has worked so hard these past few months trying to adapt to this world, and I have never once heard him complain or make a single excuse. He is the epitome of the very highest standards that we look for in our cadets, whilst you have flounced around all across the desert holding pity parties wherever you went.'

'Have you been spying on me?' I was incensed. The truth of his words stung, and yet I still felt they were unjust.

'Of course I've been bloody spying on you. You were my finest officer until you decided to act like some bloody diva. I need you back in the game and I need someone to protect Julius.'

'Protect him? Sir, if he isn't up to the job…'

'Neith, he is a Beta. A Beta outperforming most Alphas. How well do you think that is going down? He needs protection from us, not from himself.'

This shocked me. No one would harm Julius. Why would they?

'Sir, is this to do with Paul? Because I've been thinking about that. I don't think he could have been working alone, I think—'

'Stop right there. I'm not interested in wild conspiracy theories, Neith. I just don't want some fearful citizen becoming resentful of Julius' presence. I need you to help him adapt and settle in. We thought you would be the best person to help him with that. Whilst he has been in an academic environment, he has been shielding from the rest of the community. I know he'll still be working here, but gradually he will need to integrate into the community, and I don't want them unsettled by him.'

I took a deep breath and gave it one last shot.

'If he is so precious, am I really the right person for the job? My last mission was sub-optimal. I—'

'That was not your fault. I formally order you to stop picking that scab. If you persist, I don't have any place for you in the QC, is that clear? You have a new mission now, get on with it.'

And that was that. Sam put down his coffee cup and stood up. I hadn't even sipped mine, but I know a dismissal when the door has been opened in front of me. It was time to review Julius' files and work out why he kept dying and what I could do to keep him alive.

#13 – Neith

The shadows were quickly retreating as the sun rose, and I had to admit that over the past four hours Julius had proved his fitness levels. At one point he had thrown a towel to me, saying I looked a tad sweaty. He wasn't wrong. I was dripping wet and it was clear that my fitness levels weren't quite where they should be. However, like yesterday in Sam's office, he was being polite, but there was just something about it that was mocking me. It was like knowing there was a subtext, but not quite being able to reach it. We seemed to have swapped roles. Now I was the one grieving and he was the one standing back and watching. Was this all just a game to him?

So far we'd done a five-mile run, swum, jumped, crawled and lifted. In combat training, he had thrown me to the ground as many times as I had thrown him and he had landed five fatal body blows with sword, stick and bow. He could also pick a deadlock in under a minute. And failed to set off a single booby trap in the holo suite. All the while I had been shouting questions at him, social, ethical, historical, artistic, mathematical. He got them all right except for the ethical ones, and I was prepared to accept that he argued his case convincingly. Although I deducted points for describing Alphas as being unimaginative and superior. Again, the way he said it sounded like he was insulting us. I couldn't pinpoint how,

113

but I didn't like his tone. However, I decided to offer an olive branch.

'You clearly took this morning's assessment seriously and didn't stay up too late partying last night. Well done.'

He was sitting down on the sand and stretching out his quads. Pausing, he looked at me. His face seemed devoid of emotion and yet I knew he was scowling. Was it the slight tightness of his jaw?

'I didn't go out last night.'

'On your graduation?'

'I wasn't interested in being the centre of gossip once again.'

'I don't follow?'

'I think your exact words, after I gave you a hug, were, "Fuck. No" in front of all my cohort.'

Inside, I cringed. At that moment, I had been so horrified to have the worst moment of my life thrown back at me. I hadn't been thinking of anyone other than myself. What the hell was wrong with me? Stubborn mule didn't come close. I should have apologised immediately, but I was still trying to find a way to absolve myself of wrong-doing. Not a noble decision, but at least an honest one. Ignoring his comment, I changed the subject. Because that's what recalcitrant equines do.

The one thing I had failed to establish was why he kept dying so much. It made no sense. Julius was clever and gifted. Once he had been told what the problem was, he should have acknowledged it and improved, but he didn't. He kept repeating his mistake. According to the records, he had only stopped when he was given a final warning. I knew Betas were reckless with their lives, but it was just unfathomable to me. Julius seemed so civilised. These failures made no sense.

I tucked my hair behind my ears and then took a glug of water. If we were actually going to entertain the nonsense of Julius being a quantum curator, I had to get to the bottom of this.

'Whatever the reason, I'm glad to say you have passed this section of the evaluation. I looked at your records last night. You appear to have been deliberately dying. Psych records say you have no suicidal tendencies as far as they can tell.'

Attached to every one of the monthly evaluations was a note saying, "Speculative assessment based on an Alpha baseline" which was code for "How are we supposed to know?" All cadets were assessed monthly, graduates are assessed annually, although as part of my care and rehabilitation package I had attended monthly evaluation and counselling sessions. I was surprised to see Julius roll his eyes.

'Do you have a problem with the mental evaluations?'

He sighed and then shrugged. 'I guess not. It's just that I don't really go in for that sort of thing.'

'Typical QC trait, actually. The belief that you don't need help.'

'It's not that so much, it's just that, well. I don't.'

I sighed and threw him the water bottle. We seemed to be drifting off his death rate, but I was happy to follow this change of topic.

'We all need help, butt. You more than most, you've been pulled out of your environment and then for some incredible reason have been put into the final year of the QC programme.'

'Psych evaluations aren't going to help with that. I just need...' He paused and looked around him. I wondered what he was seeing, how he was seeing it. He had grown up in a flat, cold, damp, green country. Now he was in a hot dry land, yellow sands and blue seas, and a civilisation centuries ahead of his own.

'I just need something familiar. Just that, really.'

I looked at him in astonishment. 'You're homesick?'

He stood up and looked down at me. 'You know, Neith, you've said some pretty unpleasant things to me, and about me, over the past twenty-four hours, but I think that was probably the most stupid. I'm going for some food. Call me when you are ready to resume my assessment.' And he stalked off towards the park.

I lay on my back and looked up at the sky. That hadn't gone well. I hadn't had a neophyte before, but I was fairly certain that they weren't supposed to set the terms. Ben would have frogmarched us into a box of scorpions for behaving like that. But then Ben would never have said something so monumentally crass or insensitive. According to his notes, Julius had settled in well with his class and spent social interactions mixing with the rest of his team. He was well liked by some, while others were unimpressed, but he handled their suspicions well. No doubt he had been looking forward to going out last night and celebrating with them. He volunteered for activities and was always selected for team-building exercises. Except for live simulations. Understandable. No matter how much you like someone, you don't want them to kill you. It doesn't look good on your record as it shows that you also *failed* to stop them from killing you. As if being dead wasn't bad enough, you then get reprimanded as well.

None of his psych evals mentioned homesickness. Why had this possibility not been considered? Had it, but the docs had failed to recognise it? Maybe they were right. "How should they know?"

Julius was a stranger in a strange land, and I was behaving like a fool. I jumped up and ran after him.

'Yallah! Let's go to Chen's. Sticky locusts, my treat.'

'Sticky locusts are disgusting.'

'Nonsense, they're well lush, they are. What about chips then?' Carbs were absolutely forbidden during basic training. He stopped and looked at me, tilting his head. My brown eye smiling back at me.

'How about pancakes? Those thousand stars ones are delicious.'

I scoffed openly. The pancakes were stacked and drizzled with honey and butter. The juices then seeped through the tiny holes in the pancakes, making for the tastiest treat alive. 'Not a chance.'

'Worth a try. Chips it is. But it's still your treat.'

'Okay,' I said, relieved that an awkward moment had passed. 'But what I said back there. It was stupid. If you want to talk—'

'Of course I don't want to "talk". All you people do is "talk". I want chips. Okay?' He smiled, taking any sting out of his words.

'Look,' he said as we walked towards the catering units. 'What do you see?'

I looked around and shrugged. We were walking across the park overlooking the harbour, and a couple of people were queueing for food. There was a bit of traffic about, but other than that, perfectly normal.

'The Med?'

'Shall I tell you what I see? Out in the harbour, a boat has just risen out of the water and flown away. I thought it was going to hit the overhead cars, but they seemed to see each other, and no one collided. Whilst this happened, not one person looked up with alarm. Those people queueing for chips. One of them has a beak instead of a nose. I'm guessing she's a quantum curator. No one is batting an eyelid. All I can do is wonder; is she going to have an ice cream and does that mean she has a normal tongue? Lots of the men are in full-length robes but they're smoothly shaven and wearing aviator sunglasses. They could have stepped out of a Ralph Lauren photoshoot.

'There's a camel wandering down the high street over there, and the cars that are on the road have stopped and the drivers are chatting to each other. The air is full of swallows, and no one is paying them any attention.

'See that custodian over there? He's just asked some teenagers to run after a bit of litter that must have escaped a refuse point. The teenagers run immediately, chasing each other to be the first to grab it. It is the only piece of litter I can see.

'I can just about kid myself that I am on holiday and then a whistle blows, everyone on the benches stands up and all the surfaces are squirted with a jet of water and a brush wipes along the top.'

We waited for the bench to dry, sat down outside Chen's and ordered a cone of locusts and one of chips, while I tried to think about what he had said. When they arrived I peeled down the edge of the banana leaf and offered the locusts to him, safe knowing that he would refuse. Which is just as well as they really were far too good to share. I noticed he offered me his chips with the same reluctance, and I rewarded him by smiling broadly and helping myself. He gave me a mock scowl and I could feel the tension between us ebb away.

'Every time I see something like that happen, I think I'm on holiday in the most incredible, amazing, remarkable place. Then something happens that reminds me that this is not a holiday and I cannot go home. Home, where chips are made from potatoes, not taro, and no one thinks insects are tasty treats.'

'You like honey.'

He swatted me and told me that wasn't the same thing at all. I wasn't convinced, but he had a point. The culture shock must be incredible. I still think he probably did need to talk to someone about it, but I certainly wasn't qualified. All I could do was help him become the quantum curator that he wanted to be.

'Okay, look, before we go forward let me just understand your death rate. What was that about? You're not stupid, why did you keep dying?'

Julius blew on his chip and gave me a boyish grin and then sheepishly examined his fingernails.

'Yes, well, you see.' He laughed. 'The thing is, I just couldn't help myself. Those simulations were just so incredible that I couldn't help myself. I just had to explore.'

I looked at him in astonishment and choked back a laugh. 'It's not a game.'

He continued to look sheepish. 'That's just the problem. It was a game to me; the stakes weren't real.'

'So, what changed?'

'Professor Hu made it clear. If I failed, there would be no re-takes. No appeals. And that wasn't what I wanted to happen, so I stopped dying.'

'Just like that?'

'Exactly. Like you said, I'm not stupid.'

I sighed with relief. Curiosity was a good sign. The best curators had quick and enquiring minds. We needed them to problem solve whilst the bullets were flying. Now

I knew what his Achilles' heel was, I'd be able to watch out for it.

'Well, well, now. There's lovely.' I grimaced; there it was again. These strange words and sayings that meant nothing to me. 'Is this you?' I demanded and he looked at me confused. 'The "there's lovely" thing. And other weird phrases. I keep finding them coming out of my mouth and I have no idea how they got there. Is it you? Is this a side effect from the splice?'

He looked at me and laughed. 'Honestly, I have no idea how the splice works, but one of my grandmothers was Welsh and she used to say that all the time.'

'Did she also end all her sentences with "butt"? I spent a week trying to stop doing that. I sounded deranged. Everyone kept waiting for me to finish my sentence. I thought I was going mad.'

By now Julius was crying with laughter and attracting attention.

'Well, I'm not being funny, butt—'

'Stop it!' Julius was slapping his thighs and tears were running down his cheek. People were looking over and I grinned at the sudden spontaneity of his laughter. I waited until he recovered himself.

'At least now I know where these phrases keep coming from.' I moved the topic on. 'Okay then, enough of that. Let's discuss our first step. I have a few locations in mind, but have you been hoping for somewhere in particular?'

The first live step for any neophyte was handled with care. It needed to be a relatively safe environment with just an air of heightened tension. So, we needed the Beta population to be alert, to keep the neophytes on their toes, but not running for shelter as bombs rained down on their heads. It was also a good idea to take them somewhere vaguely familiar, where they would blend in. On both earths, there were lots of shared cities. Most of the major cities grew because of geographical locations, near rivers and harbours, forgiving climates, and good soil, although their rampant population growth meant unchecked urban sprawl that we didn't go in for.

'I was wondering about Britain?' Julius looked anxious, almost waiting for me to say no, but I thought it was an excellent idea. 'It's just I'm not terribly confident with the speech thing yet. So, I was hoping to go somewhere where I didn't have to think twice about the language.'

'Why not? Your Egyptian is perfect.'

Julius checked my face as though he thought I might be joking. Why would I joke?

'It's just. It just still feels a bit freaky. I'm not convinced that I can speak a new language fluently within a week of learning. I don't want to be on my first mission and wondering if I'm speaking properly the whole time.'

The language upgrade was a simple procedure that all NQCs received as well as many in the general population. It was a simple non-invasive procedure where lasers tickled the section of the brain responsible for language acquisition. With some accelerated overnight language sessions and a few chemical enhancements, the brain could pick up a new language in a couple of days.

Schoolchildren were taught the normal way as procedures on brains had to be very carefully regulated. Most of us had several languages under our belt before we turned eighteen, but if we wanted more and we needed them quickly, then a polyglot tickle was just the ticket.

'Okay, freak boy. I wasn't planning on stepping anywhere too foreign. What about the Blitz?' I was rewarded with a look of concern as he choked on a chip.

'I thought the first step was supposed to be safe?'

'Great Ra! We won't be stepping at night. Just pop over during the day, pick something up and then come straight back.' I paused, I wanted him to enjoy my next suggestion but wasn't sure how he would take it. 'I was thinking, normally on first extractions junior QCs just bring back a piece of litter. Something that won't be missed and is easy to acquire. But I thought it might be fun to pick up something that we know gets destroyed later on. It's more a lesson five procedure, but you're older than most curators and you have already been through the step. What do you say?'

He grinned, and I remembered how much I liked his enthusiasm.

'You're on,' he said, and then blew on his chip, eating it with relish.

'Okay, the first assignment. London 1940, here's what you need to know.'

123

#14 – Julius

I had spent the last three days researching the London Blitz. It was like being back in the lower fourth. Customs, fashion and cultural references, the minutiae and the global events. I enjoyed studying history like this, the everyday stuff. This was why I wanted to become a fully-fledged curator, so I could study history more intimately. Saving our greatest treasures was a bonus.

I had taken to wearing my coloured contacts to get used to them, but the dry air and the dust caused a constant irritation. By the time I arrived, I would look like I had been blubbing for a week. But at least I wouldn't look like I had a blue eye and a brown eye. I had pointed out that it wouldn't be that anomalous as David Bowie had different coloured eyes. It was then pointed out quite firmly back that David Bowie didn't exactly blend into the background either. My job was to slip in and out unnoticed. I had also taken to wearing the blue serge uniform of an air raid precaution warden, or an ARP, as I would impersonate one when I stepped through. I could only manage it for about an hour before it drove me mad. Hot and itchy woollen suits were not ideal for an Egyptian summer.

I had also asked the tech guys to update my virtual assistant's voice, they'd told me they'd found something far better for me, someone familiar and reassuring. I asked if it was David Attenborough, but they looked at me blankly. I gave up; hopefully, all would go well on this mission and I wouldn't need it.

Neith and I were both going across as ARP wardens. The idea being we would arrive in the morning and the locals would assume we were on our way home at the end of a night shift. Therefore, no one would expect us to do anything. I had thought Neith could dress as a nurse, but she said they got called on at any time of the day. A tin hat and a serge suit were just fine. Plus, apparently, she didn't do skirts unless strictly unavoidable.

Which was funny because these days I spend most of my time in a skirt or a chiton, as they call them. Apparently, Beta skirts are too tight, or too heavy, or too flouncy. I do not understand, but honestly, I have learnt to just nod when a lady says something incomprehensible. Especially a lady that knows more ways to kill me than I know how to catalogue a book. And she knows all of those as well.

We were scheduled to arrive on a Wednesday morning in October. There would be a devastating raid that night and we were heading to a warehouse to collect a copy of *A Night in London* by the photographer Bill Brandt. The warehouse held nearly the entire print run, and all would be lost to the flames. Other copies survived, so this wasn't a lost artefact retrieval. Neith just thought I would enjoy it more than a bit of masonry.

'Are you ready?'

Neith looked across at me and then frowned, telling me to control myself. I probably shouldn't have clapped my hands, but I was more than a little excited. I was going home, and I was time travelling. It was hard to play it cool.

Neith gave the thumbs up and we both stepped towards the wall. Just as in the simulations it began to flex and disintegrate and then there was nothing and then there was the entire universe. I was simultaneously cold and hot. My skin felt too tight. I was convinced my organs were floating away. I felt as weary as death and buzzing with energy.

And just before I could scream in terror, I was standing in London. The first thing I noticed was ridiculous. The second thing I noticed was wonderful. The third thing I noticed was terrifying.

The reason my first thought was ridiculous was because everything was in colour. I had grown up watching the Pathé newsreels of the Blitz and had become used to the black and white images. Now everything was in glorious technicolour. Or rather war-torn technicolour. Dust covered everything. It hung in the air. The red double-decker was grimy with dust and soot, as were the red post boxes. Women walked past in blue and green coats. London may have been in colour, but it looked like Aleppo. Buildings were completely gutted. A single wall, five storeys high, stood amongst the rubble, all that was left of a once major building. People walked past it, seemingly unaware of the inherent health and safety problems. I found myself looking out for the war correspondents; for Sky News and the BBC, for CNN to be doing a tense piece to camera. Like I said, ridiculous.

And that was the second thing that I noticed. How wonderful it all was. These were my people walking across the rubble, children neatly dressed, holding their mother's hands as they walked to school, crossing carefully along the planks laid on top of piles of bricks and debris. Everywhere smelt of stone and fire, and cordite hung in the air, as did a smell of raw sewage. Despite all that, Londoners tipped their hats to each other and stepped around craters and continued with their day.

And finally, I noticed the terrifying thing. I couldn't see Neith. Our perception filters would automatically deploy as we stepped through so that if we arrived in a busy scene, we wouldn't suddenly materialise. Rather, we would just gradually be there. We wouldn't suddenly pop up in front of someone, they would just realise that we had been there for a while. But Neith and I should be able to see each other instantly. I tapped my wrist brace and sent out a beacon. This was standard procedure. A team could sometimes be transported slightly apart. It was rare, but the procedure was simple. You just started pinging the other wrist brace until they replied. Sometimes a team could be separated by as much as a few streets or a few hours. Neith's brace didn't ping, so she couldn't have arrived yet.

'Bad night was it, love?'

I looked down at a smart buttoned-up lady. She wore a dark blue wool coat that strained across a heaving bosom. It wasn't particularly cold, but she looked the type that would wear woolly tights in a heatwave. I was suddenly aware of how much I missed my Granny Wales, who had been dead some twenty years, or not yet born—depending on how we were going to do this.

'I'm sorry?'

'Bad night. I see that expression on my Arthur's face some mornings when he comes back in. Were you over at Cannon Street?'

'Yes, I was. Rotten time.' I looked around and shook my head, playing for time. 'Blimey, he wasn't half cross with us last night.'

'I'll say. Still, our boys will give him back twice as good. Bet you wish you were up there with them?' She looked at me shrewdly. An apparently fit young man, I should be on active service somewhere, not at home with the old men, the women and children.

'I get seizures. No way they'd trust me with a plane. But gosh, the glory of taking out one of their artillery guns.'

'And die in the process? Don't be foolish, love. We're losing enough of our boys. Lost a whole pile of you last time around, don't need to lose another lot now, do we? And you're here doing your bit. Nice boy like you. Lifts the spirits.'

'That is awfully kind of you to say so.' I smiled warmly at her. I wasn't kidding, chatting to this woman was the most wonderful conversation I had had in months.

'And so nicely spoken. I bet your old mum's right proud of you?'

'Well, I do hope so.' Feeling awkward talking about people who weren't even born yet, I changed the conversation. 'I wonder if you could help? This isn't my patch; we all came running last night and I need to get back to Potter's Field,' I said naming the area that the warehouse was in. I decided that my best strategy was to head there and wait to rendezvous with Neith. I had three hours before abandoning the mission and returning home. Standard procedure.

'Blimey, you are off your patch, aren't you? You're north of the river right now. Head down here now, over the bridge, and turn left. Forty minutes should see you back home. Now mind how you go.'

With a pat on my arm, she headed off along the pavement, stepping around some fallen railings and waving at another lady across the way. All around me Londoners were just going about their business as I headed south towards Southwark Bridge. I joined the other commuters as we traipsed across the bridge and I realised that I kept looking out for the HMS Thunder Child on the Thames. The strangeness of it was getting to me, and I needed to find Neith. If any girl had her feet on the ground, it was that one.

As I came off the bridge, I noticed a few men had newspapers tucked under their arms. I stopped at a newsstand, purchased a paper and copied suit. Just as I was about to cross the busy road, two air raid wardens approached me. I don't know what it was about them, but my spidey senses started to tingle. The two men looked

129

Mediterranean, with neat haircuts. The shorter man was older and looked calm, but his companion was visibly sweating and looking around nervously. I couldn't put my finger on it, but something about them seemed wrong, and more than just their tans. I was also worried that my cover wouldn't stand up to a conversation with a pair of genuine wardens.

'I say, old bean, rotten weather we're having, what?' said the younger man.

I looked at him in surprise. What was he gibbering on about? Had I stumbled across a German spy? His accent was terrible, and his words sounded like something from a spoof Noel Coward play. The older man noticed my alarm, tapped his friend on the arm and shook his head.

'Sorry 'bout that, guv'nor. Had a tumble on the apple and pears, shook his noggin loose cor blimey, so 'e did.'

Dear God, they were curators. I had been warned about this possibility and warned in the strongest of terms. Wednesday, October 9th was a fixed point for the quantum stepper, which meant that lots of curators visited this point. So far, on my timeline, the QS had opened to this date over a hundred times. Who knew how many more times in the future it would open? So, it was imperative that we never made contact. In fact, it was a disciplinary offence.

The trouble was not so much the effects on the Beta world (of course), but how it could affect the Alpha world. What if we inadvertently told someone from the past a fact about the future and thus changed the future timeline? At this point, it all gets philosophical and ends again in the collapse of space and time. Like I said, big disciplinary offence. And here were two of them chatting to me. Clearly, they were on the "engage with the natives" part of the training run. But they had picked on me. Apparently, I blended in perfectly, so as far as I was concerned I deserved a big old tick in the "assimilate native customs". But now I had to disengage before the world ended. Or something.

Smiling politely, I unbuttoned my cuff. To anyone watching they would see a man tap on his watch, then hold it to his ear with a mild shake and then a polite shrug. But the other curators would see straight through the perception filter and note my wrist brace. Their alarm was almost comical as they looked at me in horror and stepped back onto the road, earning them an earful from a very angry cyclist. Honestly, even I was shocked by the man's language. You'd expect more from a man of the cloth.

Apologising, the two men were now in a proper flap and bowing, they moved away from me as fast as they could. The training manual says to avoid detection and slip seamlessly into the crowd. What with the bowing, the shouting vicar, the bus horn and the running, I'm not sure if they could have attracted any more attention.

I noticed that the newspaper seller was looking at me quizzically, so I raised my hand in the universal gesture indicating one drink too many. As I walked away, I even managed a reedy whistle, although my mouth was quite dry. I knew that the wrist brace would have recorded the entire event, so I couldn't possibly be reprimanded for it, and so far the world hadn't ended. I would, however, have to report it when I arrived back. No doubt the footage would be locked in a vault or burnt or analysed. I didn't know which, but I knew they had no sense of humour about potential time anomalies.

As I walked along, the heat of the day was building. Even though it was October in London and I had spent the past six months in Egypt, the woollen suit, heavy cotton shirt, and thermal vest weren't helping. I pulled my collar away from my neck, the dust in the air was mixing with sweat and my skin was chafing. As I looked at my grubby finger, I suddenly understood detachable shirt collars and neckerchiefs. The grime must have been a daily issue. I don't know if it was because I was hot, tired, and increasingly anxious, but as I looked around, I noticed small details that I hadn't taken in before. The population's chirpiness was a brittle act.

At one point a car backfired, and every single person flinched. A woman walking with her child stood still and started crying in the middle of the street, her child clinging to her leg. Complete strangers rushed over and gave her a hug, words were exchanged and then she patted her hair, gave herself a little shake and carried on. Her child walked on alongside her, holding her hand, and everyone continued as though nothing had happened. But I don't think I will ever forget watching as her other hand searched around, trying to find another child's hand to hold. I knew that for the rest of her life, in times of danger, she would throw out her hand to the little child that she had lost.

As I continued, I saw an air raid warden sitting in some rubble trying to pour tea from his flask. His hand was shaking so badly that most was spilling onto the bricks and broken shuttering. A man stopped, poured his drink for him, patted him on the shoulder and then walked on.

Wherever I looked there were signs of a community on the brink of collapse. At night they no doubt screamed and cried into the noise of the explosions, but during the day they smiled and whistled and pretended to each other that everything was okay. This was the social construct that they had decided upon, and they were all going to stick to it. What else could they do?

I felt sick. I wanted to go home. This was not some jolly school trip. This was not an exciting jaunt. This was a horrific adventure, and I wanted no part of it.

'There you are!'

I spun around, lost in my own thoughts. Neith must have already called out to me as she was looking at me carefully. 'Everything okay?'

'Yes,' I said with a smile. 'Everything's fine. Shall we get the book and go?'

As we walked, I told Neith about my encounter with the two other curators.

'Coc y gath!'

I looked at her in astonishment as she swore in Welsh. 'You did not get that from my grandmother.'

She looked at me thoughtfully as she tilted her head and tucked a strand of dark hair behind her ear. 'Julius, you don't swear, do you?'

'No. I don't think it's necessary,' I said. 'I mean, I have nothing against people swearing. I just, well I guess I don't do it much myself.' I didn't like where this was going.

'Hmm. Is it possible that you do swear, but you do it in your head?' I said nothing and she continued, the smile on her face taking on a wicked glint. 'And is it possible that, just to be super cautious, you swear in Welsh?'

I laughed and held my hands up. 'Guilty as charged.'

'Tidy. Another mystery solved. Now back to those quantum curators, I think we can safely say you have officially passed that aspect of the trainee step. Observing and identifying other QCs.'

We left the busy road and started heading down smaller streets towards the river. At one point we had to backtrack as the way was blocked by collapsed buildings. Neith deemed the rubble to be too unstable to climb over. I looked up at the shattered buildings lining the road and agreed. It amazed me they were still upright. I could see chairs hanging on the lip of a shattered floor. A bed hung down, its metal frame caught on an exposed joist, the headboard swinging lightly in the breeze four storeys up. I was happy to take the long way round.

'You're very quiet,' said Neith.

I looked across at her. What could I say? My fellow citizens had made a pact. They would keep calm and carry on, and I would not let the side down.

'Sorry. I was just running through separation protocols. I hadn't expected us to be separated by such a wide time frame.'

'Yes. Not unheard of, but it has caused problems for us. We're running late. The first step is only meant to contain an element of risk, not Level One Imminent Death. Come on,' she said as she sauntered across the road, 'there's the warehouse.'

I looked over at a plain brick building. There was no traffic and very few parked cars. There was a small, closed pedestrian door and a larger delivery door was also closed. From the smell, I would guess that the other side of this building opened onto the Thames. A perfect location for a warehouse.

'So, do we just walk in?'

'That's down to you,' said Neith unhelpfully.

I looked around and then made a point of doing so in an obvious fashion, pointing at the odd rooftop. I then took my newspaper, folded it backwards and wrote a few notes on it, pausing as I looked at another rooftop, making another note. Then without hesitation, I walked towards the smaller door and without knocking, walked in with the air of a man who had every right to be there. I even called over my shoulder, telling Neith not to dawdle.

As we both stepped inside, the space was large and dark. I blinked, waiting for my eyes to adapt to the gloom, and saw piles of crates to one side. The opposite wall appeared to be a large sliding wooden wall, which no doubt would be rolled back when the barges arrived to load and unload. In a far corner of the warehouse was a work cabin, but it looked like everything was closed for the day. Sat staring out of the window was a rather annoyed looking cat, and I wondered how long the poor chap had been stuck in there. No doubt whoever was in work today had just popped out as the front door had been unlocked.

'Okay, I can't see anyone, but we need to remain alert and in character in case someone returns.'

I said this as much for my benefit as for the transcription device. This would be submitted later as part of my ongoing assessment. I was just about to suggest that we look through the crates when a loud, plaintive siren began to wail. Everyone says the hairs on the back of your neck stand up when you hear that sound, and there's a bloody good reason why they all say the same thing. It was terrifying.

'Shit,' said Neith. 'We have to leave now. Our chronometers must be out of sync with local time. There's no way—'

Whatever she was about to say was wiped out by an enormous explosion. Almost the moment I heard the sound, I felt the shock wave. I would have fallen to the floor in sheer terror were it not for the fact that I was thrown back into the cabin door.

'Hello, Julius.' HAL 9000 sounded in my ear, freaking me out. I may have screamed. 'Your cortisol levels have jumped to unrecommended levels. Try some deep breathing or a few minutes of yoga.'

I shouted at it to shut up but realised I couldn't hear my own voice. Just a ringing noise and the dulcet tones of a homicidal medical device. 'Picture a calm sea. You are on a boat...'

For a second, or a lifetime, I sat there trying to make sense of what was happening. The sonic technologies in my earpiece meant I was still able to hear the AI even if I was temporarily deaf. The problem was the new AI voice. The tech department had managed to watch *2001: A Space Odyssey* and decided that HAL 9000 was a helpful computer, not a homicidal killer. Great.

'It's a lovely boat, with a white sail.' It wasn't helping, I was sitting in the middle of a bomb site being freaked out by my earpiece. Next time I would just straight-up request David Attenborough.

The visibility in the warehouse was now lighter but opaque, and if I had to guess what had happened, I would assume that the wall opposite had fallen down or maybe the roof had collapsed. I don't think the bomb hit the building directly, but I think it was near enough as makes no difference. Except of course that I was still alive.

'Breathe deeply. In through your nose, out through your mouth. Your whole body is a system.'

I sat there thinking I should probably get up, if only to shut up my earpiece, when Neith walked out of the cloud of dust towards me. She had blood pouring out of her nose, and her hair was white with rubble and dust, but she was smiling at me. I relaxed. Whenever Neith was here I felt good. I grinned weakly at her; I would go so far as to say that whenever I saw Neith I felt safe. Which was a bloody daft thing to feel, sat in the middle of all this rubble, bricks still falling from shattered walls, with more bombs on their way.

'___ ___ ___'

I could see she was speaking, but I couldn't hear her. Instead, I tapped my ears and shook my head, then gave her a thumbs up.

'Well done, your levels are now falling. Keep picturing the boat. The sun is overhead. You are a good citizen, contributing to the wellness of the world.'

Dear God, how could I stop this drivel? Neith grabbed my face and mimed hitting the recall button on the brace. I couldn't agree more, but I just needed to do one last thing. She shook her head violently, but I stood up and opened the cabin door to let the cat out and, grinning, I saw what was on the table.

With that done it was time to go. The crates opposite were on fire, the flames partly visible through the clouds of dust and now black smoke was billowing upwards and across the ceiling towards us. Making sure that I wasn't touching Neith, I tapped the recall and stepped back.

I have never been so relieved to see that white sterile flame-free step zone. The medics ran forward with alarmed expressions on their faces. This was only supposed to be a simple beginner's step.

Beside me, Neith was laughing. 'He saved a bloody cat!'

Suddenly everyone was smiling and laughing and there was an outburst of clapping which also seemed to please Neith. Captain Nymens' voice called out from the gantry loudspeaker.

'Congratulations, Neophyte Strathclyde. Did you also manage to retrieve your artefact?'

I was about to reply when Neith interrupted me.

'Sir, our chronographs were wrong. We got caught up in a bomb blast, so we stepped back immediately.'

'Actually…' I opened my satchel and retrieved a copy of *A Night in London*. 'This was on the table by the cat.'

Neith looked at me and her jaw dropped and then the room cheered again.

'Your adrenaline levels now appear to be rising too quickly,' admonished HAL 9000. 'Remember the boat.'

I groaned. 'I need a coffee and please can someone tell me how to shut up this bloody earpiece.'

Having been debriefed by Captain Nymens and patched up by the med lab, in that order, we headed out into the afternoon sun. Suddenly weary beyond belief, I sat down on one of the stone benches. I needed to think about what the Blitz had meant to me, but it was just too big to handle straight away. Like most of my research papers, I like to come in sideways when tackling a larger problem. And something had been niggling me these past six months.

'About the stepper.'

'It's perfectly safe.'

'Not perfectly,' I said, tapping my eye, 'but that's not my query, it's more a mechanical one.'

Neith shot me a familiar look. It's the look favoured by tired teachers the world over, it's the look that says, 'Really, again?' But asking questions is part of my DNA and not understanding the first answer given is like a popcorn husk in the back of my throat. So, despite her look, I continued.

'Isn't it all a bit odd having these random available windows? I mean, from everything I've understood, the QS randomly generates a range of portals to step through. You don't get to choose when and where you want to go to.'

'Correct.' She looked at me patiently, waiting for me to make my point.

'It has been programmed with a list of missing treasure and artefacts. And now and then, the list syncs with an opening and up opens the portal and through you go.'

'Yes, and?'

'Except for a smattering of pockets that can be simply dialled up and visited. London 1940, Pompeii AD 79, St Petersburg 1812, Beijing 1900?'

'Yes?' It was clear she couldn't see the point I was trying to make, so I tried to spell it out.

'Well, is the quantum stepper in a state of constant temporal flux, or does it have fixed points?'

'Both. Clearly.'

'Despite the fact that the lectures state that the random fluctuations are intrinsic to the apparatus?'

I was exasperated by this dichotomy. She moved closer to me and patted me on the knee. 'Look, I know it's hard to get your head around. I still struggle, and I've grown up with it. But honestly, you don't need to ask those questions, they've already been answered.'

'I'm just trying to understand because it doesn't make sense.'

'There's nothing wrong with asking questions, obviously, but ask the right ones, ask new ones. Don't keep asking questions that have already been answered.'

I thought about it for a while and pressed on.

'But what if the answers were wrong?'

'What?'

'What if the answers given were wrong?' Everyone here just seemed to learn what they were taught. I had spent the last six months with apparently the brightest and smartest people this planet had to offer. And they were. Everything I had seen backed that up. Every conversation revealed their intelligence, but at every stage, I was surprised by their lack of curiosity. They just didn't question the big picture; they didn't even question the middle picture. The only things they questioned were their day-to-day investigations. Now Neith was looking at me with concern.

'Of course, they aren't wrong.'

'But how do you know?'

She edged away and pinched the bridge of her nose.

'Your questioning is unfocused. This has been working for years and suddenly you think it's wrong?'

Now I was cross as well. 'And yours seems to be strait-jacketed. How does me asking questions threaten anything?'

'Look around, Julius. We have few wars, minor diseases, the world is healthy, prosperous and happy. Our way works. Accept it.'

I paused and then sighed. She was right. Why was I trying to make a case for a planet where poverty and violence were rampant, greed ruled all, and despair was a factor in millions of people's lives. Grabbing my bag, I turned down her offer of a drink to celebrate our first successful trip and said I'd meet her back at the mouseion in the morning. I was in no mood to celebrate. Visions of that woman reaching out for her child were still running through my head, and I didn't know how I could celebrate anything whilst she was suffering.

'Are you sure?'

'Yep. I'm stuck in Barber's second. Tomorrow I'll be in the third. Molto allegro rather than adagio if you catch my drift.'

I could see she didn't have a clue and shrugged. I didn't have the inclination to explain the intricacies of one of my favourite pieces of classical music. Right now I was sad, and I just wanted to go home.

As I got to halls, I placed my hand on the biometric door and walked into the cool of my room. I threw my knapsack on the sofa and was about to step into the shower when I saw a folded sheet of paper on my empty desk. Sheets of paper on my desk don't usually grab my attention. Except I didn't leave that there, and my door had been locked.

I walked over and picked up the note. The paper was thick and luxurious, the sort I would use to write thank you letters to my grandmothers. Except I didn't threaten my grandmothers.

Looking at the message, I felt sick. Someone was still trying to kill me, and I was running out of time.

interlude 3

The following text conversation was retrieved, during a sweep of the ghost files of the Q Zone security system. It has been added to the evidence report for Case No: 234530/H. The second party is yet to be identified.

— Do we know who was responsible for that screw-up?

— Screw-up?

— If we are going to try to remove two curators whilst on an active mission, we need to make bloody sure they don't return and tell everyone about how their chronographs were out. It's raised even more bloody questions. Too many "accidents" have been occurring around those two.

— Calm down. Everything is under control. We'll be able to get the supply chain up and running again soon.

— I don't care about your bloody supply chain. If I need to, I will expose that to the world.

— What?

— You know, selling the treasures is not the most important part of our mission.

— Your mission will be nothing if you can't fund it. What I do is just as important as what you do.

— You're planning on telling her that, are you? If so, I'll write your obituary now. In order to protect the hunt for the codex, I will throw everything to the wind. Including you and your supply chain.

#15 – Neith

I woke up the following morning with a throbbing head and just lay there, trying to decide if it was a quantum headache or a hangover. I was fairly confident it wasn't a result of yesterday's concussion. My brain had been scanned following the Blitz bomb blast and the minor swelling had been easily stabilised. I'd then spent the rest of the afternoon at the baths being oiled and massaged to within an inch of my life. I'd tried to convince Julius to join me and suggested that we go out later to celebrate his first successful mission, but he'd refused.

After my first mission I had wanted to stay at home as well, but Ben had insisted, and if I hadn't gone, I would have missed Clio's rendition of the Sunrise Dance complete with knives and palm leaves. It was months before we were allowed back in that bar.

Truth be told, I had just wanted to sit at home and dwell on my first mission. We were back in the Six-Day War during a ceasefire. The whole thing had been overwhelming, the realisation that this wasn't a game but real people's lives. Ben had said that introspection can lead to trouble and over empathising. I felt we owed them a greater duty of care, but Clio pointed out that it was impossible to solve the problems of Beta Earth. They'd had almost two thousand years of mistakes. What did I think I could do? She wasn't wrong, but looking at an individual in pain, it was always tough to stand by. But we'd all sworn on our honour not to disrupt their timeline. It was the most we could do for them.

As I stood in the shower, I wondered if Julius agreed. I know he'd have sworn the same oath I did but did it mean the same to him? It was a sobering thought. Why was he being trained as a curator? He might not see things the same way we did. Maybe though, after six months of living here, he could see how much better our way of life was.

I thought about his argument yesterday, that we didn't ask questions. I have to admit it was bugging me, like a tiny piece of grit in your boot. He had kept saying, "What if the answers were wrong?" and I just couldn't quite get past that. We were a culture of science and experiments, we tested everything, didn't we? But did we revise and recheck everything? I was certain we did, but when it came to the quantum stepper, maybe he had a point. Maybe I was just relying on the wisdom of others. Maybe we all were?

I stretched and yawned and got a mouthful of shower water. Spitting it out in annoyance, I stepped out and got ready for the day, pushing Julius' concerns to the back of my mind.

Arriving at the acquisitions department, I could see that he was already waiting for me in the foyer. Like the main archives, the acquisitions department was mainly built below ground. Most of the admin departments were above ground, with the actual artefacts kept in environmentally sensitive rooms.

'You look as bad as I feel.' In fact he didn't look particularly hungover, more sullen, but he remained silent and with a shrug I gestured that he follow me towards the catalogue stations. As we settled down at a shared table, I told him to get the book and I swallowed another VitC tab.

As Julius got up and walked over to the retrieval unit, I saw that he was walking stiffly. He really should have taken me up on the massage. I watched as he dialled in his code then presented his wrist brace. I waited for him to turn round and pull faces at me while he waited, but he didn't do that. Clio did. I looked away and sighed for the umpteenth time. I'd known coming back to the mouseion would stir up memories, but I would need to get on top of them quickly. Sam had given me an opportunity to redeem myself, and Julius clearly needed help.

'Now what?' he said as he placed the book on the table in front of us.

Was it me or did he sound truculent? Or maybe just tired? I thought we had connected on the mission, but yesterday when I had suggested a drink to celebrate he had just walked off.

'Now we issue a full catalogue record. Normally this is done by the archivists, but like all stages, you need to learn what the other teams do, just so you understand everyone's contribution and don't value your own higher than anyone else's.'

'So why didn't we do the preserving section?'

'Because this book wasn't damaged, isn't old, and had absorbed little in the way of Beta toxins. Not much to do, really. Plus, I thought given your skills you might like to start with cataloguing?'

'Fair enough. I'm being an arse. Sorry, bad night's sleep.'

Placing the box in front of us, he pulled up the cataloguing screen and began to whizz through the fields. Basic physical description: Book. Subject matter: Photography. Author: Bill Brandt. And so the list went on, with Julius flying through them. Occasionally he would forget himself and use a cataloguing shorthand from his own world and we would have to remove that but otherwise, as I suspected, he had no issues with a detailed catalogue record. He paused when he got to the supplementary artefacts field.

Julius looked at me and I shook my head. Sometimes an item would receive additional features. A sheet of music would have an accompanying audio file, performed by an Alpha orchestra. Or if the artefact was damaged by fire or impact, then we would make a facsimile of the object in its original glory if we could, to show how an item should have looked. People could then dial up either holo-copy.

He carried on typing, then stopped at the final field. Curators' notes.

'I thought we'd already submitted our mission report?'

'Yes, this is just a little appendix. A place for the quantum curators to leave a trace of their personality. It's a small code that means nothing to anyone else. It might refer to their feelings about the step, about the item they retrieved, it could even be about the weather. But usually, to anyone else, it's impenetrable. For me, I'll be adding 'Blue Skin Black.' Blue refers to my partner, skin refers to the danger level, hair, skin, blood, bone, marrow, and Black refers to explosion, main threat present. What are you going to put?'

I saw him consider what I had just said. It was a piece of frivolity, but these little notes were a way in which we could add our personality to the record. I loved doing it as it made me feel that I too, was part of the artefact.

'Adagio for Strings.'

I looked at him quizzically, waiting for an explanation. But he said nothing. He had barely said a word all morning.

'Okay.' I bit my lip. I just couldn't seem to get through to him. 'You don't need to tell me, but partners do end up sharing most stuff. Look, let me show you Clio's. It will make you laugh. She used to love leaving utter gibberish.'

I pulled up the file for a golden Mongolian crown.

'Here, look. "The red dog sings at the *something* moon." It doesn't even make sense. I asked her what the gibberish word meant, and she said it was a secret code and up to me to solve.' I turned to Julius, grinning, but saw that he hadn't found it as funny as I had.

'Can I see the object?' Finally, he seemed to take an interest. He seemed alert for the first time all morning.

I clicked on the 3D scan button, but nothing appeared, instead, an error code popped up. I hit refresh but received the same error message.

'That's annoying. We can always go over to the vaults and see it in the flesh if you want.'

'No, I…' Julius paused and looked anxious. Some of his mood was rubbing off on me, and I wasn't sure why he was getting agitated.

'Actually, now I think about it, I remember Ramin saying something about a missing file before our last mission. Maybe there's a bug in the software. Let me report this and we'll call it a day.'

I'd leant forward to log in and file the report when Julius pushed back his chair and stood up. He was suddenly smiling, if somewhat wildly.

'Do it later. Come on. Let's take a break, I'm hungry.' He all but pulled me away from the screen and seemed almost desperate to leave the building. 'Last one to Mario's buys the ice cream.'

I closed down my screen and got up. I would file the report later. In the meantime, I would humour Julius and try and work out what on earth was bothering him.

#16 – Neith

Having bought our ice creams, Julius suggested a walk and we headed off towards the far side of the lake. It was nice out here, although you never bumped into anyone so it could be a tad boring. As we sat in the shade of a date tree eating our ice creams, a figure walked towards us with the sun behind his back making his face hard to see. Not that I needed to, I would know Ramin's walk anywhere. The last time I had seen him he had been trying to convince everyone that Clio was a traitor and had been put on sand leave for his lies.

'Hello, Julius. Neith.' He smiled at Julius but when he looked at me he just nodded. Who the hell did he think he was?

'What do you want?'

'Julius invited me to join you guys in celebrating your first step together.'

I was furious. Why the hell did Julius think I would welcome Ramin's company? And how the hell did Julius know how to get hold of him anyway? I was about to ask Julius what he was playing at when I noticed he was busy writing something that he handed to Ramin. He gestured to me for silence, and held his wrist brace out to Ramin, saying that he fancied a swim. I watched perplexed as Ramin stood up and walked to a nearby tree by the lake. He came back and showed me the piece of paper that Julius had written on.

'My conversations are being monitored. Please remove your wrist brace.'

This was stupid, and I was about to say so when Ramin also put his finger on his lips and gave me one of his old sad smiles. I decided to play along and handed over my wrist brace and waited until he returned.

For the first time all day, Julius visibly relaxed.

'Right, what's going on?' I said. 'What nonsense is this? And why is he here? How the hell do you know each other?'

'I know about as much as you do, Neith. But in the past six months, I have found Julius to be an intelligent and enjoyable companion. Never once have I found his concerns to be nonsense. So, shall we let the man speak?'

'You've been hanging out?' I was livid. I was preparing to take Julius under my wing and train him up as a fully functioning QC. Nubi's balls, I'd even had notions of forming a full-time step partnership with him. Only to discover that for the past six months he'd been hanging around with a traitor to the mouseion. I was about to say more when Julius cut across me.

'Oh, sit down, Neith. Who the hell do you think has been helping me settle into life on this earth when you flounced off into the wilderness, nursing your petty hurts and grievances? Rami here took me under his wing, helped me with classes, helped me train. Hell, he even helped me socialise. Showing me what is acceptable on this dull, boring buttoned-down, repressed planet that you consider to be some sort of bloody paradise. I am on first-name terms with nearly every custodian in the area as I broke rule after rule in the early days. How can swimming at noon be a violation? Since when is having the same flavour of ice cream five days in a row a transgression? And you actually have a law about which side of the pavement you can walk on. Jesus!'

Ramin gestured at him to lower his voice and pointed to the trees where the wrist braces were. Julius had been getting increasingly agitated as he ungratefully spouted off all that was wrong with the world.

'So, you don't like it here, I get it. Why didn't you just stay in London when you had the chance if it's so awful here? I can see that having bombs falling out of the sky must be so much more appealing.'

'That's not my home either. And I love it here. I love the mouseion, I love the studying, I love the QS, God I *love* the QS. But it is possible to love a place and also acknowledge its downsides.'

I wasn't convinced. I had grown up in a loving family. Most of my memories are ones of laughter. My school advisors encouraged me in subjects where I shone, and I was surrounded by pupils that felt the same. This was a normal childhood. There were no downsides. I was recommended for the QS trials as they considered it a perfect fit for my skills, and I thrived. My country saw the very best in a person and encouraged that. And if walking on the right side of the pavement meant that the flow of people around a busy city worked more efficiently, then that was to the good. And eating too much ice cream, whatever the flavour, was bad for your health, placing strains on the individual and the healthcare system. Surely a system that monitored personal consumption and advised when you were overdoing it was a good idea? And why would anyone want to swim whilst the sun is at its zenith? These laws are to protect the individual and in protecting one we protect all. I could have said any of this, I could have been noble and grown up. I could have tried to see it from his point of view, instead, I said, 'I didn't flounce off.'

'Sure looked like a flounce from where I was standing. On my own. Stranded. I am so sodding grateful for Rami that I can't begin to tell you. He saw I was floundering and called on me. I owe him everything. And if you think he's a traitor, then we need to end this conversation right now. But frankly, I am trying to save your life and he is the only person I trust.'

It was the most that he had said all day, but he was jabbering on.

'Go on then, how you are saving my life?' I was aware I may have sounded a tad truculent.

'When I got home last night, someone had broken into my room and left a note that read "Stop asking questions about the QS. You are easy to kill. As is QC Salah. As is anyone you speak to about it." If that's not a death threat, I don't know what is.'

I was shocked. 'But that's a total violation. No one is allowed to enter your room.'

Ramin nodded. 'Seriously, that is a major concern.'

155

Julius looked at both of us, puzzled, and tried again. 'Didn't you hear what I just said? Someone threatened my life and yours. Plus, they must be monitoring our conversations.'

We then spent a bit of time trying to explain how it was clearly a prank, but that breaking into his room was a serious breach. Alphas didn't go round killing each other. He looked between the two of us and tried a different approach.

'What about the missing file then?' I could hear the challenge in his voice, as though he knew that would convince me. Suddenly Ramin looked alert and glanced back over to the wrist braces by the tree. Was it possible that he believed Julian? Were we being bugged?

'What missing file?' asked Ramin.

'There was a glitch in the catalogue when I was trying to show Julius how to submit a retrieval file. I couldn't pull the details up, so I decided to go and show him the original item and file notes rather than the holo-record.'

Ramin frowned at me and looked over at the wrist braces again and then asked in a quieter voice if I had actually done it.

'No. Julius suddenly wanted to stop for ice creams like some kid, and I figured that we could look later.' I paused, looking at each of them in turn, both with the same worried expressions. 'And now I realise that he did that deliberately to stop me investigating further.'

I glared at the two of them, feeling outmanoeuvred.

'Is there something wrong with the mouseion catalogues? Why are you treating this like a secret? How does a neo curator know about it, but I don't?'

'I don't know anything about a filing system problem,' said Julius. 'I got a death threat last night and have been more concerned about that. When you saw the missing file it just added to my general sense of unease. After all, this world is apparently perfect, but missing files, break-ins and death threats just don't figure in my idea of perfection. So, when you mentioned Rami, I realised that he might be able to help. Like I said, he's the only person I trust.'

I sighed, trying again to reassure him. The death threat was a prank, but messing around with the Alexandrian catalogue? That was sedition. It was not an understatement to say that civilisations rested on the stable foundations of the mouseion. If someone was messing about with the system, they were going to have to deal with me first. I took a deep breath, an action plan forming.

'Right. Here's what we are going to do—'

Ramin cut me off. 'Nothing. Neith, you are going to do nothing. But I am.'

I looked at him in amazement. 'What the hell are you talking about? Since when do you get to give me orders?'

'Since when did you think you were in charge?' asked Ramin bluntly.

'If there is a problem with the mouseion's catalogue, then it needs fixing.'

'I agree, just let me look into a few things first. Please. For old times?'

I paused. Every part of me wanted to trust him. Once, when we were teenagers, during a school trip, we had been playing rock jump near the waterfalls and I had slipped. It was only his speed and strength that had saved me from being washed over the lip of the falls. I had hung suspended in the water as it rushed over my body towards the rocks below. I may have survived, but the odds weren't in my favour. Only Ramin's hand wrapped around my wrist as he braced himself on the other side of the rock held me in place. We stood like that for fifteen minutes before the rescue services arrived. The entire time he kept telling me stupid jokes and making me laugh, even though the panic in my eyes must have been evident. It was that event that had fast-tracked us to the quantum academy.

'Do you remember Wadi El-Rayan?' said Ramin, echoing my thoughts.

I laughed, surprising myself, and it was the best I'd felt in months. Grudgingly, I decided to go with the flow for a bit. It went against all my instincts except the one that reminded me that Ramin was my oldest friend. He knew me as well as I knew him.

'Forty-eight hours,' I said and walked over to the wrist braces. I slipped mine back on and headed back into town. Was I trusting my best friend or a traitor?

#17 – Sam

Sam pulled the two glass cups towards him and crushed some mint leaves into them. The smell filled the room and for a moment he was transported back to his garden where he had picked them that morning. As he poured the boiling water over the leaves, the scent intensified. He completed the ritual by adding a few spoons of sugar and giving it a quick stir before passing a cup to Asha Giovanetti, head of mouseion security.

Given her rank, she did not need to wear the custodian uniform as she theoretically didn't walk the streets helping citizens directly. But here she sat in the dyed primrose robes of a custodian. As she had climbed the ranks, she'd eschewed each uniform star, keeping to the most basic of garbs. By the time they made her head of security, no one blinked an eye when their dour boss turned up for work dressed the same as the lowest ranks. You'd have to be an idiot to underestimate her, as she sat quietly and inoffensively in the corner. Easy to forget and overlook. So long as the job was done well, those in power ignored her, which had been her plan from day one.

Asha grinned at him and added another spoon of sugar.

'You are always too stingy with the sweet stuff, Sam.'

'Just looking after my waistline.'

'Well, you look after yours and let me take care of mine.'

Sam looked across. Asha may have been heading into her sixth decade, but he wouldn't challenge her to a race or an arm wrestle. Unlike a lot of senior staff, she had never been a quantum curator. She had done all the simulations as a cadet, and the one obligatory live step, but with her brains, it was clear she was destined for the engineers. Only the brightest mathematicians and scientists made it to that department. This was the department that actually worked on the quantum stepper and kept all the anomalies in check. It was a dry, boring number-crunching job but also wrestled with metaphorical tentacles and end of the world scenarios. It took a certain kind of mind to not only theorise about the maths but then actively implement it. They were also a department of high risk. The attrition rate in the engineers was almost as high as that of the quantum curators. Although for the engineers the problem was mental burn out.

Asha surprised everyone and selected custodianship. A move that many tried to talk her out of, but she had her eye on the future and the future did not look rosy. There was a problem at the mouseion that even as an eighteen-year-old cadet she had spotted. At eighteen she didn't know what it was but had worked out that the best place to find it was from the top of the security forces.

Now, several decades later, she was exactly where she wanted to be and had a pretty good idea of the problem. And the problem was cataclysmic.

'We have an issue. Well, two.' Sam sipped his tea, removing a stray leaf from his mouth and continued. 'Two days ago, during a probationary QC step, the stepper and wrist brace malfunctioned, sending the team to a slightly different time designate and separating them by over two hours.'

'Irregular, but not unheard of.'

'Agreed, but when they arrived on Beta, their wrist braces didn't correctly sync to the local time and they were out by four hours.'

'That's slightly more unusual,' mused Asha. Sam had a way of spinning out the facts whereas she wanted them all up front without the dramatic flourishes. Still, Sam wouldn't have called her if there wasn't a bigger issue and she was prepared to listen to his roundabout way of getting to the bones of the problem. 'How often does that happen?'

'One in maybe a hundred steps.'

Asha ran through the probabilities of the two failures happening at the same time, not liking the figures.

'What did the engineers say?'

'Within the levels of acceptable fluctuation. But barely.'

'Was there any issue with being four hours later than planned?'

'They arrived just before one of London's worst Blitz raids.'

Asha narrowed her eyes. An incredibly unlikely set of statistics resulting in a near-death experience. Well, that was what the randomness of the universe was about, but still, it smelled wrong.

'Which pair was it?'

'QC Salah and NQC Strathclyde.'

'Shit.' There were the bones she was looking for. She leant back in the chair and stretched her neck from side to side. This wasn't good, it no longer felt random. And once again stank of someone or something manipulating the QS, an instrument supposedly impossible to tamper with.

'You said there were two things?'

'Yes. The second issue also involves those two, but I honestly think that that is a coincidence.'

Asha tapped her finger on the arm of the chair. She didn't like people speculating on facts she was not yet aware of.

Hurriedly, Sam explained how they had called up an example file and it had failed to materialise. Neith was about to investigate further when Julius suggested a break.

'That was lucky. How do you know this?' Asha tried to work out if Neith had alerted someone by dialling up the record.

'Ramin told me.'

'And how did he find out?'

'She told him.'

'Good grief! She deigned to talk to him? What does this mean? Does she finally believe him? That he was innocent in the Fabergé debacle?'

'No, as I understand, she still thinks he is evil personified. She is so determined that Clio was innocent that she can't see the wood for the trees. But for the good of the mouseion, she has agreed to wait on it for a few days.'

'Good girl. Well, there's nothing for it, we have to bring her in.'

'I agree, but can we trust her? More importantly, do we bring in Julius? Can we trust either of them?'

'It's not about trust.' Asha leant forward and jabbed her finger on the table, 'It's about facts. And the facts suggest that Julius would have to be the most elaborate sleeper ever, and Neith would have to be the best liar ever. Julius is patently an ingenue, and Neith always speaks from the heart. But does this mean you don't trust them?' Asha was curious. Sam had spent months monitoring Ramin, Neith and Julius.

'Course I trust them. But Clio fooled me. I know nothing about who we are up against other than they have their fingers everywhere. They have to be very powerful, well connected and clever. I need to rely on more than my gut instinct.'

Asha leant back and nodded in agreement. 'A reasonable deduction. But let's rely on your gut instinct and my reading of the facts and bring them in. They have targets on their backs, so let's fix that before they blunder to their deaths.'

#18 – Neith

Julius was already in the briefing room when I arrived, and I headed over to join him. The room was busy, but I wasn't late, and people kept waylaying me.

'Heard your neo got the book in the middle of a Blitz raid. Bene!'

'Cool tactic to throw him in at the deep end. Make sure he really deserves to be here.'

Everyone was keen to compliment me and welcome me back into the fold, but it all felt hollow. It was an unfortunate step malfunction that had almost ended in disaster. The credit wasn't mine; I wasn't testing Julius' limits. We got lucky and we got the book as well.

'Looks like you and Blue are going to be a great team. Congrats,' said Piers.

'Just doing my job.'

By the third time I said it, it was getting quite jokey. If I was coming back into the fold, I had better do it one hundred per cent. I sat down beside Julius and we gave each other a polite nod. I wasn't impressed to find that he had been hanging out with Ramin and from his overly polite nod, I guessed he knew I was annoyed and in turn was mad at me. Oh well, he'd soon learn I was right.

'It seems rowdier than usual today?' said Julius in a flat voice.

I looked around at my fellow curators, smiling at a few who were high-fiving each other, some sitting on desks,

164

others peeling back bandages to compare scabs. These were my people.

'Just us old-timers and you neophytes now, but we're all quantum curators. Previously your lessons were shared with engineers, medics, curators and custodians, now it's just your tribe. The volume is bound to go up.'

Julius looked around and laughed, but I wasn't sure what was going through his mind. He was impossible to read. He was just the same as a little boy. See now. Where did that thought come from? Ugh. I would have to have a proper chat with him soon about splices and see what the hell I was picking up on.

Sam walked in and the room settled down. He ran through the normal welcome to the neophyte pairs and thanks to the seasoned QCs who had volunteered to do this essential mentoring job. He then ran through each mission, praising and criticising as he went. Mostly everyone had had an uneventful mission, although two neophytes had got into a fight with a monk and got their butts kicked. Naturally, we all found this hilarious. Another curator had got knocked down by a car. His neo pair had simply walked out into the road and he had had to push them out of the way. All members of the team were looking bashful; obviously, the pair were embarrassed, but their mentor was mortified that he hadn't anticipated their stupidity.

'And then we have Salah/Strathclyde, who went the full bull run. QC Salah, why don't you tell the boys and girls how your step went?'

I stood up and cleared my throat. Everyone was looking at me expectantly, many with friendly grins, or awed expressions depending on their rank. Time to go whole hog. I was a quantum curator; I was one of the best. I was going to shine and show off, I cleared my throat.

'Well, what can I say? As you know, Julius and I were the obvious pairing. I had killed off most of my previous team, and Julius kept dying in training. We were the perfect neophyte mentorship team.'

I looked around the room, challenging everyone that held my eye. I wasn't going to hide from the Fabergé retrieval. It was a disaster, but I owned it. That was my job and now my job included bringing out the very best in Julius so that when he was up for a permanent partnership, they would all be clamouring to work with him. As I looked around, I was strengthened by the smiles and nods of solidarity from my colleagues and if the junior neophytes looked awkward or embarrassed they would soon be out in the field and have a better understanding of my situation. I cleared my throat and continued, ready to lighten the tone.

'Julius here arrived two hours ahead of me and was just preparing to return when I eventually arrived. So far, so normal. London in the Blitz, nothing to see here. Walk over to that building, skirt the unexploded bomb, tip your hat to the locals, comment on the weather, all as straight as the Nile.'

I was warming up; I loved a good tale.

'We had just made it to the warehouse when a noise broke through our chatter.' I paused and hushed my voice. Everyone leaned in to hear me. 'It was a sound to drive terror into the hearts of adult and make children look to the skies in horror.' I raised my voice, 'It was the sound of an air raid siren.'

They were now hanging on my every word.

'Got to say. I was a little horrified myself. Julius here just yawned.'

That drew laughter.

'Now, we had already done a recce of the warehouse and located the pallets of boxes, presumably containing books, on the far side of the warehouse. But Julius here had spotted a cat sitting in the window of the interior works cabin. What should we do? The siren was wailing, the book was in reach on one side of the room, the cat was locked in the cabin on the other side.'

I looked around the room. Save the cat, or grab the book, or escape to safety? Everyone was deciding what they would do.

'Obviously, this was a first step. Just a training step, so I made the tough decision to abandon our mission and return to safety.'

I paused shaking my head in regret. Several of the neos were leaning in. The old-timers like me were leaning back, grinning.

'And that's when it hit me. Literally. The room exploded and I was thrown across the warehouse and into a brick wall. Top tip, kids, never leave home without your armoured undies, especially when visiting London. Anyway, I stagger to my feet, wondering if Julius is mush and if anyone will ever partner with me again. I walk out of the dust and rubble and blow me, if he isn't leant against the door of the cabin, nose bleeding, book in one hand and cat in the other.'

The room broke into cheers and laughter.

'And that as we say,' I shouted over the top of the laughter, 'is us just doing our job.'

I stepped back and gave a deep sweeping bow to the rest of the room, grinning as they whistled and banged their hands on the desks.

'Thank you, QC Salah. A lively report and glad to have you back on active service. NQC Strathclyde would you agree that was a valid assessment?'

I looked at Julius, whose mouth was twitching. 'There seemed to be some embellishments and I appear to have been painted in a more heroic light than was warranted, but by and large, yes. That was an accurate description.'

'Well then, well done, however, I'm afraid that none of that excuses the fact that the pair of you failed to file your paperwork properly yesterday. Please come to my office at the end of the session so we might discuss this failure at greater length.'

'Paperwork! Nubi's balls, are you kidding?' Looking around the room, the others winced. No paperwork was a serious dereliction. Bugger and balls indeed.

As Sam wound up the briefing, he headed towards the door reminding us to come straight over to his office and then left. Everyone else was commiserating with us but also congratulating us on the mission, and I have to say it felt good to be back amongst my people. I just couldn't believe Sam was being so harsh.

'This is all my fault,' said Julius. 'I'll explain everything and take full responsibility. It was me after all that suggested ice creams.'

I gave him an old fashioned look and then shrugged it off. 'I'm in charge, the buck stops with me. But after Sam gives us our bollocking, I'm going to get in touch with Ramin and see why he wanted me to wait. Forty-eight hours are almost up. That is far more important than some sodding paperwork.'

I paused, having shocked myself. More important than paperwork? That didn't sound right. Either Julius was having a bad effect on me, though honestly, he struck me as a bit of a paperwork fan as well, or what was troubling me was momentous. Still, that had to wait whilst Sam read the riot act.

Knocking on his door, we waited until he called out and then entered the room.

Almost as soon as we entered, Julius launched into an apology without waiting for Sam to speak. I'd have cut him off for lack of protocol if Sam hadn't first.

'Stop right there, Julius. There is no need to be "terribly sorry" about anything. As it happens, your trip to the ice cream stand was a smart move.

'How do you know about that?' I asked.

'Ramin has been in touch. Now, would you both sit down whilst I bring you up to speed. Coffee? Tea?'

I watched suspiciously as Sam poured three cups and beckoned us to join him on the sofas rather than at his desk. This did not have any of the standard hallmarks of a dressing down that I was used to. Maybe we were being fired? Cheers, Ramin.

'Sir, I—'

'Enough, Neith. For a while now, I have become aware of abnormalities in the system. Steps not going according to plan, glitches in the filing system. At first, it appeared minor and within the realms of statistical cock-ups, but over the past year, it's been getting worse. Following your last mission, Ramin told me about the file that had been missing. As well as other things he said, it became very clear that the mouseion has been infiltrated by someone, or rather some many, that are actively working against the spirit of our organisation. I don't know to what ends, only that they must be well placed and at all levels of governance.'

'Are you kidding? Sam, this isn't a joking matter.'

'QC Salah, have you ever known me to joke about the integrity of the quantum department?'

'Respectfully, sir, if the threat is as bad as you say, how do you know that they are not currently listening in to this conversation?'

'With respect, Neith, I'm not a bloody idiot and I have put shielding measures in place.'

The tension of the room was unbearable when Julius started singing "R—E—S—P—E—C—T" followed by an allusion to a lady called Aretha, who I thought might have been in charge of the fine art department. We both glared at him.

'This is hardly the time or place for Beta antics, Neophyte Strathclyde.'

Julius stopped singing but smiled at Sam instead. 'I beg to disagree. You appear to be arguing about an issue that doesn't exist when you should be working together. You do, after all, appear to be on the same side.'

I held my breath, waiting for the inevitable explosion and then looked at Sam in wonder as he smiled and then laughed.

'You are quite right. And I am grateful for a fresh perspective.' He turned to me. 'Neith. I would like your involvement in this and for you to meet a few other people already working on the problem.'

I tried to respond that of course I was going to help, but he held up a hand.

'This will be difficult. No, hold on. I know your record, I know that won't be an issue, but this isn't a mission on Beta Earth. This is a home problem. You may be forced to break our laws, run afoul of our security agents, you may risk death or even dishonour. I want you to consider the ramifications.'

What was there to think about? Someone was attacking my mouseion and they were not going to get away with it.

'Of course, I'm in. But what about Julius here? It's hardly right to ask him to get muddled up in our problems.'

'I rather think I got muddled up in your problems when you saved my life and dragged me through to your reality.'

He had a point.

'Okay. Tomorrow morning I want the pair of you back here. I'll put it in the diary as a follow-up consultation regarding Julius' record-keeping skills.'

I winced. That seemed a harsh cover, but Julius wasn't in the slightest bit bothered.

'In the meantime, behave as normal, have a moan about being unfairly targeted, go for a ride, whatever. Come back here tomorrow in uniform. We trust you, but if after tomorrow's meeting you want to have nothing to do with it, I would ask that you protect us with your silence. And please remember, once you leave this room, act as though anything you say is being listened to.'

I stood up, stunned. I felt like weeping. The Mouseion of Alexandria was the shining jewel of our planet. It was a paragon of all that was noble about our civilisation. It wasn't just our efforts to save the Beta artefacts or the remarkable quantum technology. The mouseion was the entire concept of academia and study. We had built a stable, happy and healthy society based on certain principles. Freedom of thought, generosity of spirit, levelling the playing field. Honouring hard work and kindness. Now I was being asked to whisper in closed rooms. I walked out of Sam's rooms in a daze, but as soon as the door closed behind us, Julius let out a deep breath.

'What an arsehole. Sorry, I mean excuse my language, but seriously. We have to come back again just because I failed to fill in a form correctly. You people are insane.'

I looked at Julius, uncertain of what he was talking about, then cottoned on.

'That's Captain Nymens for you. Paperwork is important, but yes, arsehole is appropriate.' I laughed and punched him on the arm. He was faster than me at deceiving his institutions. A natural Beta advantage and one it seemed I had better brush up on quickly.

#19 – Julius

'Why is Nymens being such a git?'

Neith and I were walking along the corridors towards Sam's office and if I'm honest I had a spring in my step. The fact that there was something rotten in the state of Denmark had reassured me, and for the first time since I arrived, I'd slept like a baby. After yesterday's meeting with Sam, everything seemed easier to cope with. I wasn't going mad, there was a problem, and I wasn't the only one that had noticed it.

Neith looked like she had gone ten rounds with Mike Tyson and lost nine of them. Now she stopped walking and looked at me quizzically, tipping her head to one side. She paused whilst I waited for her to cotton on and then continued walking, this time just a tad more formally. It was clear the idea that someone could eavesdrop on our conversation was a hard one for her to grasp.

'Must I remind you to use the proper form of address again? It's Captain Nymens to you, Neophyte Strathclyde. And I would remind you that observing the correct procedures when it comes to paperwork and the filing of documents is not to be dismissed so lightly. As you yourself should understand.'

'I know, but why blame you? It was my fault. Dragging you in for this training session seems a waste of your time.'

'Not at all. I am your mentor so if you make a mistake the fault is mine. A remedial session is in both our interests.'

We continued along the corridors playing the parts of sulky student and fed-up teacher until we reached Captain Nymens' door and Neith knocked sharply, then entered. From the corridor, you can only see his desk. It's not until you enter the office that you can see the sofas at the far end of the room. Which was just as well because Rami and a lady were already sitting there. Given that Rami was still officially on sand leave, his presence might draw speculation. I didn't know who the woman was, but Neith apparently did as her formal demeanour suddenly became ramrod. Previously, she had been acting for the benefit of any snoopers. Now, she was in earnest.

'Forgive me, Captain Nymens, we have arrived at an inauspicious time, my profound apologies. We shall return at a better time.'

Sam closed the door and the woman stood up and approached Neith.

'Quantum Curator Salah, what a delight it is to finally meet you in person.' She stuck her hand out and Neith appeared to be in a daze as she automatically shook the woman's hand. This was one of the few times I had seen Neith flummoxed, so I looked at the source of her confusion with greater interest.

The woman was wearing the standard pale yellow jumpsuit of a custodian. Her hair was cut short, she wore no make-up or jewellery, and if I saw her again in a crowd,

I might not remember her. She had no stars on her lapels, which given her age—I would say somewhere in her fifties—meant that she was either new to the job or rubbish at it. I tried to remember what I had learnt about the custodians from Shorbagy. You gained a star on the left lapel for every rank achieved and a star on the right lapel for each discipline mastered. Yellow was the colour of custodians except for the ones that wore red, and as far as I could make out these were the equivalent of private security or soldiers. I could count on one hand how many times I had seen a red uniform.

So, who was this woman wearing only one star, sipping tea with the captain, and causing Neith to be so alert? As I was studying her, I realised that she was also studying me.

'And Neophyte Julius Strathclyde, I have been following your progress with interest. I am Asha Giovanetti, head of mouseion security.'

Oh dear Lord. Giovanetti was only spoken of in hushed tones amongst the cadets. There wasn't a misdemeanour that she didn't know about, there wasn't an infraction that she was prepared to overlook. It was impossible to appeal to her better side as she didn't have one. She was a humourless, dour, devourer of souls.

'Chancellor Custodian, sorry, Director Custodian.' Dammit. I was blabbering. Now was not the time to forget the sodding nomenclature of the custodians.

'Please call me Asha, at least in here anyway.' Beside me, I could almost feel Neith's reaction, as the most dangerous woman on campus smiled at me. 'Seriously, relax. Come and join us.'

As she turned her back on us, I looked quickly at Neith, who gave a tiny shake of her head. We sat down on the sofas, and I noticed Neith had sat as far away from Rami and Asha as she could.

Asha suggested Rami pour some tea and then took in Neith's ramrod posture and let out a small sigh.

'Neith. Someone is destroying the mouseion. I don't know why or how. I don't even know who they are, but I know rot when I can smell it and Alexandria is riddled. Will you help?'

'I'm not going to lie to you, but you could start with him,' said Neith, gesturing towards Rami.

'You will not be any use to us if you persist with this stupid childlike behaviour. I have full faith in Ramin, and if I have, so should you. Gods, woman. He has been your best friend since crèche. Why do you persist in such blindness? Grow up. And why would you lie to me?'

Now Neith did recoil and I felt sorry for her. She was being dressed down in front of her boss, her neophyte, and the person she perceived as her enemy. I chipped in.

'Ma'am, if I may. QC Salah and I have had a difficult few days. The phrase "I'm not going to lie to you" is a splice idiom that she has picked up from me. So, I apologise, but like I said we have had a tough few days. Three days ago, we were "accidentally" dropped in the middle of the Blitz, then two nights ago I received a death threat via a note left in my room. It is difficult to tell who to trust at the moment.'

I smiled at Rami, just to let him know that even if Neith didn't trust him, I did.

'I can clear that up,' said Asha. 'I left the note. Some topics of conversation seem to cause people to relocate or disappear. Discussing the mechanics of the quantum stepper is one of them. I need you and Neith here, so I sent you a quick note to shut you up.'

'My room has a biometric key lock.'

'And I'm head of security.'

I paused. She had a point. I thought about the note again, I had read it as a threat but in reality, it could also be read as a warning. I wished Charlie were here, he'd love this.

'Well then, Neith, what do you say?' said Asha turning to Neith. 'You can leave now if you want, although I will of course insist you both take a memory pill. Or you can stay and help me defeat the enemy within.'

I wasn't sure what Neith was going to do and I wasn't sure I wanted to take a memory pill, but whatever she did, I would follow her lead. She had saved my life once; I owed her my loyalty. I looked at her and I swear she had never looked angrier. Oh great, I thought, scary-sounding memory pill it is then.

'What it is, is, ugh.' She paused and shook her head. 'Sorry. What I meant to say is that if some bastard is attacking my library, they will rue the bloody day they were born. I'm in.'

With a deep exhalation, I drank my tea. Poor Neith seemed to be most affected by the splice when she was stressed or challenged. Or maybe it was simply being back in proximity to me. I hadn't noticed her channelling Granny Wales much, except at moments of tension. As Asha proceeded to explain the problem of filing irregularities and missing artefacts, I noticed that no one had asked my opinion. That was okay, I was getting used to it and I listened to the chief of security as she carried on outlining the situation. It's not like I had any insight into what was going on, and Giovanetti had a lorry load.

'Obviously, it all came to a head during your Fabergé step. When you came back, I debriefed Ramin at length and he told me that the day before you went on assignment he had discovered that *The Storm on the Sea of Galilee* was missing. As far as I was concerned this was the final nail in the coffin. When he told me this, coupled with everything he had to say about the Fabergé mission, I instantly moved him to a place of safety. Incidentally, as a matter of full disclosure, I have also been watching you two as well. Your safety has been my paramount concern.'

'Not quite paramount,' I said, and she smiled at me. I wondered what her scowls looked like.

'No, not quite paramount. The mouseion always comes first, after all. You may not agree, but I know that Neith and Ramin do.'

I wondered about that. 'Really?'

'Yes, of course. They are quantum curators. They have been screened and educated for decades, they know how essential the mouseion is and all that it stands for.'

'Except the same could have been said of Clio and Paul...' I left the sentence hanging and watched as four people stared at me, puzzled. I tried again. 'Your reasoning is flawed. You state that everyone would die for the mouseion, but we know that can't be the case if you have factions working within the organisation to subvert it.'

'You're being ridiculous,' said Neith. 'In case you've forgotten, Paul and Clio did both die for the mouseion.'

'No, they didn't,' I said. 'Paul was assassinated, and Clio must have died in the crossfire. Neither of them died protecting your precious society, they died trying to protect themselves or someone they loved.'

Sam, Ramin and Neith were all quick to protest that as curators their first goal was to protect Alexandria. Only Asha looked at me thoughtfully as I carried on. 'Clio is as guilty as sin. She blackmailed Paul, probably shot him, and framed Ramin. Hell, Neith, you were probably only steps away from being killed yourself.'

'Enough!' Neith jumped up. 'I will not listen to this.'

'Sit down,' roared Nymens, his first utterance since Asha had taken the lead. 'If you won't see what is plainly in front of you, you are no use to us. Your dim-witted thinking will jeopardise everything.'

We sat in silence and watched Neith as she walked over to a far window and looked out. She stood like that for almost a minute, then rolled her shoulders and asked if there was any coffee available. The tension in the room faded away and whilst Neith still refused to make eye contact with Ramin, I knew that she was prepared to put her unwavering trust in Clio to one side. It wasn't enough, but it was a start and everyone in the room knew it.

'Full disclosure. On the day I returned from Cairo I was followed and the man following me died.' Neith let out a big breath and sat down. She'd clearly been holding on to that for a while.

'What were his final words?' asked Asha, leaning in.

Neith looked up, surprised that her announcement hadn't caused more of a reaction from the head of security.

'You already knew?'

'Of course I did. As I said, I've been keeping tabs on all of you. Even if I hadn't, don't you think I would have thoroughly investigated a violent death?'

'Were you also responsible for the cover-up? That man wasn't a cleaner.' Neith was getting angry and it was clear to me that she was close to losing her temper. Asha seemed unruffled by Neith's rising voice.

'I was responsible, but I met no resistance. It seemed like I wasn't the only person who wanted to keep this quiet. The pharaoh and the chancellor both agreed with me that it was bad for morale.'

'So, who was he? Why was he following me? Who sent him?'

'He was one of my junior custodians. So drop your attitude. I feel his loss more strongly than you do.'

Neith snorted. 'You weren't there holding his hand when he died.'

'No. But I wish I had been. Someone has been recruiting in my department. I missed that and now this lad is dead.'

'So, you have no idea who sent him?'

'None. But I would be grateful if you can recount his last few minutes. Maybe you can shed some light?'

Neith paused and nodded and then quickly ran through her actions with her interpretations as to what was happening.

'When I got to his side, I muted his wrist brace. I don't know why, but I felt I owed him some privacy in his final minutes.'

'Did he say anything?'

'He said he was sorry.'

My heart twisted. What a horrible way to die, with regret on your mind.

'Anything else?' asked Asha.

Neith quickly looked across at me and then continued with the same monotone, report-giving voice.

'He said, "Death to all angels" and then he died.'

#20 – Julius

Everyone looked at me and then paused. Neith got up and made another cup of coffee whilst Rami pulled some feathers out of a cushion. Asha and Sam looked at each other with worried expressions.

'Does anyone want to enlighten me?' I asked, and I have to say, I might have sounded a bit peevish.

'It's an old cult. To be honest, I thought they had died out years ago,' explained Asha. 'Back when the stepper was first up and running there was a lot of fear and ignorance about Beta Earth. Education helped, but some were still worried by the threat you posed.'

'How can we pose a threat? We don't even know you exist.'

'There was some nonsense about the angels that stepped over being a contamination.'

'Pensioners?' It was hard not to scoff.

'Them and the splicing. There was a concern that we were polluting the gene pool.'

I felt sick. 'You think I'm genetically dirty?'

Rami looked across at me sadly. 'Never. None of us does. It was an embarrassing little episode in our history and one that we quickly put behind us.'

'"Death to all angels?" I don't think it's as behind you as you want.'

Whilst I had been talking, I could see that Asha had been thinking and had muttered something to Sam. Now she turned to me and we all fell quiet.

'Julius, this is an unexpected development, but not one that I think is directly relevant to the thefts at the mouseion. With your permission, I am going to start looking into this, but I would like to focus on the thefts first.'

I shrugged, what else could I do.

'Neith, if you would care to join us?'

'Okay then,' said Neith, having sat back down beside me. 'But first I just want to say this. Julius, I tried to save that man's life. Had I known he was a purist; I'd have pushed him over the edge.'

I was grateful for the little hand squeeze she gave me as she turned to the others and took a deep breath.

'First things first, we need to examine the Fabergé step notes and see if that reveals anything.'

'We can't, it's classified,' said Rami.

'There may be different levels of clearance. I can sneak a peek and if I can't access it then we'll think again,' said Neith, dismissing him.

'Except the file is being monitored,' I said.

Asha looked at me. 'No, it's not. I should know.'

'Yes, it is.' I checked her face to see if my contradiction annoyed her, but she just sat quietly listening. 'Months ago, I tried to download the file and within fifteen minutes the chancellor was by my side asking why I was looking. I told him I just wanted to try to reconcile my new world with my old one and thought this would be a good place to start.' I took a sip of my tea, thinking back to those early confusing days. 'He thought that was a fine idea and said that I could, of course, view the files. And then he said with a laugh that I had been there, so actually, I already knew everything that was in the file. And therefore, didn't really need to see it anyway.'

'Did you ask again?'

'No. I know when a politician says no. Plus, what could I do? I knew and trusted no one. Neith had abandoned me, only the chancellor paid me any attention and everyone else acted like I was dangerous. The last thing I was going to do was shake my cage when I didn't know who my jailers were.' I paused. 'Can I get some coffee as well?' After a while, their idea of tea made my teeth scream for a dentist.

I walked over to the machine and watched as the four of them discussed what the implications of Chancellor Alvarez monitoring that file meant. I listened perplexed as they tried to think of explanations for the tampering of files and missing treasures. What could it all mean? They went on like this for a while until I realised they were serious. They didn't have a clue.

'Greed.' They all looked over at me confused, so I re-joined them and tried again. 'My best guess. Things are being stolen to order. These items are ending up in private collections.'

It seemed so obvious to me, and yet I was still looking at four blank faces. Even Asha seemed confused.

'That makes no sense. Anyone can dial up a holo-replica of anything in the vaults and if they want, they can purchase a permanent, perfect replica.'

'It's still just a replica, though.'

'Well, obviously.'

I tried again. 'What is it that the very richest on your planet like to do?'

'Give back to society.'

'Help use their wealth for redistribution.'

'Fund medical research.'

I was prepared to accept that this version of earth was a calmer, fairer, more benevolent version than my own, but I had met many sorts since I'd been here and I noticed that as humans we were all pretty similar. They may have fewer thieves, murderers, oligarchs, and power-mad tycoons of industry, but I bet they still had them. Now I'd discovered that they also had people that believed in the purity of a species. They weren't that much better than us after all.

'You know, you aren't all perfect,' I said and watched as they looked at me, slightly affronted. 'The fact that people have died, that the security has been compromised, that items have gone missing proves that. This isn't random. Persons unknown are behind it. If you can accept that, which you clearly can as we are all here discussing it, then surely it is only one small step further to accept that items are being stolen for personal gain. Someone is making money on the sale, and someone else is gaining something that no one else in either world has.'

'But that's so revolting,' said Sam. 'It sounds like something from a Beta melodrama.'

'Julius prefers the term Other Earth,' said Rami, who had been sat quietly listening to everyone else until now.

'Julius can prefer what he likes,' snapped Nymens. 'I am being asked to accept that my society is corrupt, and my quantum curators are riddled with thieves. I'm going to deal with the big picture first if that's alright with you?'

Privately, I cheered. Rami was a great guy and I appreciated his support, even if his timing was rank and Nymens was glaring at me.

'Doesn't matter what you call it right now. As you say, you have a bigger picture to deal with, namely that someone is treating your mouseion like Harrods.'

I took a moment to explain Harrods and saw that this was just making them madder. I could see their point. Being compared to an upmarket corner shop was beyond the pale. The idea of people pilfering the British Museum for their own private collection would make my blood run cold too.

Nymens looked at his watch and indicated that the hour was almost up. It was essential that we did nothing to raise suspicions outside this room.

'Here,' said Asha, pulling two wrist braces out of her bag. 'These two are perfect clones of your wrist braces, except they have no unusual sub-routines in them. I should like to examine the ones you are currently wearing and see if, as I suspect, they have been tampered with.

Your last step back to the Blitz was suspiciously dangerous.'

We swapped our braces over and handed them back to her. 'Also try to get used to not wearing them so often whilst on this earth.' She paused and smiled at me. 'If you are being watched, I want whoever it is to see this as a typical pattern for you. Julius, given that you can barely keep the thing on, even when on a step, I don't imagine anyone will notice a change. Neith, you will need to blend it more carefully. We don't know who is watching you.'

'But these new braces won't be bugged, will they?' I asked.

'No more than standard permitted protocol. But people may also be physically watching you. Let them see that you aren't always wearing the brace. Now I am going to start running a check on missing artefacts.'

'How will you know?' asked Ramin. 'It was pure chance that Neith and I both discovered missing files.'

'Not pure chance. You have both been partnered with rogue elements. Chances are if you went looking through more of your back record you'd find others.'

'Ach-y-fi. She's right about Paul. Remember in the briefing room he wanted you to stop talking about that Sea of Galilee painting? Now we know why.'

I watched as she engaged with Rami. Her face was alive as a part of the puzzle solved itself and firmly settled on Paul's shoulders. She turned to Asha.

'But he's right, we can't afford to tip anyone off. Paul's handler must still be on this side. What are you going to do? You're going to have to be careful and not mess things up.'

Asha looked at Neith silently until Neith suddenly remembered who she was talking to and apologised before she continued.

'Trade secrets. I have the volcanic option or the sneaky one. Let's try the sneaky one first, hey?'

She put her cup down and I could see that they were preparing to leave, which now had me worried.

'Hang on. We haven't discussed the other matter.'

Again, with the four identical quizzical expressions.

'The problem with the QS itself. The fact that it's flaky and temperamental. That it's apparently both rigid and fluctuating. The fact that it is open to manipulation.'

Nymens stepped forward and placed a friendly hand on my shoulder. 'Honestly. That is not a problem. Those are just the variables of quantum mechanics.'

The others smiled and nodded in agreement. 'We've grown up with this, it's new to you so obviously it seems odd but trust me, we have bigger things to worry about.'

Foolishly, I decided that he and the others probably knew what they were talking about. That was going to prove to be a colossal mistake.

#21 – Julius

The following morning I ran along the boulevard. The sea was gently lapping on the shore, and the gulls were wheeling overhead, curious to see what fool was up and running so early. I had had another wonderful night's sleep and had woken up full of beans. It felt churlish of me but knowing this earth had actual bad guys in it cheered me up no end. When I got to the end of my circuit, I ran back along the sand, careful not to repeat another engagement with the Chancellor.

The fact that there were people out there that viewed me as somehow polluted or dirty should have hurt more, but quite frankly, after six months of seeing this society's attitude towards my earth, I was hardly surprised.

Despite the early start, I still seemed to be running behind and by the time I got to the weekly briefing I saw that Neith was already there and laughing with some of her colleagues. It all seemed so innocent but was there someone in this room watching and waiting to take us down? I grinned at my own melodrama and, waving at a few of my friends, went and sat at our allotted table.

The door slammed and with a face as black as thunder Captain Nymens walked into the room followed by the chancellor wearing what can only be described as a look of deep fake concern. Or wind.

'Seats now,' barked the captain. 'Chancellor Alvarez has graced us with his presence today to inform us of some troubling news. He will address you after this morning's step assignments.'

I looked at Neith, who had sat down beside me and shrugged. Something had pissed off Nymens. Fingers crossed, it didn't involve us. As he read out the list of the next few days' assignments I drifted and wondered what to cook for supper. I'd invited Stef and a few of the others over so we could chat about our first missions. Maybe I could convince them to bring food if I provided the beers? Either way, it would be good to catch up. I was still musing when Neith nudged me.

'If we aren't keeping you from something more important, Strathclyde?' Captain Nymens asked icily. 'I was just informing you of your next mission. I hope that's not too boring?'

'This week?'

'Would I be announcing it in this week's mission briefing it wasn't actually for this week?'

'No, but I…' I'd thought that neophytes had their missions spaced out at the beginning with one a week maximum. We had stepped only three days ago.

'The chancellor was very impressed with your first mission. He felt that a small mission to the fifteenth century might be just the ticket for you. It is a great honour to you and to QC Salah and we…' He gestured to the chancellor. 'Would be terribly grateful if you could pay attention long enough to say yes, sir, thank you, sir!'

I was convinced that my face was bright red, but I mumbled, Y*es, sir, thank you, sir*, as quickly as I could and sat up straighter, determined not to drift off again.

'Now that you all have your assignments, I shall hand over to the chancellor who has some very grave news.'

Chancellor Alvarez stood up and approached the podium. Gripping it with both hands, he looked down at us in silence. Just as I wondered if he was ever going to speak, he drew in a deep breath.

'What I am about to say carries a Level Eight protocol.'

No one moved, but the tension became electric. A Level Eight protocol referred to confidential information. In such an apparently free and open society, such restrictions were rare and not used lightly. Although frankly, they seemed to me to be an almost daily occurrence.

'This morning I was informed of some irregularities amongst the computer files relating to the Beta artefacts and on closer inspection, at least one item was found to be missing.'

He paused, allowing the room to take in the importance of his words. Back home there would be an outcry, people calling out questions, raising hands. Instead, his words fell on a room stunned into silence.

'I called Asha Giovanetti for an explanation, but I regret to say that she cannot be found.'

People were looking around, shaking their heads, mouthing questions to each other.

'Should anyone be approached by Giovanetti or notice any anomalies, I want you to bring them to my attention immediately. Do not discuss the matter with anyone else, even your step partner. At this stage, we don't know who we can trust.' He shook his head solemnly and stood up straighter. 'This is a very sad day indeed. Any questions?'

Naturally, Sabrina had her hand in the air.

'Honoured Chancellor, are you suggesting that esteemed Director Giovanetti may have possibly, and by no means certainly, stolen some artefacts and run away?' She was almost sweating under the exertion of not actually blaming anyone for so monstrous a crime. Especially not someone that might hinder her future career.

Alvarez smiled warmly at her. 'Absolutely not, Neophyte Mulweather. I want no one here to leave with the impression that Giovanetti is a thief and a traitor who has betrayed everything that we stand for. All I am saying is that we would very much like to speak to her at this alarming moment in our history. For now though, please remember this is Level Eight, and come to me directly if you have any concerns. About anything.' He paused, making eye contact with as many people as possible. 'Or anyone.' And then he swept out, beckoning Sam to follow. All he needed was a cape.

Now the room erupted.

I turned to Neith. 'Who is this Giovanetti?' There was no way I should know anyone this senior, and I doubted it would help if anyone realised we'd been chatting just the day before.

One of the older curators leant back in his seat, addressing me directly. 'Giovanetti is head of security and, trust me, if she is guilty, no one will ever catch her.'

'Rubbish,' shouted another curator from across the room. 'The chancellor has clearly outwitted her, that's why she's fled.'

The arguments for and against waged back and forth until a tall woman with facial tattoos and dark black skin stood up, clearing her throat. The room fell quiet.

'Speculation is worthless. This is Level Eight. Keep your thoughts and opinions to yourselves. We have missions to run. Let's do what we can to the best of our ability and leave what we can't to those that can. Remember, We Preserve.'

The room cried 'We Preserve' angrily back at her and gradually left in pairs.

'Who was that?' I asked.

'Pharaoh Opisia Aroyo.'

'A pharaoh?'

'It's a nickname for the most senior quantum curator. I wouldn't be surprised if she was in the same cohort as Director Giovanetti as cadets.' Neith paused, looking thoughtful, and then smiled. 'Enough of this. As the pharaoh said, we have a mission to prepare for. Let's grab some beers and head to the beach and organise our learning strategies for the next few days. You know, this

194

is such an honour, I can't wait to prove the chancellor was right to back me like this. It is so important.'

So, we were jumping within a week. I hadn't heard that part of the briefing properly. For all Neith's smiles, that didn't sound good at all, but I played along and informed her that as senior partner the drinks were on her.

Once we were sitting out in the dunes, we removed our braces and Neith activated the little static buzzer that Asha had given her. 'Fuck.'

I had to agree with her, but I was a little out of my depth. 'Which is the more concerning issue, our mission or Asha's disappearance?'

Neith rolled her eyes. 'Giovanetti, obviously.' She shuddered slightly. 'You know I can't bring myself to call her Asha, that just seems so chummy.' Shrugging her shoulders, she carried on. 'You heard what Sam said. Being offered a proper mission so early on is a great accolade.'

'Oh, you were serious about that?' I thought she'd been acting. 'But what if it's not a great accolade? What if it's a way to get rid of us?'

'Seriously, Julius. How does sending us on a mission get rid of us? We'll be coming straight back.'

'But what if Alvarez is behind all this?'

'Alvarez?' Neith laughed delightedly and chinked her beer bottle against mine. 'What a fabulous idea. He's the world's most pompous ass, but a manipulator of time and space? A villain of pernicious intent? Inconceivable.' And she took a slug of beer.

'Do we think Asha is guilty?'

Neith turned away and looked out to sea. Her jaw clenched. 'I don't know. I've been proved to be a poor judge of character, but I think not. Last night she told us she was going to run a sub-routine to see if she could find any virus or more missing artefacts. This morning she's on the run. I think she found something or someone. I just hope that whoever it is doesn't find her.'

#22 – Neith

The sun was warm rather than hot, and the air was typically moist. I watched as little gnats drifted up from the river and small birds swooped in to dine on the wing. As was usual with northern Europe, everything was green and for once it wasn't raining.

Julius and I were relaxing on a soft green riverbank. Upstream was a ford, downstream, a small cascade, and it must have been raining recently because the river was running high and fast, catching the sunlight as it splashed over the rocks. Beyond the river, the clearing once again turned into woodland, but here in this glade the sun shone, and the trees were full of the sound of birds.

'So, that ford there and the track beyond, that's the main road from Mons to Vaucelles Abbey?'

I nodded, my mouth full of a juicy fig that I was happily devouring. I like these moments on a retrieval, especially in a pre-industrial age, where there wasn't a war or a natural disaster going on. At times like this, I could just unwind and enjoy my surroundings. For all the dampness of the air, I couldn't help but enjoy myself.

'And you're sure it's okay to just sit here and wait? We shouldn't be prepping or anything. Staking out the lie of the land. That sort of thing.'

'Relax. You know how this goes. Our incompetent servant took a rest at the inn at Mons. Poor chap had been travelling all day from his master's abode in Namur. His master being?'

'Robert of Namur, friend of Edward III.'

'And Edward is important because?'

'Because he commissioned the *Inventio Fortunata*.'

'And the *Inventio Fortunata* is important because?'

'Because it is a travel journal of the northern reaches of the globe, mainly the Arctic. It is full of stunning maps apparently and is the earliest example of bound cartography of the far north. I can't wait to see it.'

'Focus. So, what does Edward commissioning this book have to do with Robert of Namur?'

'Because Edward presented one of the seven copies he had made to our mate Robert.'

'He is not our mate,' I said, flicking my hand at him. 'But anyway, yes, he is now in possession of one of only seven copies of the *Inventio*. Or rather, his manservant is. Or rather, he was. As I was saying, having slept at Mons he may have enjoyed an evening of freedom a bit too much and has woken up with a hangover. A hangover that an opportune thief has noted, along with our chap's fancy livery and heavy book.'

'And there really isn't a monastery anywhere closer where Robert can get a copy made of his precious book?'

'When the renowned Vaucelles Abbey is only a two-day ride away? Nothing but the best for a gift from the King of England. So, the poor hapless servant prepares his horse, only to watch in horror as the thief nabs his satchel and gallops off into the woods. Our servant being unsteady of limb on account of old legs and a fierce hangover calls the guards. Who offer pursuit.'

I paused and listened to the sounds of the forest.

'Not yet anyway.'

'And when our thief gets here, we slip out of sight and wait for him to ride across the ford where the book will fall out of his bag and sweep towards the cascade?' queried Julius.

'Exactly, which is when you will dash into the river, grab the book and get back into the tree cover before the guards turn up.'

'And if the guards arrive early and do notice us?'

'We employ the time-honoured Plan B.'

'You mean we leg it.'

'Exactly. It'll be fun.'

I took another bite of my fig and threw one to Julius, who was looking distinctly nervous.

'And I go into the raging river because...?'

'Because I'm in a full-length dress and you're not. Plus, it's hardly raging. Even if you went over the rocks, it's just a few bruises. Chances are you won't even break anything. But that's not going to happen, is it? Because?'

'Because you'll come and rescue me?'

'No silly, because it's important that the book is out of the water as soon as possible. Your breaks will mend. The book won't. Imagine all those beautiful paints pouring off the page, the gold leaf lifting from the vellum. The leather binding absorbing the water and sinking to the bottom of the river.'

'Okay, fair enough. When you put it like that. And you're sure your little box of salts will dry out the water instantly?'

'Trust me. We've been doing this for a while. So long as the book only has a short dip it will be fine.'

'And how do we know this is the right time frame? What if we're late, what if we're early? What if...'

Oh dear. He did seem nervous. Maybe I shouldn't have teased him about the book getting destroyed in the river. As usual, Julius was more concerned with the object rather than the mission. But that was okay, as soon as the task was underway he would swing into action.

'Julius, I admire your attention to detail, but what can we do? The stepper deposited us here. It's 1483. The wrist brace says we have arrived an hour ahead of schedule, which is about as perfect as the QS gets. If it's wrong, there's nothing we can do about it. I can hardly call up your Google and find out the time, can I? Just chill.'

I'd forgotten how twitchy neos can be. I hitched my skirt up. The day's heat was making all these layers uncomfortable. Happily, we were just dressed as working folk so my tunic, although full-length and in layers, wasn't as bad as if we'd stepped across as nobility. I'd have loved to have gone for a paddle, but I had no idea when the thief would turn up and I didn't want to get caught unawares, trying to get my hose back on, tie them up, then get my poor excuse for shoes fastened. I was just wondering if I could push my luck when I heard distant hoof beats and we dashed into the tree line.

Sure enough, a few minutes later a rider came thundering past. As the horse cantered across the ford, it slipped slightly, jerking the rider. The satchel on his back tilted and a large leather-bound book slid out, hit the horse on its flanks and then tumbled into the water with a splash. If the rider noticed or not, he certainly wasn't stopping, and I realised the guards must be hot on his heels.

Julius must have realised as well, as he was already running towards the river. He grabbed the book out of the water and legged it back to me. I could hear more horses hoofs, two by the sounds of it, and we'd have been fine if Julius hadn't tripped, throwing the book forward. I grabbed it and shoved it in the desiccation pouch, and then the guards rode into the clearing.

'You there. Stop!'

Hitching my tunic up, I sprinted into the trees with Julius quickly alongside me.

'Do we step back now?' yelled Julius.

'No. We need to be out of sight.' It was one of our guiding principles: don't scare the natives by disappearing in front of them. The perception filter doesn't work when you are being actively pursued. Of course, sometimes curators did just 'disappear' as is evidenced by the amount of Beta folklore of ghostly vanishing characters, but personally, I just think that's sloppy.

'Keep running, the trees should slow the horses down.'

But not by much. This wasn't a gnarled old forest full of undergrowth. This was a large and open majestic beech wood. The dappled canopy high above our heads lent the forest floor a soft open aspect. The huge trees were widely spaced and, honestly, you could probably ride the entire household cavalry through ten abreast, but still, it was marginally better than being out in the open. At least our pursuer didn't have arrows.

Which, of course, is when an arrow went whizzing past my head. Our guy was a shoot first, ask questions later type. If he even bothered with questions and given that this was fifteenth century Europe, I figured that he was more a shoot first, loot the bodies later, kind of guy.

I was just about to shout to Julius to step, protocol be damned—I'd rather be sloppy than skewered—when I lurched to a halt and fell forward. I scrambled to get up and looked around in amazement at the arrow that had snagged my skirt and lodged the fabric into the leaf and twigs on the floor. I yanked it free, but now I was looking up at one of the most unpleasant faces I had seen in a while. The guard was fat and sweaty and smiling at me in a manner that even his mother would have slapped off his face. As he dismounted, Julius came running back towards us.

'Sir, sir. We beg your pardon. We ran because we were scared.'

I had already shielded the book with the wrist brace's perception filter and now pulled my tunic back down to my ankles. I made to get up, but the guard told me to stay where I was. Great. We were doing that then, were we? Part of me was almost willing him to try. If he took one step closer, I'd show him all about my own brand of medieval engagement. For now, though, I was happy for Julius to continue.

'Scared of the guard? Only an outlaw says that.'

'Yes, my lord.'

'Yes? What are you, an outlaw or an idiot?'

'An idiot, my lord.'

He paused, looking between us. So far Julius' grovelling lackey act seemed to be working. 'Hmm. And what are you doing in the clearing with this yaldish Saracen if it ain't obvious? Is she good?'

Maybe he didn't need to take a step closer. If he carried on talking like that, I was going to punch his teeth down his throat.

'Yes, sir, but a bit poxy, if you know what I mean. Leastways, that's what she says the scabs are.'

Great Ra, I nearly burst out laughing, the speed with which the guard stepped back from me. I gave my groin a scratch for good measure and then mumbled towards Julius.

'Tell the good lord about the man on the horseback. And his big satchel and how you reckoned as he might be up to no good.'

'She's right, sir, I reckon he was riding his horse so fast he must have been pursued by the devil hisself. Whatsoever he stole must be worth a fair penny.'

By now the guard was looking back over his shoulder. No doubt the other guard had ridden on, and our man here was trying to decide between riches and rape. I scratched myself again to help make his mind up. Spitting on the floor, he climbed back onto his horse and rode out of the wood and back towards the path.

As though his legs could hold him no longer, Julius collapsed down beside me.

'Sorry about the venereal disease. Wasn't sure of the best approach. I've never given anyone the clap before.'

And then he started laughing. Once the tinge of hysteria passed, I clapped him on the shoulder and told him how proud I was.

'Yallah. Let's go home and you can buy me a beer to make amends.'

We stepped apart from each other and on the count of three, hit our braces.

And nothing happened.

#23 – Sam

Sam was running through the daily paperwork. It was a tedious part of the job, but at the moment he was glad of the monotony. He was worried sick about Asha but didn't know how to proceed. Whatever report she had run must have caught someone's attention, and they were prepared to move swiftly against her. Only someone more senior than Asha had that level of clout, which could only mean that this went all the way to the top. That being the case, Sam didn't know who to turn to or what to do next. Neith and Julius were safe, and Sam had ordered Ramin to lie low until he had a plan. He knew Asha was likely to make contact once she was secure, but until then he needed to investigate quietly. After work, he would call in on Haru Giovanetti, Asha's husband. Maybe he could shed some light on everything? Sam didn't imagine that Asha had kept any secrets from her husband. Plus, Haru had a great wine cellar.

A red light started flashing above his door. That only lit when there was a problem with the stepper or during a drill. Heading down the corridor, all the warning lights were flashing, and staff were hurrying to their allotted stations. A drill wasn't on the cards, nor would there be one whilst curators were in the field as a drill always involved the shutting down and re-booting of the stepper.

As he strode into the control room, he was reminded of the incident six months earlier. Then everyone seemed to be perplexed and concerned. Today the anger was palpable. Not least because Farnaz Beckett and Simeon Jones were shouting at each other at the top of their lungs. Jones was a toadying little creep that had never knowingly used his backbone in all the years Sam had known him. Whereas Farnaz was renowned for staying calm in a crisis. That these two were literally screaming in each other's faces made Sam pause long enough to realise that all the rest of the technicians were just watching in astonishment, and all the machines were blank.

Bellowing over the top of them, both turned to look at him, and then promptly tried to talk at the same time.

'This piece of camel vomit has just switched off the stepper—'

'I want you to sanction your station head for her obscene use of—'

'Silence! Beckett, is the stepper truly offline?'

When she nodded, he looked at her in horror. Neith and Julius were out in the field with no way to get home.

'How much longer till we're back online?'

'Ten minutes, sir, but we've never switched it off whilst we've had curators on the other side. I don't know if the quantum link will still be in place.'

'Captain Nymens, it is impossible for there to be curators in the field. I don't know why she is lying.'

'Why did you switch it off?'

'As acting head of security, I wanted to test the system and see how everyone responded to an unscheduled drill.'

'When the hell were you appointed to that position?'

'Last night,' a deep baritone replied, and Sam turned to see that Chancellor Alvarez had entered the control room. 'I wasn't aware I needed your permission to appoint my staff, Captain Nymens?' Without giving Sam the chance to reply, he swept on. 'Now, Director Jones, what seems to be the problem?'

'Thank you, sir.' Jones puffed up his chest. 'I have been deeply concerned about some of the lax routines around here as you yourself have observed, and so I decided to run a drill this morning.'

'Excellent idea, but I don't understand.' He turned to Sam. 'Have QC Salah and NQC Strathclyde returned already?'

'No, sir, I understand they are still in fifteenth century northern Europe.'

'Then the machine can't have been switched off?' Turning back to Simeon, he frowned. 'Surely you checked the logs?'

'There was nothing on last week's rota.'

'I put them on the list myself just the other day. I have been much impressed by their skills, and I wanted to advance them as quickly as possible. Are you telling me that you didn't check the daily logs?' asked Alvarez, his voice getting increasingly clipped. He took a step towards the acting head of security and loomed over him. Alvarez had always used his height to bully and intimidate and knew that standing too close to someone would always remind them who was in charge.

'No, sir, I—'

'Captain Nymens, what sort of safety measures do you have in place that don't even stop the override of some bloody idiot.'

The blood drained out of Jones' face and his puffed up chest deflated just a little. Sam was furious that Alvarez was already looking to blame someone other than his brand new appointee.

'Of course we have safety protocols. Just because someone initiates a drill or a maintenance routine doesn't mean it happens. If the quantum stepper is in active use, the switch can't be triggered. You would need to physically override it.'

'Which he did!' shouted Farnaz.

Both Sam and Alvarez looked at Simeon in astonishment.

'You manually overrode the safety switch?' asked Alvarez.

Simeon's chest had now pretty much deflated and beads of sweat ran down the side of his face.

'I wanted to make conditions as real as possible. According to the logs, there was no one in the field.'

'You fucking idiot,' said Alvarez, shocking everyone in the room who had never heard the chancellor say anything stronger than fiddlesticks and whoopsie-daisy. 'Wait outside my office. You had better start asking your ancestors to stand by your side because if we lose those two curators you won't be having any descendants. Go!'

Simeon Jones saluted sharply, turned, and left the room stiffly with his head high. As he put his hand on the door panel, Sam was gratified to see it was shaking.

'Captain Nymens,' said Farnaz, 'we're coming back online.'

The room was silent as all the control panels lit up and ran the basic diagnostics. Sam kept his eyes on the far wall, where a large screen of the globe showed all active agents. Every second he waited for the green light to flick on over the Low Countries. After a minute he asked Farnaz to run a mission report on Case No 345631.2/NS-JS.

'Already on it, sir. Hang on.' As she started reading the most recent mission reports on the screen she suddenly stopped and bowed her head. Taking a deep breath, she turned to face Sam and Alvarez, her face trembling to contain her emotions.

'Mission aborted: No recovery.'

#24 – Neith

'Try it again.'

'You think the tenth time might be lucky?'

Julius was watching me, waiting for me to fix things. I looked up at the trees and watched as a squirrel ran along a branch, leaping from one bough to another. Why couldn't I just spend the rest of my days lying on my back looking up at the trees with no one expecting me to have all the answers?

'Right. You know the drill. If we fail to return after three hours past the known extraction point, our braces will be automatically activated from the other side. It can feel like a bit of a yank, but at least it will get us back.'

'And if it doesn't?'

'It will. Our braces are working. They are attached to us and we'll be going home. So long as we're alive and the brace is on our wrist, we will be going home. Trust me.'

This had never happened to me before, but I knew the principle. I'd spoken to curators that it had happened to, and they said it felt like having your body pulled through your ear canal and then back out through your nostril, which sounded about as much fun as being covered in camel vomit. Been there, done that, in no hurry to repeat the experience.

Reassuring Julius, I suggested we walk downstream and sit by the river whilst we waited it out. No point in remaining in sight of the highway.

Julius got some pebbles out of the stream and we played noughts and crosses.

'So, your language module worked a treat, but I didn't catch "yaldish" any idea?'

Julius placed a pebble in the corner and won again, grinning at me. I could now see the tactic in the game.

'Honestly, Neith, I think he was being rude.'

'Spare me. He was about to try and rape me. I didn't think he was saying anything courtly.'

'A "yaldson" is the son of a prostitute, so I'm guessing that a yald is…' He trailed off and then quickly changed tack. 'Honestly, the way the words tumble into my brain is fabulous, all my Cambridge studies seem to come up to the surface as well. I reckon if I met Chaucer now we could have a right old chin wag.'

'That would be some party trick for a corpse, he's been dead some thirty years. But yes, if you already have knowledge of a language system, the brain tickle works a treat. Although, I noticed you swap into English, try to remember to stick to French on this side of the channel.'

I'd set a three-hour alert on our wrist braces and I was gratified to see we now only had five minutes left. It was lunchtime and I was getting hungry. Much longer and I'd be training my catapult at that squirrel.

'Will we get an alert, or will it just happen?'

'I think it just happens.'

My wrist brace buzzed.

'Is this it?'

'No, that's the timer I set. Any second now though, given quantum variations.'

We both sat and watched the river gurgle past and after about five silent minutes, Julius asked in a very calm voice how long a quantum variation could be.

It's fair to say that when life is going wrong, it starts going wrong very quickly. I knew sometimes curators hadn't returned from the field. They had always been recorded as died in service, but what if they hadn't? What if they were left standing in the middle of a field, shaking their wrist brace, shouting fuck a lot? I needed to make a plan, but first I needed to sort out our immediate problem. Food and shelter. All QCs step over with everything they need for a couple of days just in case the QS sends them back a few days early. In this case, we both had our braces and a bag of coins. Enough wealth to buy us anything we needed.

'Right. Here is what we are going to do. We are going to walk to Mons and find some lodgings for the night. Chances are we'll get yanked back along the way, but we may as well do something rather than sit on our arses waiting for rescue.'

'Then what?'

'Then I'll think of a plan. Honestly, Julius, this is going to be fine.'

He looked at me and then shrugged his shoulders. 'Fair enough. Hand me the book and let's go.'

I looked at him, puzzled.

'It's a big book, I'll carry it.'

I was about to protest then realised that what he suggested made sense. I was already hampered by the full-length tunic; no point in lugging a heavy tome around as well.

Several hours later, we trudged into town. By the time we arrived, I was reminded of how much I hated medieval footwear. The shoes were basically leather slippers and the only comfortable way to walk in them was toe first. Julius said they just needed a bit of dubbin and some soap on our feet. He was ridiculously chipper.

'Could you stop whistling?'

'As you wish.'

I glared at him. Every passing minute that we weren't yanked back made me realise just how serious our predicament was.

'Why are you so happy, anyway?'

'I'm just pretending that I'm Robin Hood on his Duke of Edinburgh's. Can't do much else at the moment as my travelling companion is not very chatty right now.'

I bit my tongue. I wasn't sure who the current Duke of Edinburgh was in this timeline, nor his relevance to our situation right now, but I understood Robin Hood well enough. If Julius even suggested I was Maid Marion, there'd be words exchanged. Less, hey nonny, and more not bloody likely.

At the inn, Julius took the lead and said we were on pilgrimage. I had converted to the one true faith and we were heading to Rome. The innkeeper praised God that I had been saved from the fires of hell and then said we could sleep on the floor indoors. He also offered us supper and some food for the road for a few pennies. A deal was struck, and we settled down by the fire with two jugs of beer. Shortly after, a girl placed a large chunk of bread on the table in front of us and two bowls of stew. I noticed that she smiled at Julius but crossed herself as she looked at me. I wouldn't mind, but she didn't even try to be surreptitious about it.

I rubbed my feet and then tucked into the food with deep reluctance. The northern diet was so heavy, I always felt like I had a belly full of rat poison after eating this stuff. Julius on the other hand said the stew reminded him of school and then waxed lyrical about how 'bloody amazing the bread was' and 'that butter is seriously first rate'. And then, before I knew it, he had got up and headed over to the bar where he was laughing with the innkeeper.

A moment later he returned, and shortly after that, the girl came back with an even prettier grin for Julius and more bread and butter. This time she even managed to give me a weak smile as well, then fled in case I somehow tainted her.

I shook my head and took another swig of the warm ale.

'Something you said earlier about Rome got me thinking.'

I outlined my plan. In the spring of 1484, a wife was going to lose her temper with her husband and sell his Botticelli painting of his mistress to the first person she meets. The painting is never heard of again. The artwork was on the quantum list of missing treasures. All we needed to do was hang around the streets of Florence and wait for an assigned pair of curators to come and collect it.

'Isn't that a self-fulfilling prophesy?' asked Julius. 'They were very strict on that in lectures. We couldn't actively engage in the timeline.'

'No, the wife sells it to a tinker that decides to scrape the paint off it and re-sell the canvas and frame. He thinks the colours are gaudy. The curators will retrieve it after the first scrape. And travel home with the missing Botticelli. Plus, two extra curators.'

'But what about splicing?'

'Think it through. What do we have that they also have?'

'Back-up braces!'

'Exactly, and their braces will have an active link. We'll just borrow those and head home.'

There was one tiny problem with my plan, and I finished my stew whilst I waited for Julius to discover it.

'Doesn't that risk creating a paradox and destroying the universe?'

Like I said. Tiny problem.

'It will be fine if we come back to our own timeline.'

'And what if those curators are not from our timeline but are from two years in the future or ten?'

It was tricky. If we turned up on Alpha ten years after we had left it, we might cause some issues. If we arrived ten years before we left we could have two sets of me running around, and a Julius in very much the wrong place. Theoretically, the painting hadn't yet been retrieved in my Alpha timeline. We, theoretically, should only meet curators from the future. But so far no one had been prepared to prove that hypothesis because no one had ever returned. Which some said was proof enough.

'I guess we're going to find out because I am not staying here a moment longer than I have to.'

We fell into silence again and I waited for Julius' second question.

'But this is all theoretical, isn't it? I mean it's delayed but we could still get yanked at any time, couldn't we?'

I frowned. He had missed the relevance of what I'd said about an active link a minute ago. 'Have you checked the location monitor on your brace?'

He looked at it quickly, to any casual observer he was merely scratching his arm. The location monitor could always tell you where you were. In modern Beta Earth, it linked into their satellite network. For historical assignments, the brace used the quantum link back to Alpha and worked out where we were that way. Now it just showed a map of northern Europe and our last known location. About ten miles away from where we were currently sitting.

'It hasn't updated.' He looked at me in horror. 'Neith. Is the link broken?'

I nodded. 'I don't know how that happened. All I know is that they have no way to find us and bring us back. They don't even know if we're alive.'

The flames flickered, casting shadows on the wall, and I could see that night had fallen around us. We were the only travellers left in the room and the innkeeper had pulled out two pallets ready for our sleep. Yawning, I told Julius to try to sleep as worrying about it wasn't going to change anything. Despite all my concerns, I fell asleep within minutes of lying on the pallet and slept like the dead.

The following morning I rose to the sound of the cockerel and the serving girl from the previous evening cleaning out the grate.

'God be with you.'

She flinched, but she did smile. Dipping her head, she thanked me, asking if I had slept well. I was about to reply when Julius suddenly snored loudly and we both giggled in universal sisterhood. I made my way to the earth closet and by the time I returned Julius was wide awake, if somewhat tousled.

'Do you know, I don't think I slept a wink last night.'

'You were snoring pretty loudly for a man that wasn't asleep.'

'I do not snore.'

At this moment, the girl returned, giggling, and laid out some hard-boiled eggs and a pitcher of water.

I watched Julius blush and then laugh as he peeled off the shell from his egg, blowing on his fingers as he did so.

'Well, maybe I did get some sleep,' he said as he held the egg out to me and picked up the second one. 'But not much.'

It didn't take long to eat, and soon we were back on the road heading south. The road was now running through collections of small fields, evidently the arable land was good here. A woman walked past us driving a herd of small pigs ahead of her, no doubt off to rootle in the woods we had just left, but other than the occasional worker tilling the field, the countryside was empty.

'I've been thinking about the potential paradox, and I think I have a solution. Although it might create its own problems. But first, we need to change our clothes.'

'That will help with the paradox, will it?' Julius was chewing on a piece of bread, which was supposed to last us all day. We had money to buy more, but the innkeeper had said we were a two-day walk from the next settlement and we'd be sleeping under the stars tonight. Which was another reason for the change of clothes.

'Nope, but I am not planning on walking all the way across Burgundy, or whatever this territory is currently being called.'

When we had stepped over we were dressed in the simple and rough homespun of common labourers. If we wanted a cart or horses to ride, we needed to show that we were in a different class. Common serfs did not ride horses. Clothing was strictly regulated in the Middle Ages, but all you needed to do was fake it to make it. I explained what I was thinking, and Julius started to laugh.

'You cannot rob a nun.'

'Think it through. It's the easiest way for me to travel without drawing attention. We can either travel as nobility, or we can travel as religious people.'

'The clergy,' he corrected me.

'Whatever. We don't have enough retinue to be nobles, but if we can be clergy, no one will challenge us, and I can wear a veil and keep my hands covered so no one will stare at my skin colouring.'

Being Egyptian in northern Europe during the time of the Inquisition was a tad inconvenient. As we got into Italy, I'd be able to blend in better with the Mediterranean population, but up here in the north I was sticking out like a sore thumb.

'And what's your paradox shaking solution?'

'We go and talk to the man that first proposed a quantum stepper.'

Julius looked at me with his eyes on stalks and laughed so hard he choked on the piece of bread. This, in my opinion, was an utter waste, as he spluttered it over the path. When he had recovered, he apologised and wiped the tears of laughter from his eyes.

'So, let me get this straight. First, we rob a nun, then a priest, and then we call in on Leonardo da Vinci. What can possibly go wrong?'

interlude 4

The following text conversation was retrieved during a sweep of the ghost files of the Q Zone security system. It has been added to the evidence report for Case No: 234530/H. The second party is yet to be identified.

— What just happened?

— We're taking steps to clean up operations. I'm under pressure to get the supply line running again. I have a huge backlog of orders. After your threat to expose our operations to keep the codex hunt safe the other day, I ordered that Neith and Julius be removed from the game. I take care of the supply line. I get treasures into the hands of wealthy patrons. I take care of the whole operation, whilst you and your agents go running around looking for missing book pages. It's my efforts that fund your wild goose chase.

— And it's my goose chase that is going to change the world. Did she give you approval to eliminate Salah because I didn't?

— No. I don't need to go running to her every time I want to do something. It's called initiative.

— It's called a chain of command, you bloody fool. Have you any idea what you've done?

— I've cleaned up the mess. A mess I might say you should have cleaned up long ago. Your policy of sitting back and watching seemed lax to me.

— Whereas your policy of running in and creating chaos is a good one, is it?

— Honestly, calm down. It's worked perfectly. They've gone and they are never coming back. Giovanetti is in the frame for stealing the artefacts. Captain Nymens hasn't noticed anything untoward, and if Ramin Gamal even so much as twitches, we will prosecute him for crimes as yet to be determined. In a few months, we can start to fulfil supply orders again.

— Listen to yourself. So smug. I won't trust Giovanetti until she is dust. That she is in the wind makes her more dangerous, not less. Nymens has never struck me as a fool, and whilst I don't know Ramin, if we were going to prosecute him then we should have done it six months ago. Not put him on sand leave. But none of that is what is concerning me. What concerns me is Salah and Strathclyde.

— But I've told you. I've fixed that. They're stranded. Forever locked away.

— You fool. Do I have to spell it out? Where are they stranded?

— Northern France, I believe. I didn't go into the details; I just gave the order.

— Did you check the year?

— No.

— 1483

— Europe 1483?

221

— Ah, the penny drops does it? You have stranded a desperate curator right in the same timeframe as Leonardo da Vinci.

— Shit.

#25 – Ramin

The problem with walking into a bar where you don't know anyone is that you spend ages chatting to total strangers. Basic hospitality meant that if you saw a new face in your local, you'd say hello to them, make them feel welcome. As Ramin wandered into the bar, he tried to spot Sam as quickly as he could. However, first he had to chat to several tables of strangers who invited him to join them. Normally he loved this and was always fascinated by the people he met, but today he was trying to find someone in particular. He made his way through the busy bar. A popular band was playing on the stage and the room was jumping. Every time he stopped to decline an invitation, everyone had to shout over the noise. There was lots of laughter and miming, but Ramin explained he was meeting someone. Another time, hopefully?

Eventually, in an uncomfortable but quiet corner, tucked away by the rear entrance, Ramin found Sam sitting with his hand wrapped around his pint. As he sat down, Sam looked up and Ramin was shocked to see the change in him. He looked broken.

'Is it Giovanetti? Have they found her? Is she okay?'

Before Sam could reply, a server came over and Sam ordered another two pints. With the drinks delivered almost instantly, Ramin waited in increasing dread. He knew Sam and Asha had been friends since college, and whilst he had only ever seen her as a dry and dull person, in Sam's office the other day, she had suddenly struck him as one of the sharpest most vibrant people he had ever encountered. If she was dead, he was sorry that he hadn't had the chance to get to know this side of her.

'Is Asha okay?' he asked again. Sam's silence was worrying. 'I haven't heard anything on the news report.'

'Why would you expect to hear anything on the news? We don't do that, do we? We don't want to scare the horses. Let's all stay calm and compliant, hey?'

Ramin looked at Sam closely. He didn't sound drunk, he didn't look drunk either, but these were strong words and Ramin was concerned and relieved that neither were wearing their braces.

'Sam—'

'It's not Asha, Ra. It's Neith and Julius. They're...' He paused and with a deep groan looked up at the ceiling.

Suddenly Ramin didn't want Sam to finish his sentence. He wanted to get up from the table and leave the room. Sam was about to say something, and Rami could think of no way to stop the words and the reality behind them. He wasn't prepared for his world to end.

'Ramin. They're dead.'

He picked up his pint and took another drink, not tasting it, waiting for Ramin to respond.

'I don't understand. It was a routine step. Have you done a remote recall?'

'It's no good, Ramin. There was an incident with the stepper and their link was severed from our end. They've gone.' And Sam explained what had happened in the control room that morning. Whilst Sam spoke, Ramin focused on the details. Thinking about life without Neith would have to wait. Once he started to try and process her death, he would be no good to anyone.

'There's no way he did that accidentally. No one is that incompetent.' Jones wasn't held in high regard by many custodians, but none of them would call him stupid. 'What did Alvarez do?'

'Fired him on grounds of gross incompetence.'

'Good. But wait…'

'Exactly, now there's no need for a review of his conduct.' The implication of an immediate firing was that Simeon Jones had made a colossal mistake and the only lessons that needed to be learnt were to not do it again.

'Did he put up any appeal or explanation?'

'No, the record will simply state that by his own action he knowingly switched off the safety restraints whilst not informing anyone.'

'Bullshit.'

'Exactly.'

Both men finished their pints and Ramin waved for two more.

'What now?' It was a sense of the inevitable that neither even contemplated a way to get the stranded curators back. It wasn't possible. If the connection was lost, it was gone. Their only hope was to stumble upon some other curators in the field and return with them, screwing up the timeline. The fact that no lost curator had ever returned this way spoke volumes as to how it wasn't possible. Scholars had postulated that curators that attempted to return to the wrong timeline would just be mangled up in the quantum vortex. It was a lecture that gave young cadets nightmares.

'I'm recalling you from sand leave. I have already put in an urgent request to the high council. You are the last survivor of the Fabergé mission, as every other agent involved is now dead. For that reason alone, you need protection. I don't know who is behind this but that doesn't matter right now. It's enough that someone is, and I'm not losing anyone else. You're moving into cadet quarters and I'm assigning two of Asha's hand-picked curators to keep an eye on you.'

'Sam. Doesn't this all seem extreme?'

'Yes, but what else can I do? Paul is dead, so is Clio. She was clearly acting under someone's instructions. Asha has been accused of treachery and is now missing. Neith and Julius are lost in time. Jones was not acting independently. We don't know who is behind this and all I can do right now is protect you and hunker down. We need to see what our enemy does next.'

The band switched style and was now calling people to come and join them on stage for a bit of karaoke. A group had crowded the stage and were singing the Beta classic 'Postman Pat' with the whole bar joining in on 'and his black and white cat'.

'Incidentally, you won't be allowed to wear the red armband on campus. The chancellor has deemed that given the high recent rate of attrition the red armbands are bad for morale.'

'No. No, I won't do that. To not wear the red for Neith and Julius would be to dishonour them.'

'Ramin. It's an order. What would Neith prefer, your life or her honour? Don't fight me on this, we don't know who is against us. We have to tread on the crocodile's back and not wake him up. Am I clear?'

Ramin scowled and finished his drink. 'Can I wear it off campus?'

'Yes. Nubi's balls,' exhaled Sam. 'Yes, if you insist. But keep your head down. Tomorrow I want you to report to cataloguing. I'm not risking you on quantum service right now so you can work in the archives instead. Just be careful and if you notice anything odd or missing, let me know before you tell anyone else. Incidentally, Soliman has placed both Asha's disappearance and Neith and Julius' loss under a Level Eight gag.'

Nodding, Ramin left the bar, aware that the two custodians that Sam had mentioned were waiting across the street. He gave them a small gesture of acknowledgement and headed back to his apartment to pack up a few things.

The last time he had seen Neith he had called her a camel's arse, had sneered at her and called her names. What a sodding stupid waste of time. They had been best friends since before they could walk, they had laughed and fought together, cheated in lessons, and raced each other across the sand dunes whilst the rest of the class tried to keep up. They would dare each other to dive into the river from higher and higher rocks. When he shaved off his hair, she followed suit. He would vet her boyfriends and she would vet his, and when occasionally they both liked the same guy, they agreed to pass rather than have the other lose out. They never swapped boyfriends, but they lived their lives swapping books and insights. As they became adults and settled down a bit, they remained best friends and even if they were no longer seeing who could catch an ostrich or outrun a hippo, they would still drink each other under the table, an event that Ramin due to his greater size, would always win.

Ramin smiled all the way home, remembering his life with Neith, and didn't cry until he was safely inside his newly allocated quarters.

#26 – Julius

I was having the time of my life. Granted, my fundamentals felt like bruised walnuts, but this was still one hell of an adventure. Currently, I was riding a carthorse, hence the walnuts, and we were heading towards Rheims.

Three days earlier, we had left Mons on foot and had arrived in Maubeuge that same night, tired and footsore. Neith had asked for shelter for the evening at the abbey. In return for their hospitality, she spent a day in the laundry. She also fixed the binding on some of their books in the scriptorium and tweaked their recipe for gall ink. At the end of the day she left with some food and the various robes of a nun tucked around under her clothes and in her satchel. It was a fair exchange.

My own retrieval was less edifying. All the priests and monks I saw were in groups or pairs. Eventually, I followed a cardinal into an inn. A cardinal was a risk given that they tended to draw attention, due to their high rank, but I was getting desperate. This man of the cloth was a truly unpleasant character, demanding a free meal and insisting that he be given the best seat at the table. When he headed upstairs with one of the tavern girls for what he called a "confessional", I felt my conscience was clear. I'd wandered upstairs and drawn my knife, but when I entered the room, I saw he had chosen to remove all his clothes anyway. Given the current placement of his face, he was not in a position to observe my entrance. The young woman looked at me in alarm, but when she saw I was only after his clothes she winked at me and then groaned loudly. Grabbing the clothes, I gave her a big thumbs up and a fake blessing. Grinning, I quietly closed the door behind me.

I then waited for Neith at the edge of town, having bought two very dodgy looking nags and some food for the next stage of the journey. I named my noble steed Lightning, in the hope that he might try to live up to his name. All in all, I was very impressed that my training had paid off. Also, I didn't die, which was clearly a bonus.

By the time Neith joined me, she was beaming from ear to ear and had a bounce back in her step that I hadn't seen in a long time. When she saw her horse and heard what I had called mine, she laughed and christened hers Zephyr. Zephyr and Lightning looked at each other and then returned to chewing the grass.

Cardinal Julius and Sister Bonaventure's fabulous fantastical road trip. I even called it a road trip out loud and was instantly swatted for my troubles. For the first day, Neith insisted I remain in my rags, in case soldiers came looking for someone impersonating a cardinal but none came, and I was glad to swap the rough itchy weave for fine cotton and silk.

When we had started to travel in our new robes, Neith had suggested that I create a detailed persona and get into character as quickly as possible. I decided to call myself Cardinal Julius of Walsingham. Walsingham was a famous site of pilgrimage, which lent an extra level of prestige and credibility to my persona. Plus I'd been there on many a school trip, so if I had to talk to anyone about it I wouldn't be too flummoxed.

'The best sort of lie is one with a lot of truth in it,' said Neith. 'Your middle English is excellent, you look English, and we're far enough away from England that no one will doubt you are who you say you are.'

Now I grinned across at Neith, who may or may not have smiled back. A cart was heading towards us and she had covered her face. Every time I looked at her with the veil down, I had to stop myself from shuddering. She looked like something out of a Japanese horror movie. Her black veil was heavy and fell past her shoulders, standing out in contrast to the pale cream robes she wore. We must have made a striking sight as she sat next to my more flamboyant red robes and red hat.

As the cart came closer, the man slowed his horse and made a point of wanting to talk. Neith's idea of dressing in holy orders was a good one, but it did mean that people would keep talking to us. As I was dressed as a cardinal, Neith said it would be well within character for me to act superior and to ride on, ignoring all I considered beneath me. From what I recalled of some of the clergy in this period, I might well not stop until I met the Pope. Even then I might pause. Still, having pinched the clothes from a man of God, I felt the least I could do to atone was to act in as Christian a manner as I could. Just in case the big man was looking down.

Besides which, we hadn't seen anyone all day and it was nice to chat. Neith was gradually becoming more and more morose, and our conversations had petered away into nothing whereas I was focusing on the world around me.

I was gaining so much insight, it was astounding. I was also impressed with everyone's hygiene levels. I'd assumed everyone would smell more. Of course, it was highly probable that I stank as well and had just stopped noticing.

'God be with you.'

'And also with you, Your Excellency. Are you travelling far today?'

I explained we were heading to Rheims, where we hoped to buy a covered wagon or better horses.

'Please call me Father, I think it's more appropriate right now.' I laughed in self-deprecation. Normally a cardinal would not be on such a lowly draught horse. 'These noble steeds are better at pulling carts than bearing riders, so they are, and I think Sister Bonaventure would be grateful.'

'I'm sure the Lord will provide in Rheims. It's a large enough place, but unless he provides you with wings, you won't be there today. I'd say noon tomorrow.'

'Well now, that's a shame to be sure.'

The Irish accent had surprised me. I had channelled the old priest from my boarding school, Father Eamonn. A great man and a demon on the rugby pitch, he was also prepared to turn a blind eye to anyone caught smoking. A fact that improved his standing immensely amongst the lower fifth. However, if he caught you drinking, he'd confiscate it on the spot and report you. Unless it was whiskey. If it was whiskey, it would still be confiscated, but nothing was ever mentioned. As such, the senior school soon became ardent whiskey drinkers and Father Eamonn smiled even more. What I hadn't really remembered at the time was that he was Irish, and now his way of speaking was coming through in my persona. Neith thought it was funny. She was trying to ditch my Grandma's Welsh accent, whilst I was embracing my rugby tutor's Irish one.

'I have some apples in the cart and some dried beef if you would like some for this evening's meal, Father?'

I thanked him and went for my little pouch of small coins. The larger money bag was under my robes. As soon as I did, the poor man pulled back in alarm saying he would take nothing from a man of the cloth. I smiled, reminding myself to poke Neith about my Christian values later on.

We would have chatted longer, but Neith's horse began to get restless. No doubt because Neith had probably nudged it, but she was right, we needed to get on. As we left, the farmer warned us that the road south from Rheims had become increasingly lawless. He recommended travelling west instead, skirting the woods completely or hiring a guard to escort us through that section. I thanked him for his advice, blessed him for his gifts, and we rode on south. As the road curved out of view, Neith threw back her veil and scowled at me.

'If you mention Christian values again, I swear I will eat both apples and all the meat and you can chew on the hard crust of your piety.'

I laughed, but I could see she was serious. All this religion was grinding her down. She kept protesting how stupid the entire concept was, but I wasn't going to rise to the bait. I knew she was just trying to pick a fight. Every time she said something belittling, I would just nod my head and say she was probably right. If I'm honest, it was beginning to annoy me, but I was determined to let it go. As a lecturer in comparative religions and faith systems, I had learnt to credit everyone with their own opinion. I loved a good debate, but right now Neith was just too scared and angry. I tried to reach out.

'Okay, let's travel on a bit and make camp for the night. There's no point riding in the dark. Maybe in the morning, you will see things in a better light.'

'A better light?'

It was then that I said something woefully stupid. I know it now, and I knew it the moment the words left my mouth.

'Yes, you know. Maybe cheer up a bit.'

See? Stupid. Beyond stupid.

'Cheer up a bit?' Neith pulled her horse to a halt and just stared at me and then let rip. 'Cheer up? We are in the middle of the fifteenth fucking century, I have blisters on my arse, I am wearing the heaviest sweatiest piece of clothing I have ever worn, and I've worn armour for fuck's sake. I am stranded with a whistling idiot, riding a horse only good for dog food. I have nothing to cheer up about. You have no idea how scared, lost and isolated I feel right now.'

By now she was shouting and the birds in the nearby trees had all flown up in sudden alarm, with her horse twisting in circles as she got more and more agitated.

I jumped off Lightning and grabbed at Neith's reins trying to calm Zephyr down and telling her to get off the horse. Swinging her leg down, she pushed the horse away from her and stormed off whilst I tied the horses to a nearby tree branch. It was half an hour before she returned. Half an hour for me to stew and work myself up.

I watched as she sat down beside me and cleared her throat.

'Julius I—'

But I wasn't going to let her apologise, not until I'd had my say.

'You say I have no idea how scared, lost and isolated you feel? Have you any idea how self-centred you sound? Hello? Six months ago, I woke up in another world. Another sodding world! With no way to get home to my timeframe. When I looked in the mirror even my face had changed. For the past six months, I have been surrounded by people who think I'm a freak show. I'm patronised or stared at. I was stranded on my own without a single friendly face to help me fit in. You'd buggered off and

Rami wasn't allowed to visit me in the first few weeks. So, don't talk to me about "scared, lost or isolated".'

I was breathing heavily, and I realised, as the words came spilling out, that I had been waiting a long time to say them. The silence stretched out between us and I listened as our fragile friendship slowly dissolved within it. I wanted to undo the situation, but I couldn't take the words back. I had meant every syllable. At least it was out in the open, and if I had offended Neith, then she would have to learn to live with it.

'I'm sorry, Julius. I'm a fool. I don't like being out of control and this is about as out of control as I've ever been. Forgive me?'

I wanted to, but I couldn't.

'Forget it. Let's ride on.' I handed the reins to Neith, but she wouldn't take them.

'Please, I'm sorry. What more can I say?'

'You can apologise to Zephyr.' I know it sounded silly, but honestly, I've always had a soft spot for animals and calling Zephyr dog meat was unforgivable.

'What?'

'Say sorry to Zephyr. It's hardly his fault you're in this situation. And don't look at me like that.'

Neith tried to compose her face. 'But he's an animal?'

'Horses are very sensitive.'

'So is my backside.' She smiled, and I could see she was attempting to build a bridge.

'I'm not joking, Neith. Apologise or we can just ride on in silence.'

Neith looked at me and, honestly, I don't know why I had suddenly decided to pitch everything on that point, but I had. Defending a medieval horse had suddenly become my life's goal. I guess Neith could see it as well as she suddenly let out a groan and went over to Zephyr. Rubbing him on the nose like I'd shown her, she offered him a full and handsome apology plus the apple in her pocket.

'Thank you, Neith. And I'm sorry as well. This is a mess, but we will get through it. We'll get to Milan, we'll get to meet one of my heroes, then on to Florence, and we'll step back to your home. Then you can tell everyone how you had to endure blisters, whistlers and a bad case of the pox, all whilst dressed as a nun.'

By now she was smiling. The fight had cleared the air and we got back onto our horses, wincing a bit, and continued on our way.

'When we get to Rheims, are we getting better horses or a covered wagon because my posterior is making an argument for a nice bench seat?'

Lightning was a wonderful companion, and far more biddable than the camels I had failed to get to grips with, but he was as slow as treacle. Neith looked across at me, nodding.

'Agreed, plus a covered wagon means we can sleep in that and avoid the whole say a prayer for me nonsense, in the local taverns.'

'Yes, Sister Bonaventure.' Seeing that she was in a good mood, I decided that now was the time to grasp the nettle. 'Neith. Are you ready to talk about what us being stranded means?'

'Other than we're screwed?'

I ignored her question and carried on. 'Either something cataclysmic happened, something accidental happened, or something deliberate happened.' I ticked off the scenarios on my fingers, guiding Lightning with my knees. 'Cataclysmic seems unlikely, but you never know. Accidental seems a non-starter. The security protocols in place for that to happen would have all had to collapse at the same time. Therefore, deliberate seems the most likely to me.'

Neith scowled, but I continued.

'You and I have both seen plenty of evidence in the past six months that things aren't going to plan on Alpha Fabulous. Paul was clearly working for a third party, and that third party had to be Alpha-based. For what it's worth, I believe Rami. Paul was being blackmailed and framed, and Clio was in on it.'

I waited for Neith's customary bulldog defence of her friend, but this time she was quiet. I pushed on.

'Recently you discovered a file anomaly with the Mongolian crown. And we then discover that Sam and the head of security have been monitoring this situation for months, possibly years. The night that Asha breaks cover and runs a test on the files, she is exposed as a thief and disappears. If that doesn't stink of convenience and cover-up, I don't know what does. On the same day, you and I are selected for another step mission. Ahead of schedule and outside of standard protocol. And then we are abandoned. Do you know what my greatest worry is right now?'

Neith looked over at me.

'That Ramin is safe?'

I let out a huge sigh of relief.

'Yes. That the last existing member of the Fabergé team is safe and well. Does this mean you accept he's innocent?'

Neith had taken to plaiting Zephyr's mane as we rode along, and now she was unpicking the plaits and waving out the mane.

'Yes. No. Honestly, Julius, I have no idea. If I believe him, it means he was right, that Clio was a traitor. And I'm just not ready to believe that.'

Well, at least she was moving a bit. And I understood part of her dilemma. Rami had explained that they had been teammates from the beginning. On every mission, she had put her life in Clio's hands. They could finish each other's sentences, run into a burning building knowing what the other would do before even checking. They were a perfect unit. To suggest that at some point Clio had started to work against the mouseion, and Neith had failed to notice, was a big deal in terms of trust and friendship. As Ramin said, it would have been easier if Clio had tried to recruit Neith. Then it would only be the betrayal that Neith had to get her head around, not the deceit as well.

'Okay, she's dead anyway, so let's just leave her out of it. But can you agree someone on the Fabergé team was working with someone on Alpha? Someone that never came to light during the subsequent investigation.'

'Yes,' said Neith, 'because the investigation concluded that Paul was wholly to blame.'

'Pretty convenient, hey?'

Neith was silent and I pressed on. 'I think the fact that Asha has been framed and we have been removed from the picture is fairly damning evidence that Paul was not working alone. If we accept that Paul is the guilty party. Do you agree?'

'Yes, but it just seems incredible. That someone would be working behind the scenes to destroy and manipulate the entire framework of the mouseion just to steal an egg.'

'Not just an egg, Neith, remember *The Storm on the Sea of Galilee* and the crown, and who knows how many other things. And for what it's worth, I also don't think it's just one person. I think it's a whole network.'

Neith held up her hand.

'You go too far. One rogue element is hard enough to fathom. An entire organisation? No, we're not Betas. We don't behave like that.'

'You can accept that one person can, but not more than one? Someone had you followed, remember.'

Now she was annoying me. This devotional love of their society made Neith and her fellow inhabitants dangerously compliant. For a moment, I wondered if it was a global conspiracy to subdue the masses but decided against it. It was more likely to be a few bad eggs that knew how to take advantage of a situation.

'Okay. Let's focus on the individual then. Who's your money on? My front runners are Sam, Asha, or Alvarez. What about you?'

I waited until she had finished laughing.

'None of them for a start. Sam is as straight as the day is long, plus his wife would have his guts for garters if she thought he would do anything to jeopardise their children's future. Nope, he's a non-starter.'

'He has total access to the stepper and knows all the curators from their first days as cadets.'

'No, that bird won't bite. But I'm looking forward to seeing him again and letting him know what you said.'

I shrugged and changed tactics. She was probably right, anyway. I liked Sam, he just felt honest. 'Asha then. She's head of security. You yourself said you don't know of anyone brighter, that she could have been head of engineering.'

'Exactly. Too bright. If she was behind this, we'd be dead, and no one would be any the wiser.'

An uncomfortable but valid point, although as far as her world was concerned we were apparently now dead, anyway.

'Alvarez then.'

'The exact opposite. That man is an utter buffoon. He wouldn't have the skill or the imagination to pull this off. Great Ra, I'd tell him, but he'd only report me.'

'You wouldn't tell Asha what I said then?'

241

'Tell Director Giovanetti that you thought she was a traitor? I wouldn't inflict her wrath on my worst enemy. No, honestly, I don't rate any of your choices. But I agree, it has to be someone senior with security clearance. My money would be on someone in the high council. Someone like al-Cavifi. Oh, that would be nasty, but I think she'd be in the perfect position to get away with everything that's happened so far.'

'Nasty?'

'Because she's so well loved, she has stood for three consecutive terms. That's thirty years of growth and prosperity, under the same hand. I've heard she wants to retire at the end of this tenure so she can spend more time playing with her grandchildren and re-focusing on her work in particle engineering.'

The more Neith said, the more I thought the director sounded like a perfect candidate. Except that she was too far removed from the mouseion; she'd need an inside man. Or woman.

We rode along in silence, thinking about our current predicament. We were getting closer to the city as we were seeing more people on the road and in the fields. In one field I watched as a small child toddled through the rows of plants towards a man that was tilling the soil. The child held something up to him and he bobbed down to inspect her treasure. Their two heads were almost touching as they crouched down, gazing intently at something, his scythe creating a frame over their heads. At the far end of the field was a woman with a baby slung to her chest and another small child walking alongside her. They were collecting something from the field and placing it in baskets.

It was funny, but looking at that family group they seemed as modern and as human as either Neith or I. A small family all pulling together. I hope they all made it. This period of history was not a gentle one.

'Okay, let's focus on things that we *can* sort out. A bed for the night and a wagon for tomorrow.'

Neith had far more experience than me in shopping in a medieval city, but she was a little hampered by her habit. It would be down to me. Having successfully stolen a cassock, she felt comfortable in me buying a wagon and kitting it out for a long ride. Either that or she was desperate for a bath. We had taken the warning about thieves in the wood on board but decided that hiring guards or travelling in a convoy would draw too much attention to ourselves. We might pass a casual inspection, but after days on the road, we were liable to give ourselves away.

Stopping at the city gates, we asked where the best inn was and headed that way, securing two rooms, two hot baths and an evening meal to be served upstairs. After Rheims, there were going to be few places that offered such luxuries, so we may as well grab them whilst we could.

Saying goodbye to Neith, I asked the innkeeper where I could obtain what I needed for the road, and he loaned me one of his lads to take me to all the places I required.

By the end of the day, I was several pieces of gold lighter, but in the morning we'd have a fully stocked wagon and two decent horses. I'd traded Lightning and Zephyr and told the merchant that they were fine and noble beasts, if not the best, for riding. Looking at my two new horses, I decided to call them Tom and Jerry because I thought Dragon and Donkey might cause some confusion.

I'd even gone a little mad and bought two sleep rolls stuffed with feathers as opposed to straw, I was a priest after all, and we needed to keep up appearances. Plus, I had caught Neith wincing as she'd swung down from her saddle, and I thought she might appreciate a little extra padding as well.

#27 – Julius

The following day, I paid the innkeeper for some food for the journey and went off in search of Neith. In the yard, a group of young women were huddled intently around the veiled figure of Neith. Whatever she was saying, she had their undivided attention. I snuck up and listened in.

'The best thing you can do is get married, learn his trade, and pray he dies quickly. An old husband is best as you may be able to excite him into an early death. Then refuse to marry again and run his business yourself. If that's not on the cards, consider a convent, but choose wisely. Convince your parents that their position in society depends on the status of your convent. And remember, whatever you do, avoid getting pregnant. And don't believe any of their lies about not getting pregnant. You can get pregnant if it's your first time, if you keep one foot on the floor, if he doesn't put it all—'

I cleared my throat, and the young women sat around the veiled Neith looked at me in alarm and ran off shrieking.

'Sister Bonaventure. Do you think we can make tracks? Before the city's fathers come and burn you for witchcraft?'

Neith tilted her head and looked up at me. I couldn't see her expression, but I was fairly certain she was smiling.

'Just doing my bit for emancipation.'

'Get thee to a nunnery indeed.'

'Do I look like Ophelia?'

I offered her my hand and pulled her up. She still reminded me of a terrifying vision of a nun in some European art-house film. I think Hamlet might have snapped out of his mope pretty sharpish if Ophelia had a bit more Neith in her veins.

'Come on then, let's hit the road. The innkeeper reckons we should make it to Troyes tonight, but that we shouldn't stop at all today. The woods are being regularly patrolled by the city guards, but there are brigands in there that haven't been flushed out yet.'

Our route was set. We were heading south to Troyes and then east over the Alps to Milan, the aim being to make it by the end of summer. We had plenty of money, so when we arrived in Milan we would swap our identities to cloth merchants. Neith could then blend in far better with the other traders and, even though she was a woman, her skin colouring would add to her foreign ways. We would catch up with da Vinci—the idea still made me laugh—then head down to Florence to wait upon the temper of a wronged wife, and hitch a lift home.

As we made our way out of the city I was delighted to be sitting on a lovely, padded cushion. I felt like an old man going on about a cushion but believe me sometimes those simple pleasures are terribly important. No one else seemed to be heading out on the road today and, in fact, a lot of traders were heading in for the market.

A few called out for blessings—I duly obliged, despite the tutting to my side—and was rewarded with reports that the road was free from hindrance.

I pulled the *Inventio Fortunata* out of the satchel and began to read.

'Again? You're going to damage it, you know. It belongs in the archive.'

'It's brand new,' I protested for the umpteenth time. Every opportunity I had, I sat and read it. The author had a lovely wit, and it was an absolute travesty that we had lost this from our timeline. His descriptions of the Arctic were spot on and, despite later speculation, it was clear that he had travelled to the far north. He described the northern lights as proof of the divinity and eating fermented fish as proof of hell. He wasn't a fan.

As we rode along, I spotted an old couple on the road ahead, on their way home. They had obviously been in early to market to get the freshest stuff and now were heading to whatever little abode they had in the woods.

'Don't even think of it,' warned Neith.

'You're allowed to do your Emmeline Pankhurst bit, but I can't offer a lift to a couple of old codgers?'

'No. They could be sitting in the back of the wagon robbing us blind, they could be a lure for bandits, they could have a plague.'

'Good grief, Neith. You are being ridiculous.'

'No, Julius, I am trying to get us to Italy as quickly and safely as possible without offering lifts to any passing stranger.'

Our argument continued in hissed whispers as we passed the old couple, and I felt uncomfortable as we did so. Their loads were heavy, and their backs were bent.

'You know we're going to end up paying for that.'

'Superstitious nonsense.'

An hour later she was still deriding me for nonsense when the first arrow hit the canvas sides of the cart.

The road had opened up into a nice clearing with a river running alongside, and it looked like an ideal spot for a picnic. Or, as it turned out, an ambush. An arrow hit the other side of the wagon and two armed men stepped onto the track about ten metres in front of us. They were dressed in a ragtag of clothes, the jerkins trimmed with fur but tatty. Clearly, the original owners were long since dead. One man took a step forward and held up his hand.

'Greetings, Father, Sister. We wish you no harm.'

I wanted to believe him, but his companion sniggered, and it somewhat revealed the lie.

'I told you this would happen.' I said to Neith in modern English as I slowly pulled my staff towards me.

'Oh, you knew this would happen, did you?' she shouted back at me, also in English. With her arms gesticulating wildly, she moved her crossbow closer and nocked an arrow, ready to fire.

'I said we should give that old couple a lift, but you said no. And now here we are being threatened with our very lives. I knew we were tempting fate. This is karma.' I shouted back.

'There's no such thing as karma. I think we have two shooters, two in front, maybe another few still in hiding,' she roared at me.

'Whose fault is that? Keep shouting and let's see if we draw anyone else out.'

At a nod from the lead bandit, another arrow hit the side of the wagon.

'Now look what you've made them do!' I called, gesticulating to the two men who were now shouting at us to be quiet.

'Okay, I have a line of sight on the first shooter. Stage two.' And she stopped shouting and started kissing her rosary and praying loudly in French.

'Now then, Sister. You are perfectly safe with us. Why don't you step down, and we can prove it? We're just honest but hungry citizens. We simply want to share some of your food. A bit of Christian hospitality.'

There was some laughter in the trees away from the shooters and I figured we were dealing with six to seven men. I liked our odds. This would be my first actual fight, not some simulation or classroom battle. The cadets always fought as hard as possible and we often ended up in casualty as we improved, but it wasn't the same. I most certainly didn't like getting hurt, and the aftercare package in the late 1400s wasn't going to be great, but what other options were there? I would see if I could talk our way out of it first, though.

'Pax. Pax. I will join you and show Sister Bonaventure here that we have nothing to fear.' I pulled my staff towards me and climbed down from the cart.

'Leave the staff behind, Father.'

I looked at it in surprise. 'My crozier? Oh no, my son, I never travel without it. Besides, I have a withered leg. Without it, I can't walk.'

In truth, it was nothing like a crozier, but I'd asked the blacksmith to stick a cross on the end of it and it certainly looked more like a religious item than a seven-foot length of seasoned oak. I had enjoyed training with a stick back at the mouseion. A pole was an excellent weapon if you were wearing a skirt. Flying kicks were less effective if your feet got tangled in reams of fabric. Hitching my cassock up I stepped down then paused, leaning heavily on the pole and limping towards the leader. As I got closer, I could see he was in a bad way. His teeth were broken, and he smelt atrocious. Both men's clothes hung off them. This was clearly a small group of thieves, stealing enough to support themselves. There was no way they would let us keep the wagon, and robbing the clergy would truly bring out the city guards in force. Their only option now was to kill us and hide our bodies.

Neith called over to me in French, then switched to English.

'Hail Mary, Mother of God. Make the first move and I'll cover you.'

I turned my back on the brigand and shouted back to her. 'Peace, Sister. All will be well. And hey, this is like

250

those cop movies where the two cops start arguing with each other whilst they're surrounded by baddies.'

'What? Julius, will you please stay focused?'

'Don't you see, they are all leaning in to listen to me shouting at—'

And right then I dropped to the floor and swung my staff out wide, taking out the leader's legs. As he went down, I heard a grunt from the trees. One bowman down. Thank you, Neith. I jumped, grabbing the knife that was strapped to my breeches and, without thinking, I stabbed the winded man in the chest. I couldn't hear anything other than the blood pumping in my ears, but I saw the second brigand run towards me, his mouth wide and clearly shouting. Two more men broke free of their cover and came running towards me. I smiled in satisfaction as I watched the one at the rear fall backwards, a short arrow sticking out of his forehead. I knew that later I would regret laughing, but his expression was so surprised, I couldn't help myself.

The second bandit was now on top of me and kicked me hard in the guts before pulling his own knife. I yanked my knife out of the other guy's chest and stood slowly.

'Do you really want to condemn your immortal soul to hell?' I gasped.

He paused and I may have got away with it, but the other bandit was now running towards me and the odds had changed in his favour. Of course, as I stood there in my priestly robes, he was forgetting that I had a much greater power standing behind me. As the first guy swung at me with his knife, I dodged it and punched him in the face with the hilt of my dagger. The hilt was slippery with blood, but I kept a grip on it. He staggered backwards and tripped over his colleague who was now laying on the floor, an arrow sticking out of his chest. His arms started to pinwheel, the blade in his hand arcing in dangerous circles, but all the time he kept his eyes fixed on mine, his face a snarl of fury. Something whistled past my ear and he dropped to the floor, another arrow sticking out of his torso.

Like I said. I had a greater power behind me.

'Sorry about that. I couldn't get a clear line of sight.' Neith jumped out of the wagon and walked towards me, crossbow in her hand, ready to fire. Her veil was thrown back and her face was grim. 'Ra. I hate killing people. Are they all dead?'

I looked at the four by my feet that had stopped twitching. The blood that had been frothing out of the big guy's mouth had now stopped as well.

'They look pretty dead to me,' a woman's voice called out behind us.

#28 – Julius

I spun and saw that a cloaked figure was sitting on a tree stump, now clapping politely. Neith hadn't moved a muscle.

'Bless you, child.' I called out to the stranger. 'We were set upon by these fierce bandits, so we were.'

'Are there any more in the trees?' called Neith to the stranger, her voice devoid of any intonation.

'No, you got the only two. Both clean kills.'

It took me a second to realise that both Neith's question and the stranger's reply were in Arabic.

'Of course, you always were proficient with the bow.'

The stranger got to her feet and pushed the cape back from her face so she could be seen properly. Taller than average and ebony skinned, she was striking enough. With her long dark braids, fierce beauty, high heels, and leather trousers, she would be a sight that no one would forget. The last time I had seen her she was running towards me with her gun pointed at my head.

'Hello, Clio. Not dead then?'

'Hello, Shit Fly. Next time you stab someone, remove the blade immediately. Rookie error leaving the blade behind.'

I didn't respond. I was waiting for Neith, who still hadn't turned. She did now, and her crossbow was raised and pointing directly at Clio.

'You bitch.' Her voice was steady, almost disinterested. I wasn't fooled and neither was Clio. 'I defended you. I spoke at your eulogy. I praised you as a hero. I believed that you had fallen in combat.'

Clio took a step backwards and raised her hands. 'Put the bow down, Neith. You don't want to kill your taxi ride home.'

Neith passed the crossbow to me, which I wasn't convinced was a good idea. I had always suspected that Clio was behind Charlie's murder. Now, seeing her standing there with a cocky grin on her face and full of the joys of life, I knew that I had been right.

'Neith—'

'If she makes a move, shoot her.' Then, calling out to Clio, she told her to remove her cloak and turn around. When she was satisfied she couldn't see any weapons, Neith walked towards her old teammate. I stepped to one side to get a clearer shot on Clio. As she watched me she nodded her head. 'You've been learning some skills, I see.'

She should have probably been paying Neith a little bit more attention. Even I was surprised by the speed at which Neith moved. Her fist shot up and thumped straight into Clio's face. There was a crack as her teeth smashed together, and a string of blood and spittle flew out as Clio fell backwards. Clio may have had the advantage of height, but Neith had six months of rage behind her, and in one blow she toppled her. She stepped back, looked down at Clio and spat at her feet.

'I chose you over Ramin.'

Clio looked up, wiping her mouth and spitting a tooth out into her palm. Her eyes were furious slits, but a second later the expression was gone as though it had never been there.

'What can I say? Sisters 'fore misters. And you know that's my weak tooth. Have a heart, you've snapped it off at the peg.' She held out her palm to Neith, who stepped back towards me, never once taking her eyes off her teammate and gesturing for her crossbow, which I was relieved to return. I didn't think I could hit a woman or kill someone in cold blood, but just thinking about Charlie made me doubt myself.

'I take it Sam sent you?' said Neith.

Clio looked at Neith and then laughed. 'Sam? Yeah, alright. Whatever.'

I didn't like the sound of that, and neither did Neith. Her eyes narrowed and she took another step back.

'Is Sam alright? Have your lot hurt him?'

'My lot? Babes, you've misread the situation. Again.' She looked over at me and laughed. Putting her finger to her lips, she mouthed whoops at me. Personally, I thought she was lucky Neith didn't shoot her then and there.

'Relax. Sam's fine. He thought you'd like a friendly face.'

'So why didn't he send one?'

I'd have smiled, but I was too nervous. Clio was offering us a way home, but I wasn't certain she was going to live long enough.

'Kind of hurting my feelings here.'

'Sod off.' Neith raised her crossbow.

Clio took a step back and raised her hands as high as possible. 'Let me explain. Can I explain? I won't move, I'll just sit down here on the floor and tell you what happened. Then you can judge.'

Neith tipped her head to one side but didn't lower her weapon. 'Go on then. Explain to me how you didn't betray the mouseion, kill Paul, and set up Ramin. I'm dying to hear how it's all a terrible mistake and you got left behind by accident. How your brace must have slipped off so you couldn't be recalled. This should be interesting.'

Clio spat out more blood and then smiled. 'The thing is…' she paused and let out a deep breath. 'Ah, what's the point? Guilty as charged. I got a better offer. And before you ask, No, I am not going to tell you from who. So, what do you say? Do you want to go home or not?'

'I'll find my own way,' said Neith.

'Planning on catching a ride with the Botticelli team? Not going to happen, babes.' She shrugged and looked over at me, a mocking smile on her face. 'Ever wondered why some teams never return? This is the reason. You hitch a lift home with them, you will die and so will they. Four deaths down to you. Which is where I come in. Call it a final favour.'

I stood and watched the two of them talking. I didn't understand how Clio could be here, I couldn't see a brace and, as far as I knew, curators couldn't just step through the stepper to a time of their choosing. Especially curators that were supposed to be dead in my twenty-first-century earth. Standing in front of me was Charlie's murderer, but she was offering us a way home. To be honest, the Botticelli hitchhike had sounded dodgy, but still, I didn't trust Clio. She was a proven traitor. Why was she here? I wasn't buying the "for old times' sake" routine, but Neith was listening.

'And exactly how do you plan to get us home?'

She shrugged. 'The usual way. I'll give you both a brace and then we can all go home together. Won't that be nice?'

'Stay there, I'm going to talk to my partner.'

Clio looked and me and laughed. 'Yeah. Whatever, babes.'

For what it was worth, I think Clio had been stuck in my twenty-first century for quite a while. Babes.

Neith and I walked to the edge of the clearing, both facing Clio who sat on the tree stump, her hands on her knees as she smiled at us.

'What do you think?' asked Neith.

'I think this stinks. But what are our choices? Is she right that hitching a lift home will kill everyone? Because if I'm honest, that sounds less than optimal.'

'Yeah, it's a shitstorm. I don't know, Julius. I'm not thinking clearly right now. I want to hug her because she's not dead, and I also want to kill her because she's not dead. I'm really not thinking clearly right now.' She paused. 'Did I just say that? Honestly, Julius, help me.'

I'd have hugged her then and there, but there was no way I was revealing her emotional plight to Clio. That bitch, and I wasn't ashamed to call her that, could burn. But despite that, we needed to get home. But what was waiting for us when we got there? Had Clio's handlers overtaken the facility? Would we be arrested? Had Clio been captured, and when we got back would she be the one getting arrested? The way I saw it, someone was getting arrested.

'I have a question,' I called over.

'Are you going to shout it at me or come over?' called Clio.

Neith glared at me, but I didn't tell her what I was going to ask as I figured I already knew her answer. I just wanted to know what Clio would say.

I walked across the clearing, Neith following, her crossbow once again raised.

'You must have more control on the quantum stepper than I realised was possible. Maybe that's something you don't tell neophytes?' I waited for Clio to reply, but she just sat there smiling. I carried on.

'The thing is, I was really looking forward to meeting Leonardo da Vinci. So, I was wondering if you'd be able to take us there first?'

'Are you mad?' Clio suddenly burst into laughter. 'Neith, have you lost your marbles. Oh, babes, how desperate were you?'

Neith stood silently beside me as Clio continued to mock and wipe the tears from her eyes.

'I'm sorry. What's funny?'

'You. Oh, I'm just going to call in on da Vinci. No one calls in on da Vinci. It's one of our dreary cardinal rules, da Vinci is off limits, Do Not Pass Go, Game Over, toodle pip, night-night, go away. Those curators coming over to collect the Botticelli. They will be top-ranking quantum curators. They will be on the fastest in-and-out mission. Any steps that run the risk of bumping into the great man himself are handled with the utmost of care.'

'Why?' This was curious. I had noticed that the mouseion had no paintings or writings from da Vinci. Then I had thought it was just an oddity, now I realised it was deliberate. Were they not saved, or were they saved and then held away from public view?

'Why?' mocked Clio. 'Because on both earths, da Vinci is brilliant. Alpha Earth doesn't want to run the risk of *this* da Vinci meeting a quantum curator and start thinking about quantum physics. What horror if the Beta Earth should also develop a quantum stepper. Gosh, they might even ask for their stuff back. Worse yet, they might come over and mess up Alpha Earth.'

I turned and looked at Neith, who just shrugged at me.

'She's right. But not in how she interpreted it. Yes, da Vinci is a genius. We have a strict rule not to mess around with your timeline. Putting ideas in his head would absolutely mess around with that. Likewise, we avoid Hypatia, Newton, and Einstein.'

'But you said we were going to meet him?'

'And we were. Because I was desperate. But now we have another option.' From the look on her face, Neith didn't rate this option much higher than destroying the Beta timeline or killing four curators in an attempt to piggyback home.

Clio stood up, swept the leaves off her cloak and sauntered over. 'Good call. Now when you're ready...'

'Hang on. Wait. What about Tom and Jerry?'

Both women just looked at me, confused. 'You can't just leave two horses here, surrounded by dead bodies. What if they attract wolves or something? And what about all the belongings? All the gold?'

And then I had a brainwave. Telling them to wait a minute, I did something potentially idiotic. I unhitched Tom and, jumping on his back, told the women to give me five minutes and rode back down the road. Sure enough, not five minutes around the bend I found the old couple slowly making their way along. Pulling up beside them, I jumped down and handed the old man the reins and told them that when they came around the corner, they would find my wagon. Everything in it, including the gold, was theirs.

'Oh, and there's a book in there. Take particularly good care of it. Maybe hand it over to the local abbey?' I knew it was wrong of me, but I couldn't help myself. Maybe they would use it for firelighters, maybe not, but I just wanted to give it a second chance.

The little woman looked at me in astonishment as I detailed all the treasures in the wagon.

'But what about you, Father? Won't you need your horse for the road?'

I looked at her and laughed. 'Where I'm going, I don't need roads.' It was incredibly corny and, laughing, I hitched up my cassock and began running back towards Neith and Clio. Which is when I realised I had done something very stupid. Clio might want to save Neith, but she had zero love for me. What if she had stepped back with Neith and left me stranded? It was with unmitigated relief that I found the two women staring at me with the same sense of bemusement that I had just left around the corner.

'If we're going to do this, let's get going, we'll have witnesses in about five minutes.' Patting Jerry on the flank, I told him not to worry and that company was on the way and joined the women.

Shrugging her shoulders, Clio stepped towards us and said *now*. A second later I was standing in a desert.

#29 – Neith

I blinked and the glorious sun was warm on my face. The air was hot and dry, and I fell to the floor and watched as the sand trickled through my fingers. As far as I could see there was sand in every direction. It was wonderful. I was home. Julius knelt beside me and smiled, and I gave him a goofy grin back. I was relieved beyond measure. For all my talk about chatting to da Vinci, and hitching a lift home, I hadn't actually thought it would work, but what else could I do? And then up popped Clio. Which reminded me.

'What exactly was that? How did we get here? Where the hell is Sam and the quantum stepper?'

Clio shrugged with a smirk on her face. 'I may have me some access to a second stepper. But. You see, here's the thing. I don't want anyone else to know about it. Could you tell everyone you just woke up back on Alpha?'

'Have you lost your mind? I'm arresting you and putting you on trial for your crimes.'

Clio rolled her eyeballs and knelt in front of me.

'No, babes. You are not. I felt I owed you for old times, but I don't plan on hanging around. I just thought you could repay me the favour by staying schtum.'

I leapt to my feet at the same time that Clio did, both of us moving into a fight stance. Not that I intended to play fair. With Julius by my side, she didn't stand a chance. When I'd watched him fighting in the woods, it was clear that he was good. That had been his first genuine fight, and he hadn't hesitated. He had also done just the bare necessities. There was no blood lust, no enjoyment, he acted in self-defence only. I liked how he fought. Admittedly there had been a slightly hysterical laugh at one point, but I was happy to chalk that up to adrenaline.

'Are you going to be boring, Neith? I don't plan on hanging around.'

'Oh really, and exactly where do you think you are going in the middle of the desert?'

'Just watch.' She smirked at me. Then said, 'Okay let's go.'

And with that, she disappeared. One minute she was there, and the next minute there was just me and Julius standing in the desert with a bird wheeling overhead in the empty blue sky.

'What the fuck was that?'

'Did you hear her at the end? It sounded like she was talking to someone,' said Julius curiously.

I played the conversation back in my head. He was right. Her last words had been an instruction, which meant that someone else had a quantum stepper and it worked better than the mouseion's.

'Neith? My wrist brace is online. Who do we call first?'

I looked at Julius in amazement. Was he mad?

'No one! Someone wants us dead, let's not tell them where we are.'

'That's my point. If we try to stay under the radar, we're easier to get rid of quietly. We need to let everyone know we're back.'

Wow! Was he ever devious? I was still trying to get my head around the fact that someone had tried to deliberately eliminate me. It was only Julius' suspicions that had opened my eyes. He was right before and I was prepared to listen to him now. I tapped my brace.

'Sam. I'm not dead. No, wait. Listen. Pull up my coordinates and think up a fast cover story. Someone tried to kill us. Julius reckons we're still in danger. Yes, okay. Yes.' Honestly, if I didn't know Sam better, I'd say he was getting choked up. Hanging up, I turned to Julius. 'Right. Pictures.'

We grabbed a few snaps and then sent them out to all his year group and all my active contacts, with the message 'Good to be home. Drinks on us later.'

For the next half hour, we replied to a storm of texts. Until I knew what Sam's cover story was going to be, all our replies were upbeat but vague.

'So, a second quantum step machine. What do you make of that then? I don't remember anything about that on the course curriculum. Is this something only senior curators know about?' asked Julius.

I shook my head. There was only one machine. Centuries of research and world funding had perfected the strict formulas that da Vinci had established. His work had been passed on to Newton. Throughout history, the greatest thinkers had worked collaboratively until Einstein literally tightened the bolts and flicked the on switch. And all the scientists, mathematicians and engineers credited their achievements to the work of Hypatia, the mother of modern mathematics.

'The world worked together to build this machine. There isn't another one.'

'Except there is. But you know, as I'm thinking about it, it doesn't make any sense. If you have access to your own machine, why use the mouseion's to steal stuff?'

I sighed. This was like back in Sam's office. Julius kept going after the wrong thread. Someone was stealing artefacts and falsifying the evidence. That was the bigger picture, and Julius needed to focus.

He was stripping out of his cardinal's robes and I quickly joined him until he was standing in a pair of linen breeches, and I was in a little linen shift. I'd have stripped fully, but I was aware that Julius could be quite funny about skin. Besides, I was quite sweaty, and no one wants sandy bits if there's no water nearby. We folded our garments and got them ready to hand over to the costume department. All clothing was returned to the outfitters. You'd get shouted at if you returned their clothes burnt and torn, but if you handed over original artefacts, they would shower you in baklava.

'Is that a vulture overhead?'

I peered up, squinting at the sky. 'Reckon. But it's not interested in us.' I paused dramatically, then said, 'Yet,' but spoilt the drama by laughing. Sweet Bast, it was good to be home. But, oh boy, did I have some apologies to make.

Then I was going to expose Clio's boss and get her stripped of all honours. Every time I thought of her, I could feel myself going cold and hard. I still didn't understand why she had done what she had, but my job wasn't to understand her. My job was to stop her.

'Incoming.'

The sound of a heavy-duty dune buggy could be heard making its way towards us. Sam must have come straight across the dunes to get to us as fast as possible. A second later, the buggy crested over the ridge and Julius and I started shouting and waving our arms. They could hardly miss us, but we couldn't help ourselves. The buggy pulled up in front of us in a plume of sand and Sam stepped down from the driver's seat. At the same moment, the passenger door slammed and Ramin came racing around the back of the cab and sprinted towards me, almost knocking me over as he embraced me. He squeezed me so tightly that I thought he might suffocate me. All I could think was how badly I had treated him as he kissed the top of my head a thousand times. Finally, he stepped back from me, looking me up and down with tears in his eyes.

What could I say to him? I wanted to scream my apology to the heavens, but there were never going to be enough words to cover the depth of my regret and misery.

'I thought you were a traitor.' The emotions overtook me, and I started sobbing. 'Can you ever forgive me?'

Ramin pulled me in for another hug and then stepped back again, openly weeping as well. 'I thought you were dead, stupid. I can forgive you anything. Just never die again.' And then he hugged me again and we just stood there in each other's arms, reunited once more.

'Don't I get a hug?'

'Come here, you daft Englishman,' called Sam and gave Julius a huge hug. Honestly, seeing the panic in Julius' face made me roar with laughter, as he stoically endured the hug and even patted Sam on the back. That would teach him to try and break the tension.

Sam grabbed a blanket out of the boot and laid it out on the sand, and we all settled down.

'I think you need to debrief here, and we can work out what to say when you get back,' began Sam. 'First things first, how the hell are you here in the middle of the Sahara? When did you come back through the stepper? Why didn't you alert us then?'

Honestly, my heart shrank further, and I felt sick to my stomach.

'Clio brought us back. I'm so sorry, Ramin. I should have trusted you, not wait for proof. I don't know if I will ever forgive myself for that.'

That was at the base of my grief. I didn't believe Ramin until I had incontrovertible evidence. Ramin squeezed my hand.

'That's because you're a great curator and you follow the evidence. I'd have been the same. I just had the advantage of knowing I was innocent.'

He wasn't wrong, and yet I felt I had let him down. I could feel Julius sitting beside me, pointedly not saying anything. I knew that with his Beta values, I had failed some set of friendship codes.

'Ramin's right, Neith. Stop with this self-abasement nonsense and explain Clio.'

I laughed. Explain Clio. And so, I started to tell Sam everything that had happened.

'I thought Clio had her teeth strengthened?'

'She did.'

Ramin roared with laughter and punched me playfully on the arm. 'Atta girl. Man, I wish I had seen that.'

'Oh, she was fierce angry.'

Sam coughed and I continued with my report. I was just explaining how she had disappeared when I heard the distant whomp of a heli-cruiser. Some of Julius' paranoia was clearly rubbing off on me as I felt a momentary sense of unease.

'Sam, we're not going to disappear again, are we?'

'With all the photos and texts Julius has been sending out? Look, he's even taking and sending pictures of the cruiser.'

I glanced across at Julius, who smiled apologetically. 'I know. I feel like a teenager or an urban campaigner. I just feel safer knowing that everyone can see me.'

Ra, the Betas were a suspicious lot. The cruiser landed as Julius continued to take and send photos. Its rotors folded back, and I could see the government seal on the side of the panel. The door opened and al-Cavifi walked down the unfolding staircase. She was dressed for a normal day at work and as soon as her feet plunged into the sand, she removed her high heels and strode over to join us. She was followed by a man who I had only seen on television before. I hadn't voted for him on either occasion. As Pharaoh Tarek strode to catch up with al-Cavifi, I wondered how much trouble I was in this time.

'Captain Nymens, report,' said al-Cavifi.

'Quantum Curator Salah and Neophyte Quantum Curator Strathclyde were retrieved from the Beta Earth, via Quantum Curator Clio Masoud, formerly deceased.'

Al-Cavifi looked shocked, and Pharaoh Tarek spoke. 'Salah. How certain are you that the individual you met was Masoud?'

'A hundred per cent.' I didn't bother with sir as I noticed he hadn't bothered with my title either.

'Neith, how did Clio get you back?'

'As to that, ma'am, I have no idea. One minute we were standing in a Burgundian wood in the fifteenth century, the next moment we were all standing here in the Sahara. We witnessed no quantum displacement or effects of any kind.'

'Neophyte Strathclyde. Do you verify this statement?'

As Julius nodded, I noticed that no one seemed surprised. My world had just been rocked, the very axis that I thought our society had been built on, had tilted, but they were just frowning. Maybe this was the way of politicians, to roll with the punches and pretend that they knew all along. Unless, of course, they did.

#30 – Julius

The next few days were a heady mix of de-briefings and storytelling. It had been decided by higher up agencies that we didn't want to scare the camels. The official line was that Neith and I had been victims of operator error and stranded in the past. Fortuitously, the quantum stepper, in its weekly calibration, realised the error and pulled us back. All night shifts had been instructed not to mention it, so no one knew whose shift it happened on, only that it hadn't happened on theirs. And of course, because they were good little Alphas, they did as they were told and didn't discuss it.

Clio remained officially dead, and whilst Ramin was back on active duty, a whiff of suspicion still hung around him. Asha remained in the wind and was still connected to the filing irregularities. Honestly, the whole thing stank.

'This is insane. You are all insane.' I waved my bottle in their general direction. We were sitting by the banks of Lake Mareotis. Sam had brought a picnic and some beers, and we'd all pitched in with snacks. To all intents and purposes, we looked like a bunch of mates having a jolly by the water's edge, and indeed it was the first time the four of us had been together without other officials and dignitaries interviewing us.

'Everyone's behaving as if nothing has happened. As if this doesn't completely blow open the situation.'

'A tad melodramatic,' Rami said with a smile, 'but you're not wrong. We now know that Clio is working for someone else. A second quantum stepper is in play, items are being stolen from the archives, and we are going to stop that. That's what we need to focus on. None of us are engineers. None of us can investigate the stepper issue.'

'But it's fundamental.' I tried again as the others frowned at me.

'Julius. It isn't,' interrupted Rami, 'If a second stepper had been around for a long time you would be right. They would be using that, not ours, to steal stuff. We have to conclude that it's either new or unstable. Or both. For now, we need to focus on where our skills lie and that's the mouseion itself. Whilst you were gone, Sam and I got talking, and we think we know who is behind all this.'

'Julius thought Sam was,' said Neith with a laugh.

Sam looked at me and nodded his approval. 'Good thinking. Who else did you suggest?'

I thought about making one more push to focus on Clio but acknowledged that Rami was right. We had bigger fish to fry right now. Instead, I told Sam who my suspects were. When I mentioned Chancellor Alvarez, he smiled and nodded at Ramin. 'And why do you suspect him?'

I explained that in my eyes he was in a perfect pivotal position. He sat at the fulcrum between the mouseion and the outside world. Everything went through him. To circumvent him would require a lot more effort and more people involved, and the more people involved, the more likely mistakes were to happen.

'However, he can't be doing this on his own.'

'Well no, he has Clio.'

I agreed but wasn't happy with Clio's role in all this. Something about her simply didn't tally up.

'But it won't be just her. We don't know if they are willing participants like Clio or blackmailed like Paul. We also need to find out who he's selling them to.'

'And why,' said Neith.

'We know why,' I said in exasperation. 'To make money from people that covet those items.'

'I'm really not sure—' started Ramin, but Sam cut him off.

'That doesn't matter. We can't deal with that either. Focus people. The mouseion is our domain and we *will* preserve it.'

We chinked our bottles in salute. We had all sworn to preserve the mouseion and its libraries and archives.

'How do we prove it?'

Again, there was a lull in the conversation. I had no idea how their culture worked and was unsure of what to suggest. I was certain that we should look at the technology. They thought that was a red herring.

'We need to see the contents of Giovanetti's files. Who is in charge of her investigation?' asked Rami.

'It's classified, but since Alvarez fired Simeon Jones, the Department for Security is in something of a mess right now,' replied Sam. I found I was calling him Sam more frequently as I got to know him, but when he started barking orders, he went straight back to being Captain Nymens. I thought about what he had just said, it was very convenient.

'All the better to cover things up.'

Neith frowned at me. 'You think Alvarez is deliberately causing chaos. You don't think this is incompetence? Because it sure looks like incompetence.'

'Alvarez has been doing this for years. That Mongolian crown showed an error file from three years ago. Almost immediately after you first recovered it, Neith. I think Alvarez has been getting away with this for years. What I think we should be asking is what went wrong with the Fabergé step? That's when the wheels came off.'

Sam shook his head. 'We can't look at those files either.'

'Old school then. We need to talk to people. If we can't trust the network, let's talk to humans and see if we can find anyone who is prepared to say they noticed something odd. What about an actual curator? One of the archivists. The people that handle the physical items.'

The three of them looked at me and paused.

'It's high risk.'

'What if the person we speak to is in on it?'

'What if speaking to them jeopardises them?'

I took a swig of beer. I didn't know the answers, this wasn't my world, I didn't understand the nuances of their society. All I knew was that in my "violent, barbaric world" my life had been calm and stress free. Here it was at actual risk. Since becoming involved with them I had been shot at, spliced, someone had dropped me under a bomb in the Blitz and then tried to abandon me in the fifteenth century. This world was dangerous, and someone was quite happy killing people.

'I know someone in the archives,' I said, thinking of Minju. 'Why don't I speak to them. People are very forgiving of my barbarian ways.'

It wasn't much of a plan, but it was the best we could think of for now.

interlude 5

The following text conversation was retrieved during a sweep of the ghost files of the Q Zone security system. It has been added to the evidence report for Case No: 234530/H. The second party is yet to be identified.

— Do we have an explanation for how Salah and Strathclyde returned?

— Yes. It means someone else beat us to the codex.

— That's not possible.

— I know that, and yet what other explanation is there for all this? And who the hell is Clio working for? I thought she was one of ours.

— She was. Is? Honestly, I thought we had lost her. I thought she was dead.

— You may well have lost her, but she's clearly not dead.

— So, what do we do now?

— Personally, I'm keeping my head down. I sense a massive storm brewing and I have no intention of getting caught up in it. The stakes have changed, the codex is everything now. Don't think she hasn't noticed who gave the order to strand Salah in 1483.

— I can't be held responsible for that.

— Great Ra, woman! Of course you can and trust me. She does.

— Well, what do I do now?

— Keep a very close eye on all your assets and do nothing.

— Should I start looking for clues to the pages of the codex?

— Are you insane? Does that sound like do nothing?

— But I have to do something? I need to redeem myself in her eyes.

— You won't redeem yourself by interfering with my side of the operations. If you are exposed, they will be crawling over everything you did. No one is looking at my side. Do nothing and let's hope that this all blows over. For now, we have our orders. Watch and wait.

#31 – Julius

The following morning I headed over to the mouseion. There was a nice breeze blowing in off the Med, and the awnings and canopies along the boulevard were busily flapping. Students were leaning on sheets of paper, laughing as they occasionally ran after a page. The custodians would be busy today handing out littering fines. I saw Shorbagy in the distance and was pleased when he waved at me before carrying on with his patrol. They were small steps, but I was slowly settling in and whatever was going on here, I wanted to help end it. This society, for all its faults, was worth saving.

Sam had told us to focus on the artefacts, but I still couldn't get over the issue of the stepper. If there was a second quantum step machine, why bother infiltrating the curators? Why not just steal directly from the mouseion? Even more puzzling, why had Clio and Paul tried to steal the egg whilst on the mission. This was also a change in pattern. I was certain that if one anomaly was explained, then both would be. There was always a cause and effect, but the others seemed too focused on their specialisms. I know that's how their culture worked, but it was playing right into the hands of whoever was pulling the strings.

As I approached the mouseion, my heart lifted. I loved libraries and museums. There was just a sense of walking into the best place in the world. The area was busy with tourists and academics alike, all here to study or admire the exhibits saved from my world. I strode across the atrium to the main reception and saw the same receptionist that I had encountered on my first day on Level B5. Taking a deep breath, I decided to rise above any perceived pettiness, waited my turn, then stepped forward with as engaging a smile as I could manage.

'Neophyte Quantum Curator Strathclyde, how may I serve you today?'

Got to admit, I rather liked the change in tone. Either the first time I had startled her out of her manners, or news had got around about me rescuing a cat during the Blitz. That story had really travelled. Or it could have been the fact that Neith and I had been saved from the fifteenth century. But my money was on the cat.

'Good morning. Greetings and health to your house and heart.' I had decided to go fully formal. 'I'd like to have a word with Minju Chen. Could you tell me where she is working today?' Whilst I'd been working on my final project I'd often found Minju in the Roman remains, but sometimes other archivists were working in that section.

'Minju Chen?' The receptionist looked at me and said Minju's name in a surprised and slightly disapproving tone. Dammit, I'd been doing so well, I wonder what I had done wrong? Maybe she didn't know who I meant.

I tried to clarify. 'The one with the tail?'

'*With the tail*,' repeated the receptionist in astonishment.

Yep, I had definitely said something wrong that time. If I was home, I'd assume it was the physical reference, but here it wasn't an issue. Or so I thought. I waited silently, trying not to put my foot in it further. She looked at me with a puzzled expression but pulled up her holoscreen.

'B5 – Romans – Gaul.'

I smiled, thanking her formally, and headed off towards the lifts. I'd have to find out from Neith or Rami what I'd done wrong later on. In the meantime, I needed to ask Minju about missing files without making her party to anything that might land her in trouble.

I zipped along the corridors and arrived at the reception booth. It was empty, and I headed around the desk to the back offices. As I did, I heard voices from inside, so knocked and waited. A minute later, Minju came to the door. Over her shoulder, I noticed a door closing. Beaming up at me, she stuck her hand out for a formal handshake and then ushered me in, inviting me to join her for a cup of tea. I sniffed the air, and she laughed, assuring me that she didn't mean mint tea. I smiled, but that wasn't what I had smelt. Only one person I knew wore aftershave that obnoxious.

'Have I interrupted a meeting with Chancellor Alvarez?'

Minju's shoulders tensed, then fell as she continued to spoon leaves into the teapot. She turned to look at me with a worried expression.

'Not an unwelcome interruption at all.'

I frowned. Minju was a total sweetie. I bet she would be easily intimidated by a bully like Alvarez.

'Here, sit down whilst I play mother.' I laughed as I saw her pull out a notepad. 'It means I'll pour the tea.' As she sat down, I started to get the cups together, pouring hot water into the teapot. 'What did he want? If you can't say, don't worry.'

I pottered about and gave her time to collect her thoughts. She seemed genuinely put out.

'At first he was talking about the necessity of storing all these Roman artefacts. Maybe we should ship them out to a secondary mouseion? Maybe the one in Sudan? Like a secondary Beta Archive.'

She fiddled with her tea and I stopped her after she put in the third spoon of sugar. No wonder she was agitated. Removing the Roman remains sounded like a serious demotion to me. Not necessarily for her, but for the subject and, like any decent archivist, that would bother her more than her own personal standing.

'That's out of order. Why not just build more tunnels if it's a storage issue?'

'He said that wasn't the main problem and then started going on about site security and that he wanted all levels to have upgraded security. Level B5–Romans has few facilities, we don't even have holograms, but I thought that was an argument for improved facilities, not removal?'

As she spoke, I felt a sense of dread.

'What else did he say about security?'

Minju looked up from her cup, wincing at the sweetness. I picked it up and poured it down the sink, pouring her a fresh cup and prompting her again about the security question.

'He wanted to know if I had noticed any missing artefacts. But how would I know? It's not like we do an annual inspection or anything.'

I thought about that. This was the perfect way for me to question her. But if the chancellor had already been down here, it meant that he was trying to tidy things up. Too many people had already died. I didn't want Minju to disappear as well. Time to play the curious student.

'How do you know if anything is missing?'

'Why would anything be missing?'

'Well, I don't know.' I paused. Obviously I didn't want to say stolen and alarm her. 'What if someone had been examining an artefact—'

'The hologram?'

'No, the real thing.'

'Why would they want to do that?'

'Just play along with me. So, they pick it up and it's a glass bowl, and they drop it, and the glass shatters.'

Minju's face paled, and she reached for the sugar.

'Let's say that person sweeps up the glass and doesn't tell anyone. When would anyone find out?'

'Julius, have you broken something?'

Oh dear, I should have seen that coming.

'God, no, but I was just wondering how it all works. Back home we do an annual stock take, check that the item is properly stored, hasn't deteriorated, that sort of thing.'

I could have added borrowed and not returned, which was a frustratingly regular event. You would often wander into some senior professor's rooms and find a priceless artefact either on proud display or being used as a paperweight. Some professors could be very proprietorial and just felt that if it was in the college archives, then it was sort of theirs anyway. The best way to deal with it was to issue a "return slip" reminding them their borrowed artefact was now due its annual clean. If that didn't work, we'd just go into the rooms when they were out and simply remove the item. If they noticed, they never complained. The worst incident we'd ever had was when we found the Royal Imperial crown robes from the Tang dynasty being used as a dressing gown by the Dean of Modern Languages. But I decided not to tell Minju that. She'd had enough shocks for one day.

'I just wondered if you do annual inspections as well?'

She shook her head. 'We don't need to. All the artefacts are stored in an airtight unit. Meaning there is no issue with degradation. It's why we use holograms and 3D printers, so that the original artefact is rarely, if ever, handled.'

'How would you know if the glass bowl was missing?'

'We wouldn't. Not unless someone made a specific request to view that item.'

'And that would be logged?'

'Yes.'

'Even if the original curator requested it?' I was running on a hunch as to how items were being removed without drawing attention or leaving a trail.

'What's that?' She looked at me sharply.

'Oh, nothing, but QC Salah was showing me how to fill in the catalogue form and said that curators could always revisit their old items using their QC codes. Would that be logged as well?'

'Well, no,' she conceded, 'they retrieved it after all. We don't need to bother a member of staff to retrieve it for them. They can go and look at it themselves.'

'Do many?'

She paused and looked a bit surprised at my question. 'Do you know, I have no idea? I shouldn't have thought so. It's just a hangover from when the system was first set up. Certainly, I've never heard of a curator wanting to come and have another look.'

I sipped my tea and thought of home.

'We are very different, and so much the same. I am sorry for bothering you with these questions, it's just lovely to chat to a fellow academic.'

For a second Minju looked annoyed, and I realised that she probably would prefer to be known as a curator, or archivist, rather than an academic. I decided to leave before I blotted my copybook any further. Just as I got to the door, a thought occurred to me.

'If the database lost the digital file, then you'd have to go back to the original, wouldn't you?'

Minju looked at me, considering, her tail swaying in agitation.

'Great Ra, Julius, that would be cataclysmic, but yes. Then we would need to retake the hologram. Ugh, what an idea. Do you know, you've quite unnerved me.'

I felt wretched. First, the chancellor threatened her with the Roman artefacts, and then I made her feel ill. Scaring grandmothers was probably a low point in my career. I pulled the scooter out of the racks and smiled reassuringly at her.

'Look, ignore me. I'm a silly old Beta. Now, if you need any help with persuading anyone that the Roman pieces should stay here, then just let me know and I will stand in your legion.'

I saluted her in the Roman style and was relieved when she returned the salute, laughing as I sped away down the hall crying, 'Veni, vidi, vici.'

#32 – Julius

It was half past noon by the time I made it to the banks of Lake Mareotis. Rami and Neith were already there and waved me over to their table. Since returning, we had tried to meet in public surrounded by people. I know they thought I was being paranoid, but I just felt witnesses would be a good idea. They had chosen a spot on the edge of the park, by one of the walkways so no one could hear our conversation. It was a smart position and I wondered who had chosen it.

I ordered the whitebait and a pitcher of water and came and joined them.

'Guys, I think we have a serious issue. We need to move now.'

Just as I was getting ready to tell them about my morning, I could see Stef and Sabrina walking towards us with an old guy I recognised from the QC briefing room. I really wanted to catch up with Stef, but the timing stank. I was worried about Minju and felt that Soliman was gearing up to escape. I wanted to tell Neith and Rami what I had learnt. It was clear that I was going to have to wait.

I could see that Stef looked excited, but Sabrina was nervous. The man leading the way seemed the very picture of serenity, and both Neith and Rami got to their feet. There was certainly a culture of respecting your elders over here, but I wasn't used to them standing. Whoever this man was, he was clearly important to them.

Smiling at me, he walked straight to Neith and gave her an enormous hug. He then kissed her on the forehead, and on each of her hands.

'Of all the treasures in the mouseion, you were the one I valued the most. I am so pleased to see you again.'

Stef looked at Sabrina and mouthed wow to her. Sabrina looked no less flabbergasted but tersely shook her head at him to shut up. The old man then turned to Rami.

'And your absence has been like a wound in my jaw. I am glad to see you back here where you belong.'

Finally, he turned and smiled directly at me. 'And the misplaced jewel. Hello, Julius, it is my honour to meet you.'

I was slightly nonplussed, and Neith jumped to the rescue.

'Ben, please join us. Julius, this is my old instructor, Ben Wakandi.'

I tried to be diplomatic but laughed. This kind, benevolent man was the terror of her neophyte year? I had pictured someone between Cruella de Ville and Darth Vader. Not Morgan Freeman. Luckily, my whitebait arrived, and Ben's eyes lit up as he ordered another portion for himself, and a plain salad for Sabrina and Stef to share.

'I can see Neith remembers her lessons well.'

'I remember being grateful if you even let me eat salad.' She winked at Stef and Sabrina. 'Don't worry, you must be doing well if he's letting you eat a mixed salad.

Clio and I were only allowed plain locusts and green leaves in our first few months.'

'Ah well, you two were easily the worst students I had ever had to train.'

Neith thumped him lightly on the shoulder, her affection shining out of her. 'That's not fair. What about Marco and Reynolds? They actually put their foot through a Van Gogh.'

We all started laughing as Ben told the tale.

'But you see, they never had the greatness that I saw in you. I just had to work on you harder because you were so reluctant to shine. And look at you now.' As he finished his whitebait, he turned to his current students. 'If you can rise to be half the curators that Rami or Neith are, I will have done my job well. If the world were ending and everything was in chaos, I would want Neith Salah standing in front of me, because then I'd know that we would be saved.'

It was an oddly dramatic sentence, and everyone fell quiet until Stef could bear it no longer.

'Why didn't you pair those two together?' he asked, gesturing at Neith and Rami with a carrot stalk.

Obviously, his pairing with Sabrina was causing him some friction, and it was clear from Ben's raised eyebrow that he also knew the source of Stef's question. From the attentive way that Neith and Rami sat, it was clear that they had never heard the answer and were waiting to see if he would say anything.

'Well now,' he said, 'I do wonder if that was a mistake. But Clio was so talented. We could all see she was amazing, so full of fire and energy. But she also had a wild streak running through her, and we felt that the only curator that had a chance to harness that spirit was Neith. And we were right.'

I felt Neith stiffen beside me, and Ben leant across the table and held her hand. I watched as he gave it a small squeeze.

'No one could have done more. No one has ever questioned what happened.'

Then, abruptly, he dropped her hand and smiled at all of us. 'Now it is time that I leave to write up today's report and let you young folk chat. NQC Mulweather, NQC Seidel, I will see you tomorrow morning at five out by the lighthouse. Bring your diving kit.'

And with that he strolled off, waving at people as he crossed the park.

I offered some of my fish to Stef who lunged forward, but Sabrina slapped his hand, hissing at him and looking over her shoulder in Ben's direction.

'It's okay,' said Neith. 'View it as a gift. Ben accepts that. Clio and I had to rely on many "gifts" in the early days. After all, we curators are supposed to look after each other. In fact, I think it builds camaraderie. Ben probably does it deliberately.'

Sabrina looked worried, but then her tummy rumbled, and, with a groan, she followed Stef's lead.

The three of us were laughing as Neith and Rami began to tell horror stories from their early days of training, and I enjoyed teasing Neith that she was now also a venerable teacher. Rami said I was screwed. We were having good fun, but I noticed that Stef and Sabrina were reluctant to join in the conversation. I decided to try to include them; even though I was an outsider, I was the one bridging the gap. Maybe it was another respect thing for senior curators?

'You're unusually quiet, Stef. Are you trying to figure out how to convince me to buy some more food?'

He grinned but remained uncomfortable, only relaxing as Sabrina spoke. 'It's just the whole Level Eight edict. The rules are very clear.'

I thought she was being typically ridiculous, but Neith looked at her and nodded her approval.

'Quite right. But it was the mission that was restricted. You can talk to us or about us without any censure. And I'd be pleased if you did.'

She said it with a smile and then laughed. 'Talk to us, that is, not about us. Although you can do that as well. It's always nice to get to know the new intake of curators. And any protégés of Ben's will be worth getting to know, even if I am biased,' she concluded with another laugh, and I could see Sabrina visibly relax and preen herself just a little. Or maybe I was being unfair.

Soon they were swapping notes and the pair of them were asking Rami and Neith their suggestions for certain scenarios. We could have continued all afternoon, but

Neith reminded them they were diving in the morning. Ben would expect them to know all their tables for blood oxygen and nitrogen levels, not to mention specifics of underwater retrievals. Alarmed, the pair of them suddenly got up from the table and, thanking us for the food they left. As they walked off, I could hear they were already drilling each other on the decompression rates of a body at various depths.

'So that's the famous Sabrina?' said Rami with a smile. 'She's not as dreadful as you made out at all. I think she's got the makings of a great curator.'

'Especially with that hunk of a warrior by her side,' grinned Neith.

'Not my type,' laughed Rami, fooling no one.

'Fair enough,' said Neith. 'You won't mind if I see if he fancies a drink. We can discuss advanced combat positions.'

I cleared my throat. It was good to watch these two banter, but we did have other matters to deal with. I described my meeting with Minju.

'It sounds like Alvarez is beginning to get twitchy,' said Rami. 'We need to talk to Sam and tell him what you've discovered. If the chancellor is making a move, then we need to stop him.'

interlude 6

The following memo was retrieved during a sweep of the ghost files of the Q Zone security system. It has been added to the evidence report for Case No: 234530/H. The sender is yet to be identified, although we can now safely establish the recipient.

Sir, as requested.

I met with NQC Strathclyde today whilst on a drill with my mentor, QC Wakandi. Strathclyde was with Salah and Gamal. He appeared agitated, and I felt that he was anxious for us to leave. The three were friendly, but I felt that they were discussing something that they didn't wish to be overheard.

I will try to arrange a meeting with him separately and see if I can get him to confide in me.

My apologies for such scant information. I shall do better next time, and I remain grateful for the opportunity to distinguish myself.

#33 – Julius

'I have some of Asha's files!' Sam had waited until we were all settled in his office before he made his announcement. As he pulled up her notes on the holoscreen Neith and Rami leant forward.

'How did you get these?' asked Rami, whilst Neith was busy reading. 'Are you in touch with her? Is she okay?'

Sam shook his head. 'I haven't heard a thing from her. I've been in touch with her husband daily, but he hasn't heard a thing either. Or at least he says he hasn't heard a thing. He probably doesn't trust anyone right now.'

'How did you get these?' repeated Rami.

'Would you believe, the post?'

I laughed and was pleased to see Asha thought like someone from my world.

'There're over fifty items missing!'

'How did she discover them?'

'Hang on,' said Neith as she flicked the screen back and forth. 'Oh, that's clever. Look, she simply ran a weight calibration. On her first sweep of the European archives, fourteenth to sixteenth period, the database found fifty-two archive boxes with a significant weight variation.'

Much sneakier than switching the whole thing off and on again, I thought. But still, she must have alerted someone. Despite all her smart sub-routines, someone had already had the system monitored and that bothered me because I didn't think Alvarez had the smarts for that.

While I watched, I noticed that Neith was still tapping away on Asha's file, and then she pushed it away from her in disgust.

'Ach! Fifty-two objects, and out of hundreds of quantum curators, only a handful of pairs were assigned to all of these items.'

'What does that mean?' I asked. I had a good idea but wasn't as au fait with the system as the others.

'If you want to borrow a physical item from storage, you need to requisition it. Unless you were on the original retrieval team. Then you can go and get it yourself.'

'Which curators?' asked Rami.

'Manu Pasternak and James Raju, Gretchen Cook and Sara Cleeve—'

'No bloody way that Manu is a thief. Although James doesn't surprise me,' said Sam.

'Hang on, there's a few more names here.' Neith read them out with increasing disbelief. 'And finally, of course, there's Clio Masoud and me. And I know I'm not a thief. We can't assume all partnerships are corrupt. This is just a screenshot of a small area of the archives, there may be more people involved. And we have no idea how far this goes back.'

'Gretchen and Sara are both dead. They died on a failed retrieval three years ago, so if those artefacts are missing, then we know this has been going on for at least three years,' deduced Sam.

'Do you think that explains why their mission failed?' said Rami.

Sam looked angry. 'It's certainly a new dimension.'

'But why would these curators take the risk? The minute it was discovered to be missing, you would just track it back to the last person that looked at it,' said Rami.

'I know, it would be logged, right?' agreed Sam, and Rami shrugged. Looking at them, I realised that they weren't aware of this aspect of the storage system.

'Actually, it wouldn't.' I watched as the three of them looked at me in surprise. 'I asked Minju about this, and she said that she didn't think those retrievals were logged. As she put it, *why would anyone bother*?'

Sam looked at me curiously, but Neith spoke first. 'Which makes it more likely that these few names aren't a coincidence. They are the thieves. Someone told them what to steal.' She leant back in her chair looking at Sam. 'I can't believe it.'

'It's worse than that,' said Rami with dawning realisation, 'it means that those curators were actively assigned to those missions, so they would be able to later remove them from the archives with no one knowing.'

'Which leads us back to Soliman Alvarez,' I said.

Sam frowned at me. 'He's the bloody chancellor!'

'Exactly, who better?' I could see he was uncertain, so I tried again. 'Okay, well, let's go over who else there is. They have to be senior, yes? Someone capable of manipulating the roster.' I looked at Sam. 'You could do it. Who else?'

'Alvarez. Anyone more senior than him would also have the authority, but it would look odd if they did.'

'And who changed the roster and sent me and Neith back to northern France?'

'Alvarez.'

'Okay. When the angel was sent back during the Fabergé affair, you told me that the cameras had been wiped and the guard was killed. Who could have done that?'

'Now that wouldn't be Alvarez. He has no skills in IT or security. That would be Asha or senior members of her team.'

'Okay.' I thought about it. 'When Asha ran, who reported the file anomalies?'

'Simeon Jones,' said Neith, chiming in, pulling up the information from the records.

'Ah.' I smiled. 'And who switched off the QS when we were on the other side?'

'Simeon Jones,' repeated Neith with a matching smile.

'And who appointed Simeon Jones?'

This time, all three said Alvarez.

'There's more. I think Alvarez is trying to destroy the evidence.' I recounted my meeting with Minju to Sam.

'And you believe that "Minju" was also concerned about Alvarez and acting oddly?'

I noted that Sam had said Minju with the same surprise and exaggerated air that the receptionist had done, which bothered me. I decided I would circle back and ask about that later, for now, I needed to keep on track.

'Very much so.'

Sam paused, nodded his head twice, and then rapped the table with his knuckles.

'Right. Alvarez it is then.'

'Just like that?' Neith looked surprised. 'What changed your mind?'

'Minju did,' he said with a laugh. 'If Minju is suspicious about Alvarez and was prepared to say as much to Julius here, then that's pretty damning as far as I'm concerned.'

Now it was my turn to look puzzled.

'Do you know her?'

'Small Asian lady, striped tail?'

I nodded and was surprised when Neith and Rami looked at me in alarm.

'Your friend Minju,' said Rami incredulously, 'sweet timid Minju, that likes British teas, is actually Chancellor Chen, Head of Egypt's mouseions. Scourge of curators, the creature in archivists' nightmares, the librarians' nemesis. That's your jolly little friend?'

I was perplexed. She had never mentioned her title, and I had never asked. She certainly didn't come across as a scary and disagreeable character. She was a total poppet. 'Is there more than one Minju with a tail?'

By now the three of them were laughing at me and Neith was shaking her head incredulously.

'Do you remember that time she summoned all the QCs in to test their basic skills in placing artefacts in retrieval boxes? She was so disgusted with us, she failed the entire year and put us on rations for a week and made us write out in longhand the rules and procedures for artefact retrievals.'

'But all cadets—'

'We weren't cadets, some of us had ten years in the field. And you call her Minju.'

'I didn't even know she had a first name,' laughed Rami. 'I can't even imagine her as a child, playing with her toys.'

'Sweet Bast, can you imagine? Teddy! Your fur is creased. You are a disgrace to the toy box.'

Neith looked across at me and stopped laughing. Tucking her hair behind her ear, she regained her composure and gave me a huge grin.

'Honestly, Julius, here was I worrying about you fitting in to our world, and you already have the fiercest people wrapped around your little finger.'

I wasn't quite sure how to respond, but I felt protective of Minju and wanted to move the conversation on.

'So, we're agreed that Alvarez is involved.'

'If this is how items are being retrieved from the archives, why go to all the effort of Clio and Paul trying to smuggle the egg back? That doesn't make sense,' said Rami.

'Maybe whoever wanted it was prepared to pay to have full exclusivity so that it didn't even make it to the hologram or 3D printer?'

'Incredible,' said Sam. 'I can't even fathom that sort of greed.'

'Trust me. You have murderers and thieves, so why is it so hard to believe you also have people that don't want to share?'

'You think Alvarez was randomly selling these items? Or do you think someone was telling him what to target?'

It made sense to me. There was a published list of all the treasures that the QS was programmed to monitor, it could be treated like a shopping catalogue. In fact, why stop there? What was to stop an unscrupulous curator from pocketing other stuff whilst they were over on my earth? It didn't have to be on the QS list to still be worthwhile in the eyes of a greedy Alpha collector.

'Only one way to find out. We need to break into his house and see if we can find some evidence.'

I looked at my wrist brace as it alerted me to an incoming message. 'Speak of the devil. The chancellor has just invited me to join him at tonight's poetry recital. Do you think we can come up with a plan that saves me from his iambic pentameter?'

#34 – Neith

It was a silent, moonless night and the Milky Way glittered in the sky above. Julius and I were sitting in a small punt tucked into the bulrushes on the river. Bats were flitting around our heads, and a cold breeze blew along the river. The conditions were perfect for a night-time excursion.

I spoke softly into my wrist brace, 'Julius, Ramin, Sam, report.'

Ramin and Sam replied across the brace, whilst Julius just nodded at me.

'Julius, I need you to report into your brace so that I know Sam and Ramin can hear you.' He had the grace to look embarrassed and quickly added his voice to the four-way intercom. If tonight's mission was going to succeed, I needed perfect communications.

'Sam, let me know the minute you have eyes on the chancellor. Ramin, are you in place? Please confirm your locators are switched off.'

Both men confirmed, and I nodded to Julius as we waited to raid Alvarez' home. When the chancellor had invited Julius to the monthly poetry recital that evening, we'd decided that the timing was too good to pass up.

We talked it through, and a quick and theoretically foolproof scheme was hatched. Julius would tell Alvarez that he would see him there. Then, minutes before the recital was due to start, he would send a text saying he had a sudden bout of illness. Sam was going to be stationed at the poetry recital instead, to keep a visual on the chancellor, and warn us when he left. Julius had been surprised that I was taking the lead, but it had been years since Sam had been in the field on a regular basis. I then deployed Ramin to watch the street in front of Alvarez' house. Finally, Julius and I would break into the house the minute Sam told us the chancellor had arrived at the recital. Alvarez had left his house twenty minutes ago. We should be hearing from Sam any minute.

The chancellor's house was out to the east of the city on the other side of the Nile with river frontage. It was a large mansion in an area of other large mansions, all discreetly spaced out to provide privacy for their occupants. It's always so much easier to break into a house without neighbours tapping on the window. We were also blessed that the chancellor felt he didn't need to share his life with anyone, so we wouldn't have to stun any partner, child, or pet.

'Okay. He's here.' Sam's voice drifted over the intercom. 'He's being greeted by lots of people. Yep, he looks relaxed and happy. Let's destroy the thieving, murdering, bastard.'

I nodded. 'Julius, send your apologies.' I watched him hit send on the text and then spoke to Sam. 'Any reaction?'

'Hang on. Okay, a small scowl, but someone has just brought him a glass of champagne.' Sam paused. 'And he seems like he's staying.'

Right, I took a deep breath. Breaking into someone's home was an unforgivable crime. We would almost certainly receive a curtailment sentence and would have to wear a daily brand once we were released. Our faces would be broadcast on all media platforms and, of course, we would lose our jobs. The fact that we were breaking into a chancellor's home made the crime even more heinous. I'd be lucky if I got a job scrubbing down the camel ranks.

Carefully, Julius and I edged the punt towards the pontoon and climbed out. A startled owl launched itself out of a nearby tree. Its large wings were silent as it swooped across the lawn and off in search of quieter surroundings. Julius nudged me to point it out. I nodded in acknowledgement, but it was hardly relevant to the mission. I signalled in the direction of the house, and we crept up the lawn. We were both in full black for a covert Beta retrieval and it helped settle me. Julius was convinced the chancellor was at the heart of this, and I was prepared to back his assessment of the situation.

One of his back windows was ajar, and Julius boosted me through it. He climbed up the brickwork and hauled himself in through the window behind me. His foot struck a small table, and I reached for a vase that toppled alarmingly. The noise from its base was the only sound in the room as it rocked from side to side. I stretched out and caught it just before it fell to the floor. We both lay on the floor in the pitch black, waiting to see if any alarm was raised or if there was anyone in the house we were unaware of.

I lay there assessing the silence. It looked like we'd got away with it, although I currently had another slight problem. I mean, I wasn't bothered, but I knew that in about five seconds Julius was going to freak out.

'Neith!' Julius whispered in alarm.

'Yes?'

'I think there's a body on the floor. I can feel something soft.'

'That's my breast, Julius.'

Julius recoiled so fast that I was forced to lunge past him to save the other vase as well.

'Oh my God. I am so seriously sorry.'

'It's okay, I caught it.'

'No, I meant your, ahem, your...' He spluttered off into a paralysis of embarrassment.

'It's a breast, Julius. I have two. Now go and secure the windows so we can switch the sodding lights on.'

We had blackout and soundproof filters with us, and Julius went around the room, having finally remembered to switch on his night-vision goggles. He placed a filter at each window, then activated them whilst I turned on the lights. As I turned to look at Julius, I could see that he was still blushing. Good grief.

'Is everything okay?' Ramin's voice came over the brace.

'All good, although Julius groped my breast and then reacted like they might bite him.'

'Biting breasts. That could be an interesting modification.'

'Could we focus?' snapped Julius.

I laughed. I loved the adrenaline that ran through my system during a retrieval. I had my crew, and they had my back. Time to see what was what. We had come into some sort of reception room; there were lots of soft chairs and sofas and the room appeared to be modelled on a Beta French salon. Rococo on rococo. I think it was meant to be elegant, but honestly, I didn't always get Beta fashions right.

'Dear God, this room is appalling.'

Ah, appalling, not elegant. Of course, Julius being British might view French styles with an air of judgement. Those two nations seemed to spend every century bickering with each other. That said, the chancellor must like it, so I deferred to Julius' judgement.

I sent out a mapper drone and a few minutes later, having scanned the entire house, it returned and displayed a hologram projection of the property. That was curious. In the room we were standing in, the drone had mapped a door, a staircase, and a large void beneath our feet. Julius was already looking at the wall where, apparently, there should be a door. He was about to tap it when I stopped him.

'We don't know if it's alarmed.'

'The windows weren't.'

'That's because no one has alarm systems. Burglary just isn't a thing. But then neither are hidden cellars in the building of someone we suspect to be a smuggler.'

We stepped back and looked carefully at the wall. It was hung with gilt-framed art pieces in the style of Fragonard and Boucher, each bearing the replica stamp in the bottom right-hand corner. The yellow wallpaper was in a heavy flock pattern—like I said, high rococo—but nowhere was there an obvious door, until I spotted an odd seam in the wallpaper. I checked the wall again. Each roll of wallpaper appeared to be a metre wide all around the room. Except for this one section. The seam started at around fifty centimetres. And it was almost exactly where the mapper drone said there should be a door.

'Full protocols.'

Julius nodded. We were both wearing full combat curator suits that covered all of our skin and we manually deployed the neck and hood section. The suit could do this automatically, but there was no harm in being one step ahead of the situation. The suit was good for explosions, electrocutions, drownings, poisonous gas and, in one famous incident, a rhino rampage in the Tower of London.

Once I was happy that we were covered head to toe in protective covering and the suits agreed, I scanned the wall until I realised there wasn't even a lock. There was a large painting hung over the seam, and I signalled Julius to remove it. I stepped back, ready for any trap to spring, but nothing did. He placed the painting against a sofa and came back to join me as we both looked at a small porcelain finger plate at the height of a door handle. Julius smiled at me through his vizor.

'Ladies first?'

I nodded and spoke into the brace. 'Stand by. We have found a hidden door. We are about to try and open it. Let me know the minute either of you notices anything at your end.'

Just as I had stood back when Julius removed the painting, now he stood back, ready to react to any traps that I might spring. I gently pushed against the hand plate and watched as the entire panel of wall clicked and slid automatically to the side. In front of us was a simple, well-lit set of smooth marble steps leading down.

I checked our suits, but we didn't seem to have triggered any defence mechanisms. I grinned back at Julius, and we started downstairs. There was a door at the bottom with a standard handle and, just as I reached for it, I could hear Sam's voice across our intercom.

'Whatever you've just done has freaked Alvarez out. He was on stage in the middle of reading one of his new compositions, when he looked at his wrist brace, stuttered his next line, and then walked off stage. I'm following him now, and he's heading towards the car park at speed. I'd say you have twenty minutes.'

Okay, I thought, game time. 'Rami, shout the minute you see him approach. We've found a secret staircase leading down into a cellar room. There's a door at the bottom. About to see what's behind it.'

I turned the handle and the door swung into a large room that looked like a large antiques exhibition space. The lights flicked on automatically, revealing walls covered in paintings and display cabinets running down the central aisles. At the far end was a large oak and leather desk, and a few armchairs. The floor was carpeted, and all that was missing was a fireplace.

'Bloody hell. Is that a Degas?' Julius was pointing to a small bronze statue of two ballerinas dancing.

'Suit protocols first, Julius.'

Apologising, he checked his. When we'd both agreed the room was clean of any dangerous gases, we folded our helmets back into the suit collars and drew a deep breath.

'Sam, Rami. There's enough here to convict Alvarez instantly of theft.' I was wandering around the room. 'This place is full of works of art, every single one of them is a Beta original. Sam, I'm looking at a porcelain bowl by Adelaide Robineau. I like Robineau and don't remember there being any bowl on the QS list. Can you quickly look that up for me?'

As Sam went off to double-check, I made my way to the desk. Resting on top of the green leather-topped desk was a heavy, handwritten ledger. I opened it up and started to read. In the first column was an item description, followed by the sale price and the buyer. My eyes blinked at the sums involved. Then I saw one or two names that I recognised from the media feeds, and I went weak.

'Sam, sir! I have a list of people who have been buying this stuff. Sam. The sodding President of Sudan is on this list, and I'm only on the first page.'

There was enough incriminating evidence in this one ledger to bring down entire governments.

'Okay. Stay calm. I'm sending the custodians over.'

'How many?'

'All of them.'

'Tidy.' This ledger revealed a corruption far bigger than anything I had anticipated. Being surrounded by all these stolen treasures was bad enough, but now it was clear that this wasn't simply a nasty habit that the chancellor had got into. This was grand larceny.

'Plus, I'm going to have to inform Director al-Cavifi.'

'What if she's in on this? This is huge. No way Alvarez was doing all this without a vast network in high places. Sam, I'm not going to lie, we could be screwed.'

'Okay, Neith, stay calm and hide. If you need to, barricade yourself in, but do not let Alvarez get to that ledger.' I looked over at Julius who nodded at me, his expression grave as he agreed with Sam.

Sam continued to give instructions. 'I'm on my way, I have his tail lights in sight. Rami, when Alvarez arrives, don't try to stop him, but follow him into the house without alerting him. We need him cornered, but we also need to protect Neith and Julius. Only intervene if it looks like he's about to kill them.'

I looked around the room in stunned silence. This was far beyond anything I had imagined.

'It's like Aladdin's cave, isn't it? Sam's right,' said Julius as he picked up a ruby tiara. 'Alvarez will have to kill us, but he'll need to find out who else knows about this. All we need to do is hide long enough for the cavalry to turn up.'

Hiding didn't seem very proactive. I wanted to wave this evidence in Alvarez's face and arrest him then and there, but without backup, he would probably just shoot us. The man was a thief and a killer. There was nothing to be gained from us cornering a desperate criminal.

'Lights approaching,' said Rami over the intercom.

We were out of time. I ran up the steps and closed the wall door. There was bugger all I could do about the painting, and Alvarez would spot it immediately, but it would slow him down. He might even think we had left.

I ran back down into the basement, closing the door behind me. Julius and I stood on either side of it, ready to attack him as he walked into the room.

Ramin's voice now broadcast into the room, giving us a running commentary. 'Bloody hell, the chancellor can run fast when he wants to. Hang on in there. Oh, wow!'

There was silence for a minute. I looked at Julius, who looked equally alarmed. This was like fighting blindfolded.

'What?' I hissed into the wrist brace, worried about making any noise. 'What is oh, wow? Is he in the house yet? What the hell is happening?'

Rami's voice was breathy, and I could tell he was running to keep up with Alvarez.

'There are three heli-cruisers arriving. One has already landed on the lawn. I'm leaving them and following the chancellor. Bloody hell, someone is coming up the drive on a sodding motorcycle.'

There was another pause, and I started my yogic breathing. Julius' face was hard. Normally he was so animated, but now it was just all sinews and tension. Ramin's voice continued.

'Oh good grief, did you know Sam has a motorcycle? I thought they were banned?'

'Not banned, just require stringent permits,' said Sam joining in the radio conversation. 'Neith. Ramin and I are now together, we are heading into the house. Stay tight. I am now opening the comms so anyone can listen in.'

I watched as Julius nodded his approval. The more people who witnessed this, the safer we would all be.

'Please be advised, this is an all wavelength transmission. I am Captain Sam Nymens entering the house of Chancellor Soliman Alvarez. I believe he has stolen artefacts from the mouseion on his property. I believe there is also a ledger detailing all his co-conspirators. I have two operatives already in the property, QC Neith Salah and NQC Julius Strathclyde.'

As we listened over the braces, we could hear Sam had finished his opening statement and was now challenging Alvarez, who sounded shocked and surprised to see him. Whilst Alvarez was in the middle of his bluster, I could hear al-Cavifi shouting at Sam. She must have arrived on one of the heli-cruisers. Now the chancellor was getting very agitated. Demanding everyone leave his home. False alarm, home invasion etc, etc.

I opened the lower basement door and realised I could hear their voices without my earpiece. Alvarez must have run straight into the rococo salon.

'Sam, is there a painting propped up against an armchair?' I whispered into my brace. I listened to him and carried on. 'Okay, find the painting of a woman in a blue dress on a tree swing. When you think it's safe for us to appear, remove that painting and be prepared for Alvarez to do anything.'

Julius and I crept to the top of the stairs and listened whilst the chancellor continued to demand that everyone leave. He also wanted Sam and Ramin to be arrested for slander and trespass. Ramin suggested that the chancellor be arrested for crimes against poetry, and I swear I heard the director laugh. The next thing I heard were shouts from further away. Sam wasn't kidding when he said all the custodians. I recognised the chant of the red custodians.

I had considered applying to the reds, but in the end, decided that the discipline was beyond me. Those guys were incredible, but they didn't go in for mavericks or flights of fancy. Show me a brick wall and I'd think about how to get over it or around it. Show them a brick wall and they'd just destroy it. They were effectively our army and, if they were here, then so too was the high council. This could get messy. If the reds perceived us as a threat to the pharaoh, they might negate that threat by negating us.

Sure enough, I heard al-Cavifi greet Pharaoh Tarek who was now demanding that everyone leave the chancellor's house. Tarek then fired the director. It was unclear on what grounds.

'Sam, this is escalating too fast. Tell them you have proof and for Bast's sake, move carefully.'

Julius and I listened as Sam shouted over the competing voices. I listened as he told them he could prove that the chancellor had been stealing from the archives and then selling those artefacts on. Now Director al-Cavifi declared that she was firing Sam, but the pharaoh overruled her.

Sam, speaking loudly, said that he was removing the picture and placing his hand on the finger plate. Julius and I stood side by side with our hands in the air. I was confident that everyone would recognise our uniforms, and some may also recognise who we were. No one would mistake us for random burglars and shoot us, claiming mistaken identity. Just in case though, we had our helmets deployed.

The door slid sideways, and we stood very still as we peered our heads around the doorway and looked into a room bristling with custodians and civilians all staring back at us in disbelief. I took stock of the room without moving a muscle trying to spot a friendly face. I could see Julius' friend Custodian Shorbagy, but he, like the other regular custodians, was avoiding all eye contact. I couldn't blame him; this was a terrible situation. If we were deemed to be traitors all Shorbagy's interactions with Julius would be reviewed and I understood there were a lot of them. I kept scanning the room and then saw who I was looking for.

'Red Custodian Githumbi, greetings and health to your house and heart.'

There is a staircase behind me leading down into a display room twenty by forty cubits. It is full of original artefacts as claimed by Captain Nymens. With your permission, Neophyte Quantum Custodian Strathclyde and I will step aside, and you can send someone down to investigate.'

Luisa Githumbi and I had been cadets together. I had to trust someone right now, and as she was the person in charge of the most guns, it may as well be her.

Luisa gave no indication that she recognised me, which was tricky. On the other hand, she didn't shoot me either, so weighing things up I felt ahead of the game.

'Step aside. Keep your hands raised.'

We stepped into the room and raised our hands enough so we could still quickly grab our stun guns if needed. Luisa looked at me sardonically, and we raised our hands to the ceiling. I noticed that two red custodians were also standing on either side of the chancellor. I wasn't convinced it was for his own protection. As one of the reds came back upstairs, he nodded at Luisa, confirming my claim.

The dynamics of the room changed immediately.

The pharaoh demanded that Alvarez be arrested and silenced, but Alvarez started shouting to everyone in the room that he hadn't mentioned the book.

'They don't know about the book!'

I looked at him in disgust. 'Not your lucky day, is it, Solly? The book was on top of the desk. We know all about your co-conspirators.'

I expected him to look worried, but he just laughed at me. 'Not that book, you idiot. The codex.'

That's when the lights shorted, and the room was pitched into blackness. My suit went into automatic protection mode, as did Julius'. We heard shouting as the reds tried to contain the situation. Less than a minute later, the lights came back on. I could see several reds hunched over their designated targets, protecting them from any threat. All their uniforms and those of the custodians were now also battle hard. Ramin waved at me from behind a sofa. Ramin's suit was in auto mode as well, and he was currently protecting Sam who was dressed in his normal clothes. Everyone who had a gun had it drawn and was looking around trying to identify the threat. In the middle of the room lay Chancellor Soliman Alvarez with a large hole in his head, no longer offering a threat to anyone.

#35 – Neith

After that it got a bit ugly. Every red pointed their guns at us and insisted we all drop ours. Sam and Luisa Githumbi started roaring at each other as Sam pointed out that it was just as likely that a red had killed Alvarez. The impasse only ended when Luisa fired a shot at Sam's feet and told him the next one would be the end of the argument. Furiously, Sam holstered his stun gun and raised his arms. Luisa then told us all to stand against the far wall. This included the pharaoh, the various directors, the yellow custodians, and us. Once she was happy we were all secured, and that five of her team all had their guns trained on us, she inspected the chancellor's body.

'Shot with a Beta weapon.'

All eyes turned to Julius, who glared back.

'I do not own a gun. I've never even used a gun. Check my hands for residue if you don't believe me.'

'Of course, because why would you forget to use a cleansing wipe to remove the residue?'

Julius turned to me, now curious. 'That exists, does it? A way to mask gunshot?'

'Yes,' I hissed. 'Focus.'

'What about trajectory?' piped up Julius again, and I swear I saw Luisa roll her eyes.

'Neophyte Strathclyde, we will of course be taking that into account. But it would appear that the shot was fired from the garden. No one heard the glass break because it seems that filters had been placed on the windows. Presumably by yourself or Salah when you entered the building.'

She was right. In all the chaos, I had failed to notice a cool breeze had entered the room. This didn't put us in the clear though, as we could have easily signalled to an outside party. As could anyone else in the room.

Whilst we stood and waited, Luisa deployed reds to search the garden, then called for further backup, plus a body bag.

The director tried to take charge, so I pointed out that her name was on the ledger as being a buyer, and therefore part of the corruption. The pharaoh went pale but ordered that the reds arrest al-Cavifi. Everyone started shouting again until I suggested that Luisa get one of her officers to bring up the ledger. As she did, the minister for transport tried to run out of the house, and the director of urban hydration fainted. At that point, the reds arrested everyone, including us.

Three days later we were once more back in Sam's office, although this time we were joined by Asha, who had been able to return from hiding. She was still wearing the pale yellow robes of a junior custodian, but I noticed that she was also wearing a red star on her collar.

'I'm wearing it to honour and acknowledge their achievements over the past few days. I have never been prouder of my custodians achievements.'

The fact that this situation hadn't spilt over into outright anarchy was down to the calm and efficient way that the reds had seized all forms of judicial and civil authority, and then just as promptly returned it to the newly appointed interim government. The public had been told that various members of the government had stepped aside due to behaviour unbecoming to their station. Fresh elections would take place the following year, but for now, those acting in a temporary capacity would do so to the best of their abilities. It was also announced that the chancellor had died after a brief illness. I conceded that having a hole in your head would make you ill, but also that illness would only be for a short time. Over the past few days, various heads of state and captains of industry had stepped down from their positions, and there were a few more brief illnesses that might also be described as suicides.

I poured a cup of tea for Giovanetti and handed it to her. Despite her request, I couldn't bring myself to call her Asha, even in my head.

'I have been in touch with Githumbi the whole time. The minute she heard that I was due to be arrested, she got in touch and I went into hiding.'

'What tipped them off?' asked Sam.

Giovanetti frowned. 'That I don't know, although I have a few ideas. I'll need to start looking at all the files and reports before I'm prepared to speculate openly. It would be fair to say in a corruption this widespread, we have not uncovered all the principal parties.'

'But the mouseion is secure now though, isn't it?' I couldn't bear the thought that it was still vulnerable.

'I would say it will now be virtually impossible to remove anything from the mouseion in the future. Although I suspect that you won't appreciate the increase in paperwork, Neith.'

I gave a mock groan, but it was worth it.

'What about Beta Earth? What's to stop curators stealing when they are over there?' asked Julius. I stiffened. I wanted to protest, but the past few weeks had made it exceedingly clear that curators had been doing exactly that, acting like common criminals.

'Protocols will be in place, Julius. All curators will now be required to strip before they submit their reports.'

There was nothing false about Julius' groan when he heard that.

'Yes, I'm sorry about that, Julius. I appreciate how much that protocol appals you, but it will be a necessary measure. You will also need to strip in front of two technicians selected at random.'

'Quis custodiet ipsos custodes?' asked Julius.

It took me a second to translate. 'Who will watch the watchers?'

He wasn't wrong. The entire network was riddled, and we now had to treat each other as suspects. Along with dignitaries and heads of state, we'd also lost a few more curators. Alvarez had been meticulous in his note keeping. We knew who had snatched what, and we knew whether they had been bribed or forced. It was also apparent that some things had never made it to the mouseion at all. These artefacts attracted a premium and explained the "failed missions". Their worth was in the fact that no one else had seen them and no copies were available. True rarity.

It was also clear that Clio had been working directly for the chancellor for years, and that Paul had indeed been coerced. It made for very grim reading.

'It's not over, you know,' said Giovanetti as she sipped her tea, the steam curling the wisps of grey hair around her temples. 'He wasn't doing this alone. I don't think any of this was his idea.'

'But al-Cavifi…'

'The director was up to her neck in this, but I sense a stillness at the centre of all this.'

'But if she knew who else was behind this, she would have said by now. And she hasn't so there isn't anyone,' I said.

'Or there is someone and they've been smart enough to not let anyone know about them,' said Ramin.

Giovanetti looked at him appraisingly. 'Being under suspicion for six months has been good for you. A little bit of paranoia is a good thing.'

'Do you know,' he said, looking at me, 'when you put me on lookout duty outside the chancellor's, I had a terrible flashback to that awful scene in London when Julius' friend was killed.'

I nodded. 'So did I, but I couldn't think of a better way to apologise to you for my stupid misjudgement.'

I looked over at Julius, who was looking sad. My best friend had killed his, and I wasn't sure if he would ever forgive me for that. As he looked up, he must have guessed my thoughts as he raised his bottle to me and called me a wally.

Well, there's lovely, I thought and grinned. I was getting used to the voice of Julius' grandma now, and at least I no longer felt the need to fold socks. Just knit them.

I raised my bottle in return and called out, 'We Preserve,' which was taken up by the others in the room.

We had unearthed a ring of thieves, ousted a bunch of corrupt politicians, and preserved the integrity of the greatest mouseion in the world. Not a bad day's work.

'What do you think he meant by the book?' asked Julius, breaking the reflective silence. 'He clearly didn't mean the ledger, and all the books he had stolen were accounted for. And how did Clio get us home? If she had access to a second step, why wasn't the chancellor using it?'

Apparently, everyone who was arrested, from curators to directors, had just looked puzzled when the possibility of a second stepper was mentioned. As al-Cavifi had pointed out, if there had been a second stepper, she wouldn't have to be dealing with all this bloody nonsense right now. The director was not going to go down without a fight. Despite the overwhelming evidence.

Julius said this was a common pattern of behaviour amongst the truly guilty. I just thought they were idiots. Julius conceded that, in his world, that sort of entitled behaviour worked. Despite our clear superiority in so many areas, I had a feeling that Julius didn't quite approve of us, and it was a nice change when I could see his wholehearted support for how we ran our planet.

'And look,' he said, 'we have no idea who killed Alvarez. It's unlikely to have been on the director's orders. She could see already that her goose was cooked. Someone clearly didn't want him to say anything more about a codex.'

I yawned and then apologised. The past week had been exhausting. 'Can we think about the "codex" and "Clio" tomorrow? I think we've achieved quite enough for today, let's not go looking for more trouble,' I pleaded with a laugh.

We'd turned to happy small talk and speculations of who knew what and how things could have gone wrong when Sam's intercom buzzed.

'Excuse me, sir, there's a man in reception. He says his name's Arthur Pendragon, you've stolen his sword, and he wants it back?'

We looked at each other in confusion until Julius started laughing. 'Ask him what it's called?'

'What what's called?' said the disembodied voice over the intercom.

Julius was now grinning broadly. 'The sword. Ask him what his sword is called.'

The four of us looked at each other uncertainly. There was a moment's pause, then the voice came back.

'He says the sword is Excalibur and when Albion needs him, he will rise once more and answer their call.'

Before we could react to that statement, a tall blond man materialised in front of us causing everyone to jump back in alarm. On his head he wore a golden crown studded with jewels. Thick wavy blond hair fell around his strong chin, which framed a thick blond moustache and beard. He was wearing some sort of loose mail vest, and a red cloak with a lion on it was draped over his shoulders. The cloak seemed to move gently in a non-existent breeze, adding to the sense of power and majesty. The armoured theme continued to the metal braces on his legs. This man was a warrior and a leader, and I suddenly felt myself blushing to be present in his shimmering majesty.

The moment was broken as Julius started to laugh.

'So that's how Clio did it.'

'Sorry? How she did what?' demanded Giovannetti, as disturbed as the rest of us. 'And who in the name of Anubis, is this?'

'Let me explain,' said Julius, laughing as he waved his beer bottle at the beautiful man. 'The gods are back in town.'

'I don't understand?' I pleaded. 'You're not making sense.'

'Everything makes sense. Finally. Six months ago, as far as I was concerned, there was just one earth. Then I discovered there were two. But who's to say there isn't another one? Or a million more? Maybe even an earth where the gods aren't just a figment of the imagination but are actually real. You wanted to know how Clio could flick back and forth between our two earths, well maybe she hitched a ride?'

I knew Julius was speaking words, but none of them made any sense. I just wanted to carry on staring at the beautiful man. Julius didn't seem to have the same problem though, as he turned to him with a frown on his face.

'Although, Arthur, I have to ask? You aren't a god, so what's with the divine appearance?'

Suddenly the glow from Arthur seemed to slip, and I noticed that there were some crumbs of food in his beard. Also, he looked a bit embarrassed.

'Yes, about that. The thing is, I may need your help with a bet.

#Coda

A man and a woman sat on a park bench overlooking the waves as an amber sun sank towards the horizon. She had chosen this location for its privacy and, as usual, she had swept it for listening devices, including any her companion may have been wearing. She hadn't got to where she was by taking risks. If the whole pack of cards fell around her, she had taken great pains to ensure that she would walk away, untouched and unnoticed. Only two people knew her identity, and she was certain of their loyalty. Plus, if they so much as twitched in the direction of betraying her, she would have them assassinated. They knew they had her unwavering support, and they also knew she had a bullet with their name on it. The dynamic worked perfectly.

'So that's it then?' said the man, his voice tired.

'It is for the supply chain. It's a shame Soliman stored so many stolen treasures at his house, but there were still some in the cargo bays. I had them moved and we can sell them off to raise funds. For now, though, we won't be able to remove any Beta artefacts from the mouseion.'

'May I ask? We're not short on funds, are we?'

'No, not in the slightest. It's just an irritation.'

She paused and leant back on the bench. A gull flew past eagerly watching the pair in hopes of a bit of food and then, seeing none was forthcoming, continued along the boardwalk back towards the families playing in the sand.

As the gull passed, the woman pulled out a small paper bag of sweets and offered one to her companion. She knew he had more questions and waited to see what was on his mind.

'And al-Cavifi?'

'Yes. I have to admit, losing her is annoying. Giovanetti is now officially investigating the mouseion thefts. There isn't much that she misses. I presume your communications with al-Cavifi were secure? It would be annoying if attention started to be focused on you.'

'It would be more than annoying.'

'For you, maybe. But I care little for your incarceration. I only care about the codex.'

The man felt the threat in her words and sat very still.

'My communications with her were secure and you must know I frequently stressed to her that relying on Soliman may be a mistake.'

The older woman flicked away his protestation in annoyance. He paused and then continued.

'You must know my loyalty to this project. We must have the designs for the stepper. We need our own quantum stepper, and then we can visit the Beta world without worrying about all the ridiculous safety protocols for Beta lives. Why wait until they lose something? Better we take what we want when we want. They're bound to lose it or destroy it at some point anyway.'

'I quite agree. But it's much more important than just securing more treasures. You know their old saying. 'He who controls the past controls the future.' Well, I think it's about time we installed a little control.'

She pulled out another sweet and began to chew on it as they watched the sunset, her long silver tail gently twitching in anticipation of the task ahead.

Author's Note

Alternate histories are great fun to write because there is so much freedom, but there are also minefields to try and traverse. I hope I haven't unwittingly set some off in this story but it's very hard to tell. The key thing to remember is that this is fiction.

My two earths split shortly after the fire at the Library of Alexandria in 48 BC. Incidentally, it didn't burn to the ground, but it was well and truly singed. Julius Caesar now takes to the water as he becomes engaged in the Egyptian civil war. Whilst at sea a storm blows in and the ship sinks, taking Caesar to the bottom of the sea. Or at least it does in this world.

With no Julius Caesar, the tides turn in Egyptian fortunes. Cleopatra loses her fight for the throne and her brother now rules. Removing Caesar from the timeline at this moment allows everything to change.

For the purpose of this story, the next momentous change occurs over in Judea. It's been fifty years since Caesar drowned and the political climate in Judea is less volatile. Rome hasn't made it a client kingdom and interferes less in how it runs its business. The religious and political leaders are secure, people are healthy and prosperous. It's a time of stability and there is no great driver for political unrest. Jesus may or may not have been born but his life is unrecorded.

And now, as they say, we are off to the races. The next two millennia are not shaped by an ever-expanding Roman Empire, and when it fades there is no Christian Church ready to continue the empire's structure.

Without the church, something else must fill the void and so science and philosophy step in. Now is the rise of the chancellors and universities and the great mouseions.

Who knows? Historians may well line up to tell me that I'm wrong and it wouldn't happen like that. And they may well be right. But can they prove it?

Coming Soon

Book Three
The Quantum Curators and the Missing Codex

Available for order now — or read the first chapter at the end of this book.

Thank you for reading.

Getting to know my readers is incredibly rewarding, I get to know more about you and enjoy your feedback; it only seems fair that you get something in return, so if you sign up for my newsletter you will get various free downloads, depending on what I am currently working on, plus advance notice of new releases. I don't send out many newsletters, and I will never share your details. If this sounds good, click on the following: **https://www.thequantumcurators.com**

I'm also on all the regular social media platforms so look me up.

@thequantumcurators

and finally...

That's the second book down and it's been a blast writing it. I'm really getting into my stride and I can feel a whole load more books ahead of me. I've also started to assemble a great team, who quite frankly turn my fevered scribbles into something worth reading. You have to understand, I consider my first draft to be perfection. It's these guys that ensure you aren't forced to read it.

Many thanks to Anna, Anna, Steve and Al who all read every word and somehow survived.

Thanks also to my editors, Mark Stay and Melanie Underwood, and my proof-reader, Anna Gow.

And finally, thanks to you for reading my books and for joining me online. It's great that you're enjoying Julius and Neith's exploits. Without you, I'd just be scribbling in the corner, idly wondering if I would ever eat again.

Now it's time to get on with book three...

The Quantum Curators and the Missing Codex

Day Zero - First Engineer

First Engineer glanced up from his desk in surprise. It wasn't time for the midday briefing, yet Second Engineer stood in front of him tapping a print-out against her thigh. An alarming item in itself. Files were only printed when the digital copy had been deemed so harmful that it had been completely wiped and a single hard copy made, to be filed or burnt at a later date.

'Report.'

There was no need for pleasantries. They were engineers, their job was to ensure a smooth running of society. Let the other departments clamour to be the best. Engineers were silent and knew the truth of things.

'This tripped our protocols as it ran through the security filters. It's a lecture for the neophytes.'

All staff who worked for the Mouseion of Alexandra started at the same place. Whether they would go on to be curators, custodians or even engineers, they all started as neophytes. Then their skills were assessed, and they were allocated to the correct departments.

'A neophyte lecture? What on earth could be in that to have triggered an alert?'

'It was written by Curator Strathclyde.'

First Engineer frowned and held out his hand for the offending transcript. When Strathclyde had first arrived through the quantum stepper, First had argued vehemently that the man could prove to be highly dangerous. He had been overwhelmingly outvoted. The other departments had been charmed by Strathclyde and could see no threat in his friendly ways. They were treating him like a project or an interesting pet.

Despite First's objections, Strathclyde graduated as a curator. Now, he was being considered as an occasional lecturer in Beta Studies. First wondered when the rest of the mouseion heads would realise what a threat to the stability of their society Strathclyde was. Who knew what dangerous ideas he might try and inseminate? His eyes flicked across the paper.

Who amongst us hasn't wondered if we are not alone in the universe? He stared at Second and looked back over the paper, as he began to read aloud. *'If we can have a parallel existence between your Earth and mine, why not multiple universes?'*

With a shaking hand, he took a match from his desk drawer and set fire to the paper, placing it in his bin.

'Do we know if he discussed the contents of this paper before he wrote it?'

Second shook her head. 'We've pulled all the audio files from any neighbouring wrist braces, and nothing was detected.'

First frowned. 'What about his own?'

'He doesn't always wear it. He's not impressed by the *wearing it for the common good* argument. Also, according to the notes, in his monthly assessment he commented, *that as it wasn't mandatory, he'd rather not.*'

'That's ridiculous.'

'In his defence,' said Second, 'he *was* tracked and spied upon through his wrist brace.'

'But that was unsanctioned. He would never have known about it if we had been doing it.'

'I don't think he sees it the same way. And, of course, he doesn't quite see the *for the good of society* the same way we do.

'This is not news to me, Second.'

She flinched. Repetition of information was an unnecessary waste of time and unworthy of her rank. She waited to see what First was going to recommend. At this point, she felt her next suggestion would be at odds with his. She felt that Julius should be more closely monitored. He was an excellent example of a Beta mind and she wanted to study him.

'I have determined that Julius Strathclyde is a threat to society of the first order. He is an unresolved paradox.'

Second betrayed no emotion. First's reasoning was sound, but where Strathclyde was concerned, Second felt that First may be slightly conflicted.

'In order to protect the citizens of Alpha Earth, I will arrange for Julius to be removed from it.'

Second nodded her assent. She felt sure that they had lost a research opportunity, but First was within his rights. Julius Strathclyde must die..

Read On…

Made in the USA
Monee, IL
21 April 2022

95174904R00198